JACOB

A Novel of the Nightsiders

David Gerrold

for Adam-Troy and Judi Castro,
with love

Monsieur

Dark returns and I am awake.

The first few hours, I keep to myself, as usual. Since the invention of electricity, since the invention of gaslight, since the invention of candles and oil lamps, since the invention of fire, humans have rolled back the dark.

Not a problem. The first few hours, I keep to myself, listening.

The dark is filled with noise now.

Not so long ago, I could lie still and alone, drinking in the sounds of the world, crickets ticking away the heat of the day, owls questioning the darkness, and sometimes the skittering of tiny feet in the woodwork. Now, no. Instead, all the different voices, both silent and raised, sometimes quietly intense, more often screeching insanities—underneath it all, the distant howling of machines, everywhere tinny attempts at music as if to drown out all the other noises.

And the dark is filled with light as well, prowling fingers of light like the yellow eyes of huge black beasts. Cruising through hardened shadows, glaring at the dark around, they leave trails of acrid stench.

But the dark is my world, not theirs. Eventually, the beasts return to their caves, they slumber. The dark grows still again and I am free to walk the streets alone, tasting the air.

Sometimes, sometimes, long years of sometimes, I lie alone in silence, lost in dreamtime.

And sometimes I awake, curious again, hungry again. I move through darkness alone, a shadow within shadows.

And finally sometimes, I seek out those last uncertain pools of life, those three-in-the-morning lonely outposts, the last diner or gas station on a lonely road, standing brave against the pressing dark.

I seek the gatherings of those who circle the glare. Like moths, they sparkle only for an instant, then fly toward the light—they crackle into smoke and disappear.

———— ✦═❮◆❯ΌΟΧΟ❮◆❯═✦ ————

The pages work their way around the group and finally back to me. Mark and Larry nod their approval. Janice purses her lips, frowning over a phrase that bothers her, she'll come back to it later. Her scrawny little brother utters the inevitable, "Real vampires don't sparkle," as if it's his own sudden profound insight. Everybody ignores him.

Jerome is the one who's actually been published—therefore he has *credential*—sucks at his coffee. "I like the rhythm. It sets a mood."

A couple others chime in with half-formed ideas, nothing useful, and I realize what I'm missing is the acknowledgment that the piece *works*. No one has actually said, "This is good. I want to read more."

And in that moment, I realize how much I hate writers' workshops.

We don't want honest criticism, that might hurt—what we really want is a standing ovation and a gold trophy shoved into our hands. But we don't give honest criticism either, because we don't want to be cruel. We don't want to lose our friends. So we all just play patty cake with each other's bullshit and pretend we're real writers.

Camellia—not her real name, but the one she writes under—usually goes through each manuscript like a third grade teacher correcting punctuation. Her prose is methodically precise, perfectly bland. She grabs for the parsley and misses the meat and potatoes.

Jerome sits, he types, he sells. There's no secret to it, he says. Just sit, just type. He has a genius level IQ and the social skills of a hyperactive beagle. But it's not arrogance, it's enthusiasm, getting that award nomination for that first short story was the first time he ever got validated for anything. He finally has a piece of evidence that he's good at something. Self-esteem issues die hard. When you're small and smart in high school, you don't get girls, you get swirlies. If you're gay, you don't get girls either.

Patty writes fan fiction. That's the polite phrase. She doesn't bring pages to the meetings anymore. And she won't upload anything to the Facebook group either. Most of her stories end up with Kirk and Spock professing their undying love for each other. Sometimes one is hurt and the other comforts him. Sometimes they end up in bed, sharing the most embarrassing pillow talk before fucking each other's brains out. Larry was unimpressed, he told her bluntly, "*Star Trek* is about reaching for the stars, not your vibrator." She hasn't spoken to him since. Occasionally, however, she still argues that *everything* is fan fiction. She justifies that notion, arguing that all writers are reworking personal fantasies into their stories.

Jerome says that women writing about male-male sex isn't much different than men fantasizing about lesbians. Maybe that's the point. What Patty writes is for herself, not anyone else. And if that's true, then Larry is right as well. Me—I'm not going there anymore. It's argument without end.

Michael is working on an epic. He hasn't shared any of it. Mostly, he sits and grunts and offers insights that he borrowed from "the big guys." Michael has read every book on writing he can find. He wants to be perfect, he wants to write the greatest book ever. He's been working on his epic since middle school. His claim to fame is a letter he received from the editor of a major magazine. He submitted his fifty page outline. The editor wrote back, "You should learn how to lance a boil before you attempt brain surgery."

Michael waves the letter around as if it's a validation. The editor wrote back. A personal note. No one has had the heart to tell him he's had his legs cut off at the ankle with one of the most elegant cheap shots since Mark Twain (allegedly) said, "I did not attend the funeral but I sent a nice letter saying I approved of it."

Gil and Emma always come together, but they're not a couple. Gil rides a motorcycle, so he dresses in leather, Emma wears skirts over jeans. Is that some kind of a statement or does she have the fashion sense of a Republican? Maybe she's transgender, nobody is sure, nobody is impolite enough to ask—but she has a feminist mission. Does it pass the Bechdel test? Is there unconscious sexism in the structure of the story or the way the characters are presented? Does it challenge the bubble of white male privilege or does it reinforce the patriarchy? Her stories aren't narratives as much as they're screeds about how the world would be better off without men. One day, Larry is going to punch her. And that will prove she's right about men and violence. It's not that anyone disagrees with her militancy, we wouldn't dare anyway—it's just that she can't talk about anything else.

Gil doesn't write. He comments. He annotates. He informs. He explains. He deconstructs. He is erudite. And that's why nothing in the world satisfies him. He only sees what's wrong. That's why no one will go to the movies with him. You come out laughing and joyous—"That was fun!"—and Gil will immediately begin speaking in that intense manner of his, explaining how the filmmakers conned us, manipulated us, and ultimately cheated us. Too often, he's right. And after he's through, you don't know if you want to punch Michael Bay or Steven Spielberg or Jar Jar Abrams. Or just Gil. Behind his back, Larry calls him, "Mister Buzzkill."

Oh, and Blaze—why do women choose such silly names for themselves? Blaze is a dithering idiot. Not my words, Larry's. She's short, she's fat, and she loves to pretend she's a profound thinker. She speaks in that meticulous fannish way, halfway between Asperger's and booorrrring, annotating aloud every meticulous detail of the minutiae of her existence. Today she pretends she's a writer. Next week, she'll pretend to be an artist. The week after that, I don't know yet—but eventually she'll cycle back to pretending she's a writer. We had to ask her not to bring her guitar—that was when she was pretending to be a filker. She sings almost as well as she plays. She knows two chords.

Me? I'm the guy who...I don't know. I'm still trying to figure it all out.

I want to be the guy who takes this business serious. At least, that's the way I see myself in my own personal movie. That means I'm the quiet shy guy. The listener. The observer. How others see me? I'm the spear-carrier, sometimes the sidekick, sometimes the comic relief, in their movies.

That also means I'm *that* guy—you know, the one that everyone else explains things to, so the audience will get it. They see me as the stupid one. I am surrounded by self-appointed explainers.

In the movie, when you need some necessary exposition, there's always Murray-The-Explainer. He's an archetype, like Morgan Freeman always plays The-Magic-Negro. He's usually a scientist, more often a computer nerd who types fast, sometimes a specialist of some kind, like a paleontologist or an expert in epidemiology.

Murray-The-Explainer is never the hero. He's always scenery. In my case, all those Murrays are also a lot of useless and annoying noise. There was a time when I appreciated the attention. Now, no. So I've learned how to smile and nod.

Maybe I'm being arrogant—

No, there's no maybe at all in that. I am arrogant. I have to be to be a writer. Whatsisname, that guy who spoke at the college last month—he said writing *is* arrogant. You have to be at the very top of the arrogance ladder to believe that what you write is so important that trees should be chopped down.

"What about those of us who only publish eBooks?"

"Even more so—you're burning coal to create electricity. You're contributing to the heat-death of the planet. That's even more arrogant."

So yeah, okay. I'm arrogant. Arrogant enough to have a derogatory opinion of dilettantes and dabblers, doodlers and dawdlers, and especially the danglers who don't do anything useful at all, just hang on like dingleberries. And every bit as useful. They suck the energy out of the room. I take this shit serious. If I'm going to kill a tree—or a planet—I had damn well better make sure it's worth it.

It's not just about putting words on paper—not anymore anyway. Mostly they're marks on a screen. The last time I printed something out, it was a term project. But it's not about the words, it's about the thought pictures, the moment, the mood, the feelings, the experience. It's time-telepathy. A storyteller takes something out of his head and puts it in yours. It can't just be to entertain—it also has to enlighten.

And that's really the bottom line. Who the hell am I to enlighten anyone else? I can barely boil a cup of Ramen.

In my existential moods, I ask myself why? Why is any of this important? Why am I spending all this effort? Why? Just why am I doing this?

Because it's a great way to be with people without having to be with people—?

I don't know.

Except—and this is something Michael shared—it stuck with me for some reason. He said that people who read, especially people who read a lot, they have more empathy than people who don't read. And it's his theory that empathy is a necessary condition for true sentience and from there, true sapience. It sounds good. I like it. It's a useful justification to hang onto while I figure out the real reasons. And if he's right, maybe someday I'll find out what enlightenment looks like.

Anyway.

The coffee shop stays open all night, so it doesn't matter how late we stay. Sometimes we sit and argue until two in the morning. Sometimes, we don't. Sometimes we even go home and write. Sometimes I open up my laptop and type a few notes to myself, maybe even a whole paragraph, and later on—when I realize I've done five or six pages, I look up and see I'm all alone. The others have left.

Tonight, I'm not alone. The new guy is still here. The one in the black hoody. I don't know his name. He told it to me when we shook hands. His hand was very cold. I remember that, but I forgot his name. I close the laptop. "Can I ask you something?"

He shrugs.

"I mean—I don't mean to be rude, but I have to ask. Are you an albino?"

He shakes his head. A hint of a smile flickers in his eyes. "No. I'm just extremely allergic to sunlight. It's a very rare condition."

"Ah." Jacob—that's his name, now I remember. "You don't say much. Do you write?"

He scratches his cheek with one well-manicured nail, thinking it over. "No, I don't write. But I'm interested in writers."

"Why?"

"Why not?"

"No, I mean—I guess this is a strange thing to say, but my experience of writers? I mean, even myself. Especially myself. We're pretty screwed up as people. We're too fat or too skinny, too short or too tall. We're awkward, we're weird, we're dancing with insanity, with two left feet. And you don't even want to know about all the weird sexual experimentation—"

"Precisely," Jacob says. "That's exactly what makes writers interesting." He moves his chair closer to me, he leans forward, stares into my eyes. "People. Think about it. The great mass of men lead lives of quiet domestication. Like animals in feeding pens, they shuffle meekly from one cubicle to the next, school, school, school, work, work, work—until you die. But writers..." Now he smiles. "Writers—the good ones anyway—are always looking, listening, sniffing, tasting, touching, experiencing the whole world with all their senses. They're exploring, discovering, learning, sharing. They're pushing the limits of what they know. They're going out beyond the safety of the firelight into the darkness. They're going into the risk zone. They're breaking taboos. The good writers anyway. They're *interesting* specifically because they're *not* safe and comfortable and normal."

"Okay. That makes sense. It's the kind of thing you hope it's true. If you're a writer."

"It is true. The evidence is there."

"So..." I push my empty coffee cup to the edge of the table, just in time to catch Millie, the waitress, passing by with a fresh pot. She refills my mug, Jacob's too. I turn back to him. "So, what I wrote—? It's crap, right?"

He shakes his head. "No. It's just...naïve."

"Naïve? Why do you say that?"

"Because it is." He leans back in his chair, hooking one arm over the back of it. "I used to be an existentialist—that's the polite way of saying 'I don't care and I don't care that I don't care.' But there's a—a way of looking at the world. 'What is, is. What isn't, isn't.' As if that means something. It doesn't. Or, if you dig even deeper—'Life is empty and meaningless. And it doesn't mean anything that it doesn't mean anything.' You like that kind of crap? It sounds profound, doesn't it? It's not. It's just a clever way of disassociating yourself. If you don't have to care, you don't have to take responsibility."

He holds up a hand to stop me from replying, a very pale hand. "No, there's more. Let me finish. The whole point of that word salad is to say that if you want life to have meaning, you have to make it up yourself. Because you're God inside your own universe of experience. So if you follow that train of thought, toward its illogical solipsistic endpoint, everybody is alone."

I can't help myself. I ask, "So what does this have to do with vampires?"

"Everything," he says. "Being a vampire is the ultimate loneliness. Everyone you know grows old and dies, you might be immortal, but you're alone."

"But you can make other vampires, can't you? To keep you company?"

"You've never been married, have you?"

"No."

"After the first fifty or sixty years, you've had enough. You're just waiting for her to die. Now think about what it would be like if neither of you could die and you're stuck with each other for eternity...." He pauses. "When you get to the point that you can finish each other's sentences, when you know each other's jokes, when all you have are each other's memories, when you can tell each other's stories, when there's absolutely nothing new to say to each other—"

"But if you love her—?"

"Really? What is love?" Jacob asks.

"Uh—"

"Yeah. That's the point."

"I have to think about this. I always thought love was when two people fit together so well they become two parts of a larger whole."

"Like Romeo and Juliet? Two addlepated teenagers fall in lust and three days later, six people are dead—Mercutio is stabbed, Tybalt is stabbed, Paris is stabbed, Romeo poisons himself, Juliet stabs herself, and Lady Montague dies of a broken heart. Not the best demonstration of a healthy relationship, is it?"

"Now, you're just being cynical."

"Am I? Are you arguing that the hormonal responses of two barely post-adolescent persons are a strong foundation for a lifetime relationship? Think about it. Do you really want to spend eternity with this person?"

"Uh—yeah. Okay. I see your point. But not every relationship has to be permanent, right? I mean, you make new friends all your life, don't you? As you grow older, as you meet new people, as you move through new circumstances. So wouldn't the same be true for vampires? You could make new...I don't know, what would you call it?—relationships?—without necessarily having to turn them into immortal companions, right?"

"True. And you can get a new dog, but it's not the same dog, is it?"

"Oh." That one I knew. Too well.

Jacob says, "Let me finish my earlier thought. One of my favorite philosophers says that everything is a conversation. Everything. There is no *is*. There's only the 'is' that we assign to things. Let me say that another way. Maybe there really is an objective reality. But we're not designed to experience it. So all that any of us really knows is our own subjective experience, our own conversation about what is. So there's no 'is', there's only the *is* we speak. And when we speak it, that makes it real—for the person speaking, and for the person listening, at least for as long as he's listening. What do you call it? Taking a thought out of your head and putting it into someone else's? You do it when you speak. But you do it when you write as well. And if you're really really good at it, your *is* becomes the other person's *is*."

"And you're telling me this because—?"

"Because you asked me why I said your story—your fragment of a story—is naïve, and I said, 'Because it is.' And no, I don't mean like a subjective *is*. I mean it like an objective, can't be argued with, 'is.'"

"Okay. You say it's naïve. Can I ask why?"

Jacob nodded. "What do you know about vampires?"

"The same thing everybody knows. They're—"

"Right. You know nothing. Because until a vampire sits down and writes a memoir—a real vampire, a real memoir, not a work of fiction—you know nothing. No one knows anything. It's all make-believe."

"And you know better?"

"Do you?" Jacob's gaze is intense. He studies me. "Have you ever met a vampire? Has anyone?"

"They're fictitious creatures. That's why it's all make-believe."

"Ahh."

"So everybody creates their own *is*. About vampires, I mean."

Jacob nods agreement. "Now you're getting it. But—" He stabs the air with a forefinger. His eyes flash with a conspiratorial gleam. "What if there really were vampires? What if there really is something there—some condition that people have misunderstood for centuries?"

"Yeah, and what if there were no rhetorical questions?"

He ignores it. Properly so.

"Here's what's wrong with most vampire stories," Jacob says. "Most of the time, anyway. The writer isn't telling us about vampires. He's telling us what *he thinks* vampires might be. He's telling us what he believes, what he fears, what he wants. He—or she—hasn't really thought about the experience of being a vampire."

"And you have?"

"I'm not a writer. You are. What's interesting about your pages, your little fragment, is that you're trying to put yourself into the experience. Other writers—" He shrugs. "They're trying to redefine the experience in their own terms."

"Maybe I'm doing the same thing...?"

"Maybe. Maybe not. Walk it out and see. Tell me what you think a vampire is."

"Well, traditionally—"

"No, not traditionally. Realistically."

"Umm, okay." I lean back in my chair. Visions of Dracula dance in my head.

"Here's a clue. Think about the eco-system."

"Oh, well in that case." I lean forward again. "It's obvious. The vampire is the apex predator." Frowning, trying to remember all those Discovery channel documentaries. "That means you need at least, damn I don't remember, but its hundreds of herbivores, maybe thousands, just to maintain a healthy breeding population *and* support the carnivore families that feed on them. The size of the herbivore population determines how many carnivores can survive. But it's more than that, you need the carnivores to weed out the sick and elderly, the slow and feeble. The carnivores help keep the herbivore population healthy."

"Uh-huh." Jacob looked pleased. "You're on the right track. Forget vampires for a minute and think about eco-systems."

"Okay, I'm thinking."

"Who's the apex predator on Earth right now? I mean, without vampires."

"We are. Humans. We're eating the planet down to the bone. One day there won't be enough for everyone and we'll have riots, wars, and eventually a massive population crash."

"Unless—?"

"There is no unless."

"Yes, there is. Think about it."

"Oh, okay. Massive farms. Not the sprawling acreage, but city-farms. Big greenhouse things. Hydroponics. Meat-tanks. Stuff like that."

"Yeah, if humans get hungry enough, that's what they'll build. Because the market will make it profitable. And yes, you will get that hungry, so it's inevitable. What did you have for dinner?"

"A hamburger."

"Where did it come from?"

I laugh and point toward the kitchen.

"Before that—?"

"Probably that huge cattle feed lot up north—"

"Uh-huh. So now look at it from the point of view of the cow, they're in bovine paradise—they get to be part of a huge successful herd, tens of thousands of friends and companions, with lots and lots of good food for everybody to eat, they're encouraged to stuff themselves and be happy, and best of all, they don't have to worry about predators—wolves, coyotes, mountain lions, bears, or even bad weather. They have a nice warm barn in the evening, they get vaccinated against all kinds of diseases, and they get inspected regularly to keep them healthy. A very low-stress existence. Eat all you want and never have a stampede. From the cow's perspective it's a nice life."

"Until you're a hamburger."

Jacob smiles. "Well, yes. There is that—but the evidence of modern civilization is that most people have already made that trade."

"Really?"

"Really."

"So you're saying the human population is a giant feed lot, managed by vampires?"

He grins, a quick flash of his very white teeth. "Parts of it, yes. We still have a lot of wilderness left. For those who still like the hunt."

"Ha ha. Very funny. You're a vampire?"

"Oops. Did I say that out loud?" He laughs, too easy.

"Yeah, you did."

Jacob waves it away. "There's no such thing, remember?" Then, more seriously, "Don't panic. This is just a thought experiment. For your story."

I notice he dodged the denial.

I type something into the laptop. *Vampires. Apex predators. Feed lots.* Then back to him, "So, okay—if there are seven billion people on the planet—"

"Seven point five—"

"—then how many vampires will that support?"

Jacob leans back in his chair, steeples his fingers. "You're asking the wrong question. No. You're asking that question before you have all the information you need to answer it. First you have to establish the life cycle of the vampire."

"The life cycle?"

"The traditional idea—the Dracula fantasy—is that if you drink a vampire's blood, you become a vampire too. What does that suggest?"

"An infection."

"Obviously."

"So it's a disease—a disease of the blood."

"Uh-huh. And...?"

"If it's a disease, then it's not supernatural. It would have specific symptoms and conditions. And also...maybe it's curable. Stoker hinted that it was—with transfusions."

"Specific symptoms and conditions...?" Jacob looks at me expectantly. "Like for instance?"

"Um, okay. Well, anything that would help contribute to the mythology. The vampire mythos says that vampires have great strength. And we know that the human body is capable of impossible feats of strength. It's called hysterical strength—it happens with whacked out PCP-users—so that gives us some idea what the human body can do when it's pumped full of— well, whatever it takes to create that kind of enhanced ability. So, if I were speculating—oh, I am speculating—but I'd guess that the condition lets the patient trigger that kind of hysterical strength on demand. It wouldn't just be muscle strength, it would mean faster reflexes too. All kinds of physical abilities would be boosted—climbing, running, lifting, fighting, but probably not flying. That's too much a stretch."

"Not bad," Jacob nods. "Can you figure out the rest of it?"

"Well, sure. It's obvious—well, obvious to anyone who knows anything about physiology. That's a lot of work for a body to do. So any kind of super-strength has to use up a lot of energy—like a cheetah can only run so far before his body temperature rises dangerously, then he has to stop. So, I'd say that someone with the condition would have only short bursts of super-strength available, then he'd need to stop and recover, as if he'd been running a marathon. Ahh—that's it. Maybe super-strength uses up so much energy that the body needs a really huge amount of recovery. Maybe the person would have to go into some kind of deep dormancy so his body can rebuild its reserves of energy, a sleep so deep he can't be roused, at least not easily—it would look like death. So he'd need a very quiet, very safe place—a place where no one would find him and disturb him."

"Like a crypt?"

"I was thinking more like a dark basement. A bedchamber with heavy curtains. Okay, yes—a coffin would be ideal. Oh, wait—that suggests something else. If the vampire needs a very quiet resting place, then that might mean he has extremely heightened senses, to the point of sensory overload—I think it's called hyperesthesia. So he'd need a place that's very dark and very quiet. A coffin in a basement would be a good resting place."

I'm on fire with the idea. Jacob waits for me to continue.

"Y'know—that could explain Poe's story, 'The Fall Of the House Of Usher.' Both Madeline and Roderick are infected, only Madeline much more so. Roderick knows what's coming. He knows she's not dead, but he lies to the narrator and says that she is—he really does love his sister, that's why he wants her to die in her coffin because he wants to spare her the horror he believes must inevitably follow—"

"Nice," says Jacob.

"I don't know if Poe was aware of the vampire mythos. He never wrote a vampire story, did he?"

Jacob shakes his head. "Not that I know of."

"But he might have been aware of the symptoms. It would explain a lot. I know he had a fear of being buried alive. And madness—" I lean forward, frowning. Another thought.

"What—?"

"I'm thinking that...well, it makes sense to me...I mean, think about it. If the condition, whatever it is, creates enhanced strength, then it might also enhance the person's reflexes, so that means it affects the nervous system too. That could account for the hyperesthesia...."

"And...?"

"And that would probably, I mean I'm just guessing here, but I think it would probably trigger hallucinogenic episodes—I'd guess most often related to the bursts of super-strength, but maybe other times as well—like when the person gets hungry. I'd guess the condition would require a lot of energy to sustain itself, and that would probably mean incredible cravings. Let's say some kind of hunger-induced hallucinations. Maybe to a primitive mind that would seem otherworldly—maybe the hallucinations might show up as a hunger for blood. Or flesh. But like I said, I'm guessing now."

"Those are good guesses. They're consistent."

"With the facts?"

"With each other. Anything else?"

"Um. Well, if the person has hyperesthesia, that would show up as... um, a..."

"Yes...?"

"Severe allergy to sunlight—" I stop.

Jacob grins. Again with the teeth. I'm not sure I like that.

"Um."

Jacob reaches over and gently pushes my laptop shut. "Let's go for a walk," he says. "A nice walk in the dark." Seeing my expression, he adds, "Oh, don't be silly. I just had a steak sandwich and coffee. I'm good for now." He tosses some bills on the table, paying for both of us.

I slide the computer into my knapsack and follow him out to the parking lot, out past the light to the park beyond. Under the trees, where the night is even darker—here, there's only a trace of moonlight to hint at shape and form.

"Let's talk," he says.

"Isn't that what we've been doing?"

Jacob stops, turns and looks at me. "Mostly, you've been talking. Now, it's my turn." In the pale darkness, he seems to glow. "You're not the first to figure it out—that it's not a supernatural thing. Some of us are scientists. Some of us asked to be...*turned*. So they would have enough time. And so could study the condition from the inside."

"Is it curable?"

"You're assuming we might want that. I'm not sure that any of us do." Jacob explains, "Our research is secret. Our resources are necessarily limited. But...we're beginning to understand ourselves. And our condition.

"It's a parasitic symbiosis, an infectious mutation, a transformational phenomenon, none of that and all of that. Remember that movie? The one with the big green pods. You fell asleep for a while and then, when you woke up, you were *different*—it's like that. Only it isn't."

He sits down on the stone bench. "You did miss one thing, though. It does extend the lifespan. We're not immortal, but for all practical purposes, we might as well be. We age so slowly it's imperceptible."

"May I ask? How old are you?"

He pats the bench next to him. An invitation. I sit.

"I am very young," he says. "I was born in Seattle. In 1858. My mother died in childbirth. My father died at sea. He was a fisherman, his boat sank in a storm. I was an orphan at thirteen. I became a street rat, and a peg-boy—"

"I'm not familiar with the term—"

"Be grateful." He pauses.

◆ ◄═❖◆♦�‖♦◆❖═► ◆

I was...used by men. It kept me alive.

You might find this hard to believe, but many of them were kind—even tender. Later, when I grew older, the customers were rougher. So...I went into another line of work. One day—well, let's just say I wasn't as good at picking pockets as I thought I was. I chose the wrong target—or maybe the right target. I thought he was just another old man, a strange one because he moved so slowly, but—he could move a lot faster than me. Later on, I understood why, but the moment it happened, I was paralyzed. He had a grip like an iron bear-trap. But he wasn't angry. He was amused. He pulled me around in front of him and stared into my face and said, "I admire your courage."

I was too shocked to say anything. I didn't have to. He leaned down and whispered into my ear. "I will give you a choice. Would you like to share my dinner? Or *be* my dinner?"

I don't know how I knew, but—I knew he meant it, every word. Something in his voice, not the sound of it, but the way he said it. He had a very soft voice, almost womanly, very musical. I think that's why I went with him. His voice.

He took me to a place down by the wharf where the fishing boats came in. I hadn't been there since my father died, it wasn't that I was afraid of the place—I just associated it with bad luck. But that night—it was a different world, bright with gas lamps and cigars, painted whores and boisterous sailors. And us—tucked away in an upholstered retreat, on the second floor of an ancient but still expensive eatery at the shadowy end of the boardwalk. I had salmon and scallops and a big bowl of crab chowder, potatoes and beer and finished up with cake and coffee, more food in one place than I'd ever seen in my life.

He ate too, but not as much. Mostly, he watched me. I figured he'd probably want me to share his bed later. It wouldn't be the first time I'd been picked up on the street. It was a rougher life than sitting on a peg, but the pay was better. You didn't have to give half of it to the whoremaster. And I had already figured that if this man was as gentle as his voice, it wouldn't be so bad. You get pretty good at recognizing who's safe and who isn't—although sometimes they fool you. With Monsieur—that's what he told me to call him—I wasn't sure, but I belonged to him now, for as long as he wanted me. At least it would be a bed.

"And that was when he turned you?"

"Oh, hell no." Jacob laughs. "No. My...transformation came later, much later."

"I don't understand—"

"Of course you wouldn't. It's a trope that lazy writers use—that the people of the dark are so eager to recruit they have no sense of taste, pardon the pun. Maybe you don't give much consideration to your choice of meals—or life partners—but the men of The Community do. Especially where eternity is involved. There's patience, even wisdom. The careful distinctions of time and possibility. That's something else you haven't thought out. Once again, the mythology has obscured the reality."

I retreat to the safe question. "What am I missing?"

"Only the obvious. Probably because you're too young to see it. The same way I was. Stop and think what it means to have an extended life-span. You were smart enough to recognize the hallucinatory aspects of the condition—are you smart enough to realize the rest of it?

"What do you think the world looks like to someone who moves through it unchanging? Meanwhile, everything whirls around you, decade after decade—a century passes, another starts, and you're still young and vibrant, still hungry for experience. What do you do? Seek out endless pleasure? At first, maybe. But you have no idea how quickly that becomes boring, an endless merry-go-round of sensation. No thanks. Delight and wonder are spices that add flavor to life, they are not the stuff of life itself. A hard lesson for children to learn.

"No. Here's what you do instead. You read voraciously, you attend concerts and seminars, you explore the details of the city, you scour the libraries and museums, you attend courses at the university, you travel and observe, you seek out knowledge and understanding—and you seek out people of intelligence and insight. All those things for which you have no time—suddenly, you have all the time.

"Do you know why it's such a pity that human beings are so short-lived? It takes you too long to figure out how to live—and just about the time you do, you die. And all your preciously gained knowledge and experience dies with you. You can spend a lifetime becoming an expert in science or medicine, history or philosophy—and then, in the blink of an eye, you're gone, *it's* gone, all that learning disappears from the world. Lost forever.

"Do you want to know what the real hunger is? Not for blood—that's for beginners. No, the real hunger is knowledge. Experience. Insight. Enlightenment. Levels of understanding that surpass what's possible in a single lifetime—levels so far beyond simple mastery they have no name. That's the only real justification for...for this." He holds up his hands, pale in the moonlight. "Yes, I'm hungry. For the deeper sustenance of the soul. So, I ask you now—why would I, or anyone else so blessed, so cursed—why would any of us want to spend even the most fleeting of moments with an unfinished, inexperienced, incredibly naïve adolescent? A teenage girl or boy? Ignorant, uneducated, and mostly uninteresting. Why? Where's the attraction in that? Her beauty? At best, it would be a passing fancy, a casual engagement, a distraction, a diversion, a bit of novelty, a momentary confection. But a relationship? A life-partner? Please. Endless romance is an adolescent masturbation fantasy."

Jacob stops and takes a breath. He turns back to me, eyes hard. "Does it happen? Yes. Sometimes. And the results are usually horrific. Turning a child creates a monster. An adolescent—the condition affects their hormones—they get caught in uncontrollable lust, they have to create other monsters like themselves—for their blood-orgies. It's not romance, it's insanity. Those are the ones who end up with stakes through their hearts, with their heads cut off, buried at crossroads, burned alive—those are the ones who have created the mythos, the crazy ones."

He holds up his hands again. "Look. See the way I shine in the dark? Yes, we *do* glow." He laughs. "But it's the way we reflect light, that's all. I'll share a secret with you—it's not so secret anymore—but we're changing the narrative.

"It used to be, we wanted the world to dismiss the tales as ignorance and superstition. Unworthy of serious scientific inquiry. That worked, to a degree, it allowed us to stay safely undiscovered in the shadows, but it also made us objects of fear. Predators. Enemies.

"Not too long ago, a generation perhaps, you would not have accepted my invitation. You would not have walked into the darkness willingly with me. We would not have sat and talked. No, you would have retreated, repelled, horrified. You would have trapped yourself in your own fearful loneliness. And I—I also would have been alone. You would have learned nothing from me. I would have learned nothing from you. Both of us—we would have been denied the discovery of each other.

"Today, we are objects of sympathy, people are interested in us. People identify with us. People even care about us. A generation from now, maybe two, who knows? Perhaps we will someday have our own pride parade down Bourbon Street—at midnight, of course. It will be an interesting time. However...I do not see myself coming out of the coffin any time soon. Based on the hysteria of you short-timers, I think it likely I will be safer remaining in the shadows." Jacob falls silent, thinking about a future I will not live to see.

Finally, I ask, "So if Monsieur didn't want to turn you—?"

Jacob shakes his head and smiles, remembering.

Shall I describe him now? Yes, I will.

He was not what you would call tall. But he was a good height for the time. He had a stocky build, like one who had worked with his body for most of his life. But his skin was curiously pale and his hands had returned to the softness of an easier life.

His eyes were paradoxically both dark and gleaming at the same time. His features were even, neither coarse nor soft, neither rugged nor feminine, but with a hint of all those qualities, depending on the light as well as his expression.

Mostly, however, he seemed to have an undefinable attraction. The more he spoke, the more I wanted to listen to him. The more I looked into his face, the more I wanted to continue looking.

We talked. I should say that mostly I talked. He asked questions. I hadn't realized I'd been through so much, but he extracted my entire life story in a very short time. Even the worst parts. The parts I didn't want to discuss. But he had that power to draw it out.

Later, I realized Monsieur had been interviewing me, studying me. Finally, over cake and coffee, apparently satisfied, he offered me a job. Room and board and a few dollars a week. He needed someone to manage his house during the day. He said he could not bear the sunlight, so his waking and sleeping hours were inverted from those of other people.

He needed a daykeeper. Someone to manage the minutiae of the place while he retreated from the glaring eye of the sun. At first I suspected his intentions, who wouldn't? But winter was coming in hard and my resources were already meager. And Monsieur wasn't bad-looking, he was clean, and he seemed gentle enough. How could I not be tempted?

He reassured me at great length that his intentions were honorable. He simply needed someone to manage the housekeeping of the day, bring in the mail, accept deliveries from the local grocers, sign for occasional shipments, that kind of thing—and firmly turn away all morning and afternoon inquiries. "Do you have an appointment? No? Well, please leave your card. Monsieur will get back to you at his pleasure." Or, "Monsieur is resting now and cannot be disturbed. Please come back after sunset. Monsieur will see you then." I had to bathe every day, wear clean clothes, and never leave the house while the sun was up. At sunset, I would prepare the tea.

But that was only the easy part. There was another requirement as well. Every day I had to read a book from his library, any book I chose. He had an amazing collection of books, most of them shipped from New York and London. In the evening, he would come down from his chambers—I was forbidden to enter his rooms during the day—and we would sit together and we would discuss what I had read. If I hadn't kept up with my reading, if I hadn't paid close enough attention to manage a real discussion, he'd catch me out quickly.

The first time it happened, he made it clear that the reading was the most important part of my job. He wanted a companion worthy of his intelligence. Very gently, he asked me—if I didn't like reading, would I be happier returning to the street? Because if I wasn't going to read, if I wasn't going to hold up my end of the discussion in the evenings, why should he keep me around? I never skipped a day of reading after that. When he was satisfied that I had learned something from the book, we would go out to dinner. I knew he was trying to teach me, of course—but the other part of it was that he did not want to leave the house until after the evening bustle of the streets had subsided. But the sessions were useful. I began to sense that there were farther horizons in the world than I had ever considered before.

Later, after he was satisfied that I was capable of study, Monsieur arranged for tutors, all kinds. They taught me history and philosophy and the manners of a gentleman. He bought me clothes to match my new demeanor. I learned to speak French, play the piano, and even studied a bit of medicine as well.

It was a grand time, it was the grand fruition of the enlightenment— the world was changing, recognizing the advancements of science and industry. It was ironic as well—because this great enlightenment had also encouraged the people of the dark to turn their attentions inward and begin studying themselves. Ourselves. That was when a few brave souls even made themselves known to certain men of medicine. It was foolish and courageous, but necessary. But—I digress.

Monsieur was grooming me, first to be his keeper, later his companion. But for most of that time, I think I was merely his...his pet. His guard dog of the moment. I don't think he had any plans to turn me at the beginning. Later on, I was an interesting experiment. Could a daykeeper be brought up?

From time to time, Monsieur would entertain visitors, gentlemen like himself. I would lay out meats and cheeses, wine glasses and decanters of port or sherry, most of which they would leave untouched. Sometimes they would allow me to stay in the room and listen to their conversations, but I didn't enjoy that much. The way they treated me, it felt like they were patronizing me, as if I were a child—or worse, some kind of marvelously well-trained animal, a specimen for their amusement.

I recall one of these gentlemen remarking that it was both dangerous and foolish for Monsieur to trust me so implicitly. Another agreed, but said he could understand the attraction. Often, they spoke about me as if I was an object of some kind, something without comprehension or feelings—as if I were not even in the room.

Later, after they left, usually in the last thoughtful hours before dawn, Monsieur would excuse their unconscious rudeness, explaining that they had come from different times and different places, and did not yet understand the new world as well as he did.

From time to time, we would visit the homes of one or another of these same gentlemen. It made me realize that Monsieur was an exception to the rule. Some of their apartments were dark and curiously bare of the details of daily existence, the rooms maintained solely as an illusion of mundanity. Some of the men shared accommodations and their homes were meticulously immaculate. This latter observation was my first clue to the heightened sense of smell that all of these individuals enjoyed—or suffered from. You cannot imagine how badly a city can smell if it is not well-tended. Two or three of Monsieur's acquaintances had housemen of their own, mostly to manage the same chores I had. One looked at me skeptically, as if he disapproved of my existence. Another gave me a conspiratorial wink, as if we both shared the same secret—but a secret I did not yet know.

For the most part, however, Monsieur and I lived a life apart from that particular social circle. While he never specifically said so, it did seem to me that he took little pleasure in those occasional gatherings, attending more of necessity than affection. I did not know then what they discussed in private, but it was quickly evident that these gentlemen also shared the same disability as Monsieur. Later, when I was allowed to attend myself, as the newest member of the club, so to speak, I quickly understood his disaffection. But I also found it a useful colloquium, a seminar of mutual purpose, a school for survival in a world of massive disagreement. But at the time, I knew nothing of this. Only later.

At least once a month, usually in the darkest part of the lunar cycle, Monsieur's behavior would become unpredictable. For several evenings in a row, as the hours lengthened toward midnight, he would become restless. He'd start to pace, he'd become irritable and unapproachable. I learned to recognize the signs and remain as unobtrusive as possible.

Finally, almost in anger, he would reach for his great dark coat and walking stick. At first I'd offer to accompany him, insisting that it wasn't safe for anyone of wealth to be out and alone in the city, especially not this late at night, but Monsieur always dismissed my concerns, similarly rejecting my offer to join him, saying that he said he needed to take the night air alone. He bade me stay in my room, get a good night's rest, and not to worry, no harm could ever come to him. I couldn't help but notice the strange way he phrased that. No harm *could* ever come to him. Not *would*, but *could*.

Sometimes I would wait up for him—usually to his great annoyance.

Sometimes he came home disheveled. Once his clothes were viciously torn, and I thought I saw blood on his shirt, but he waved me away, saying it was nothing for me to concern myself with, as he stumbled up to his room.

On other evenings, when we stayed home together, he often displayed a curious tenderness. Sometimes he would visit me in the bath, often bathing me like a father with his only child. His touch was affectionate, never untoward, but he seemed fascinated with the appearance of my flesh, openly admiring the rosy color of my skin, made even more red by the heat of the bath water—though I had become much paler now for spending so much time indoors. It was a curious behavior on his part, yes, but I'd experienced much worse at the hands of lesser men, and after a while I came to enjoy his attentions as a sign of his affection.

I had been with Monsieur for almost three years, and I was beginning to feel safe, even comfortable, perhaps for the first time in my life—but I had also begun to experience a growing unease. I was feeling incomplete, if that is even the right word. Perhaps it was an emotion without a name.

Monsieur must have sensed my disquiet for he asked me one night what troubled me. It was a cold rainy night, we were sitting in front of the fire, and I felt bold enough to ask Monsieur why he had brought me into his house if he found me so unattractive. He looked astonished and asked me what I meant by such a question. I told him that he had never once placed a hand on me, never once invited me to share his bed, never once even asked me to remove my shirt. The only time he expressed any interest at all in my nakedness was when he visited me in the bath.

It puzzled me greatly. I had initially thought that he had chosen me because he recognized my nature—but now I had no idea why he had taken me into his household, I could only assume that whatever interest he might once have had, must have long since faded, or perhaps even worse, perhaps he now found my nature somehow embarrassing or even abhorrent. He would not be the first to feel that way. Prior to my engagement with Monsieur, I had met and serviced gentlemen who sought out the pleasures of boys or other men, but pretended to the more typical interest in female bodies—

I did not get to finish. Monsieur interrupted me with that great gentle laugh of his. He reached over and placed his hand on my arm and reassured me that no, that was not the case. First, he told me not to be ashamed of my nature. Many men prefer the company of other men, women hold no attraction for them. He gave me the key to the locked bookcase and told me that I should read some of the histories of ancient Greece and Rome. And medieval Japan as well. He said that as I read more, I would learn that I was in august company. I shared the same nature as Plato and Socrates, Michelangelo and Leonardo. Great thinkers, magnificent artists. I should be proud of that shared spirit.

So why then did Monsieur not caress me or fondle me? Did he not share my nature? Did he not appreciate it? Again, he laughed. "Dearest boy," he said, "I find you painfully attractive. There is nothing I would like more than to lie in your arms and enjoy the sweetness of your kiss. But I must not. It would not be fair to you."

"Not fair? Please, Monsieur," I begged. "I would be your willing servant in all things. Even in your bed."

"And I would have you be just that, if I could," he said. "But I dare not. For if I were to be so foolish, I would do you irreparable harm. And I care about you too much to cause you that kind of grief. Trust me, Jacob."

I fell to my knees before him, sobbing. I buried my head in his lap and cried at great length. Monsieur said nothing. He merely sat and stroked my hair, it fell down past my shoulders, I'd never had a haircut, he'd never allowed me to. He just stroked my hair and waited until my grief subsided. Finally, I looked up at him, met his dispassionate gaze, and begged him as if I were begging for my life, perhaps I was and didn't know it, but I was overwhelmed with emotion, I felt as if I might go mad if he wouldn't tell me the truth of why we couldn't consummate our passion, why we had to impose such impossible restraints on ourselves. If I surprised Monsieur with my desperate outburst, I surprised myself even more. I had never felt such desire for another person in my entire life.

⊶ ⊷

Jacob interrupts himself. "Oh, yes—that's something else you missed— the attraction."

"Huh?" I had been so caught up in his narrative, it was almost a shock to return to the present.

"The monthly excursions—you know what those were for, of course. No, we don't have to feed every night, we don't have to feed at all, but we do have a lunar cycle of our own, and in those days—before anti-depressants and mood-altering substances, we were often caught up in our own hormonal storms. Our own bipolar madness. That part has never made it into popular lore, has it? Of course not, real biology complicates things. The facts get in the way of masturbation fantasies, eh?

"But that's key to understanding the *other* thing—our unnatural pheromones. Yes, we have pheromones. It's part of the condition. And they're strongest at those times of the month when we're hungriest. It's a chemical lure that serves to overwhelm any fear you might experience. You experience it as irresistible attraction. Male or female. The more you are exposed to one of us, the more you are—oh, what's a good word here— enchanted? Fascinated? Enthralled? Captivated? *Held*. From the predator's point of view, it's a very useful adaptation. Wouldn't you agree?"

Jacob smiles. He shows his teeth. The chill of panic starts in my groin and spreads outward, rising like a wave, up through my belly and my chest, expanding outward in a rush, but almost immediately it turns into a surge of heat—or something—all the way up through my throat and finally to my eyes. I wipe the moisture off my cheeks.

Jacob reaches over with his incredibly well-manicured nail and touches the top button on my shirt. Without a word, I fumble it open. I'm ready to undo the next one, when Jacob leans back, smiling but wagging his finger at me as well. "See, what I mean?"

I swallow hard. Regret as much as relief.

Jacob gives me a look—is it pity? "That's just the barest intimation of what I was feeling for Monsieur."

Monsieur must have been moved by my tears, because he said, "Jacob, my son—yes, that is how I regard you—as the son I wished I could have had. You have given me more happiness than I ever believed I was capable of. I have trusted you with my well-being for almost three years now, a blink of an eye for me, half a lifetime for you. It is time for you to know just how much I trust you.

"'You know that I cannot abide bright lights of any kind. It is why I must avoid the daylight. It is a condition of the blood. There are other disabilities as well, far more severe, and I shall discuss those with you as it becomes necessary. But for the moment, dearest boy, please understand that my candor on this matter is a gift of enormous trust—were I to succumb to my attraction for you, were we to consummate our passion, you would very likely be exposed to suffer the same disabilities in time. I simply cannot risk that. I dare not pass this condition onto your shoulders. Not at this stage of your life. At least...not yet. As much as you have begged me for physical attention, I must with even more intensity beg you to resist—resist with all your heart and soul, as if your very life depends on it, because it does. My denial is not a rejection of your spirit, dearest Jacob, but an affirmation of it.'"

Of course, his words only increased my distress. I was heartbroken—now that I had spoken my affection and Monsieur had spoken his as well, now that I knew the depth of his feelings, the situation was even more untenable.

I was caught up in his pheromones, of course. But Monsieur understood all too well why he dared not expose me. At that stage of my life, still barely a teenager, I would have become a monster stuck in a post-adolescent hormonal storm, a captive of my own relentless lust. I would have created monsters around me.

Such an event was not unknown to The Community—that regular gathering of Monsieur's associates—in the past, the community had acted immediately to destroy any such monsters that might have been inadvertently created, quickly before such a plague could flame out of control.

But Monsieur had not yet shared any of that with me. Perhaps he thought I would imagine him insane and go to the authorities. Perhaps he feared it would destroy my affection for him. Instead, he simply assured me that it was for my own good that we not share a bed. Despite my hormone-driven pleas, he insisted. I even told him that I would not mind sharing his disability, but—he argued just as fervently—who could we trust to protect the house and the both of us during the day?

It has been repeated so many times and in so many places that knowledge is power, that most people believe the statement without ever questioning it. But my experience demonstrated to me that it couldn't possibly be true. Not always. Certainly not here.

Some knowledge drains you of power, leaves you feeling empty and helpless. Staying in the same house with Monsieur became intolerable—I spent long hours in distress, my mind churning, even to the point of considering that if I wanted to preserve what was left of my sanity, I should leave his house forever.

Monsieur could not have been unaware of my anguish. He was suffering considerable misery of his own. Night after night, he went out into the darkness, staying out till the first rays of dawn, often returning as feverish and wild-eyed as an escapee from an asylum. I had never seen him so crazed. When I asked him if there was anything I could do, he only glared at me—I cried out in alarm, he must have misunderstood, for he flung me back against the wall in anger or some other unidentifiable emotion—but he gave me a look of such rage I did not dare to speak.

The next evening, as soon as the last rays of the sun disappeared from the drawing room, he came rushing downstairs, wearing only his dressing gown, disheveled and grief-stricken. He clasped both my hands in his and begged my forgiveness for his fury of the previous night. He had no excuse, he said, only that sometimes his condition, as he called it, sometimes drove him into fits of madness, an uncontrollable lunacy. He believed he had been managing it well, but obviously he had become over-confident—last night had shown that he had not maintained himself as well as he had hoped. He was so terribly terribly sorry that I had suffered the brunt of his fury that I felt his anguish as my own.

Of course, I forgave him. How could I not? But as we sat there together, alternately apologizing and forgiving each other, it was clear that we were both struggling with the situation. We whirled about a common center of turmoil—the same way the Earth and moon rotate around a common center of gravity. But because the Earth has much greater mass, that center of gravity is actually located a thousand miles deep within the surface of the planet, so while the moon swings around this world, the combined center of gravity follows it, rotating around inside the planet's core, relentlessly stirring the mantle—and so, the Earth wobbles in its orbit.

That was the effect I had on Monsieur, disturbing him in his own eternal course. Like the moon, I circled him, always keeping the same face to his ever-changing moods, my presence pulling him first in one direction, then another. Around and around we circled, a strange and terrible dance in darkness.

Finally, one late night, as I rested sad and alone in my bath—even after the water had lost all warmth, I felt no urge to withdraw—I realized that Monsieur had done me no favors. All the tutors, all the lessons, had produced only one terrible result—I had grown educated enough to experience true despair. I knew too much of life, too much of the world, to accept anything less than all of it—and all of it was what I could not have.

As I lay there, lost in the slow dissolution of my soul, my head devoid of purpose, my mind wandered into territories I thought I had left behind.

Suspicion overwhelmed my soul. I began to wonder on Monsieur's intentions when he left on his solitary walks. Unaware of his true nocturnal purposes, I could only imagine him tangled in the arms of some other boy, perhaps one of the familiar boys of the streets. I still saw them from time to time, whenever Monsieur and I still went out together. Monsieur must have noticed them as well with his extraordinary awareness, but even to an ordinary mortal the boys of the street were unavoidable—they postured languidly against a lamp post here or the corner of a building there, not-so-discreetly advertising their availability.

Show a bit of calf, bare a sleeveless arm, it was enough—the nocturnal dances were a healthy business in those days, albeit short-lived. If a boy had looks, if he was wise enough to avoid the ravages of disease, he could survive a while, until he finally grew strong enough to find a place on a fishing boat or cargo vessel or some other useful trade. In that business, a young man's attractiveness would dissipate all too quickly. Escape was always a desperate avenue.

I'm sure the boys must have noticed us as well. Those few who might have remembered me from my days among them must have assumed that I was now serving only a single wealthy patron as a kept boy, but I had no desire to explain or justify my situation to anyone, so I ignored them. But as I said, they could not have escaped the notice of Monsieur.

But when I examined my jealous thoughts, holding them up to the cold light of logic, I fell into a most curious argument with myself. If Monsieur would not want to risk passing his condition onto me, then surely he wouldn't want to expose any of the boys on the street—but if he had no affection for those fellows, why would he care if they were exposed or not? And if he wasn't out there looking for a bit of horizontal refreshment, then what was he looking for? I did not know about the possible creation of monsters at the time, or I would have been reassured that he was not soliciting the custom of the street.

* + ⊹⊱⊰◦➤◯◐◯◦⊱⊰⊹ + *

Once again, Jacob interrupts his narrative, giving me a sly smile.

"Yes, now I know what Monsieur was doing. He was feeding. Unable to satisfy his sexual appetites, his blood-lust had surged. Flared. Fortunately, Seattle was a rough seaport then. It still is. Dead bodies were not uncommon. But…Monsieur was not sloppy. He did not need the city plunged into the same kind of panic that later paralyzed London when Jack the Ripper roamed free. I'm sure he feasted well. I am equally sure they never found the bodies—"

On that particular night, as the stillness stretched into the last hours before dawn, as I lay cold in my bath, waiting for I don't know what—perhaps even death would not have been unwelcome—finally I heard the sound of the front door and footsteps on the stair. I recognized the gentility of his step, Monsieur had returned.

It was his custom to check to see if I was awake. Sometimes we would share a bit of bread and sausage, cheese and wine before he retired. This night, not finding me in my bed, he came to the bathroom next. Finding me unexpectedly in the tub, he became alarmed. He put a hand into the water and withdrew it quickly, startled. "My God, it's colder than me. How long have you been lying here?"

I said, "I don't know. Forever, I think."

My reply further alarmed him—as it revealed my disassociated state of mind. Without regard for my nakedness, Monsieur pulled me to my feet, lifted me from the tub, and wrapped a heavy towel around me. He grabbed another and toweled my hair, my neck, my shoulders, my arms and back and chest, lower down as well.

When he was finally satisfied that I was dry, he put me into his own dressing gown. He scooped me up in his arms—I'd known he was strong, I hadn't known he was that strong—and carried me to my bed. Once he had settled me among the pillows, he looked at me very sternly. "We cannot continue like this, Jacob, can we?" No, we cannot, I agreed.

He sat down on the edge of the bed, I remember every detail of the moment, how the mattress creaked, how it gave beneath his weight, how I felt myself pulled toward him. He looked away from me then, studied the wainscoting of the wall, looked beyond it as if he was seeing something a thousand miles away.

In the silence that followed, a flurry of emotions swept through me. I felt cautious and skeptical, hopeful and afraid—because even as I feared what he might say next, I hoped for the strength of his wisdom.

And yet, at the same time—I was also beginning to fear Monsieur. Despite his own erratic behaviors, more so now than ever, I still believed in him. But I did not trust his friends. I didn't like the hungry way that some of them looked at me. And if these strange men were his friends, then what did that say about Monsieur? We are known by our friends, are we not?

Finally, Monsieur turned back to face me, with such an expression of sadness on his face that I immediately wanted to pull him to me, but I had long since learned not to engage in such open and enthusiastic expressions of affection, he always pulled back alarmed. But tonight, he surprised me. He reached out and took my hands, holding them gently between both of his. "Let me ask you this, dear Jacob. Have you given any thought to your future?"

I didn't answer his question, I couldn't—because the future had been all that I had been thinking about. That black unknown tomorrow I had been fearing for so long had pushed me beyond anguish into despair. I had come to the terrifying conclusion that I would have to finally leave this house. Although I had experienced so much comfort and wonder here when I was younger, now there was only distress. The tension between us had become unbearable. But I couldn't tell him the truth. I couldn't speak at all. Instead, the tears rolled down my cheeks unabated.

I'm certain Monsieur must have known my thoughts. If ever it was possible for one person to read another's thoughts, Monsieur must have known mine as clearly as if they were engraved in fire. My feelings were loudly betrayed in the pageant of my expressions.

"Dearest Jacob," he began, "You cannot have missed the confusion and disarray I have been experiencing in my own thoughts. I have been considering this problem at some length. And—" He stopped himself. The words were painful, even for him. "I have no choice, in this. It is for both our sakes. No stop, don't speak—"

He put a finger across my lips to keep me from protesting. "Please, Jacob. Let me finish."

I bowed my head in submission. One of the lessons Monsieur had been trying so hard to teach me was that of thought before speaking. Too often, he said, we open our mouths and release the words that are floating at the very surface of our feelings. We would be better served to hold our tongues and consider our words before we released them. We might then make wiser choices. His point was that we must never speak from our emotions, because such outbursts were never rational and rarely wise to speak aloud. This was one of those moments—my protests would have been from my heart, not my brain, even though my brain had already reached the same inevitable conclusion. But I felt I had to protest anyway—because I feared the words that would certainly follow. Monsieur speaking them aloud would give finality to the decision. I wasn't prepared for that. Not yet.

Monsieur waited until I regained some small composure. "Jacob, do not pretend with me. You understand as well as I. We cannot be together anymore. I must send you away from here—before we destroy each other.

"Stop now. Stop and listen. Please, Jacob. I need you to understand something. All this time, all these years—these three short years, watching you grow toward manhood, watching you discover the vast horizons of the world around you, it was a revelation to me. It was something I never expected to have, because of my condition—the opportunity to nurture a child and see him become a worthwhile adult. Do you think I am without feelings? Do you think I want to send you away?"

I didn't answer. I couldn't. He spoke the truth. I hadn't thought about his feelings at all, only my own.

"Remember how I caught you? Did you ever think how easy it was for me? You thought you were stalking me? On the contrary. I saw you studying me even before you knew what you intended. I watched you with some amusement. Your oh so casual approach, your studied nonchalance. You were a terrible thief, Jacob. It's a good thing you did not pursue that career or you would have spent much of the last three years behind bars."

I started to protest. "That's not true. I was—"

"—clumsy. And slow. Inept." Monsieur finished the sentence for me, leaving no room for argument. He stared into my face. "I saved your life. That wasn't my immediate intention, but I admit that I was charmed by your ambition—and yes, amused by you as well. I watched you follow me from a distance and I wondered if that single-minded determination might be put to some practical use? I suspected you might have a heart of some value. Yes, Jacob, you were an experiment—at first. I was curious what you might become if you were nurtured. Later—I realized you were something more. Much more. My mistake. Had I realized the journey we would find ourselves embarked upon, had I realized the inevitability of this moment, my rational self would have—would have taken the easier course."

He fell silent a moment, looked away, looked back. "There were opportunities along the way. Many. And I will admit, there were moments when I argued with myself—what am I doing? Why am I letting myself care? My companions in The Community—they made eloquent arguments against you, that you represented an unprecedented danger to myself, first one kind of danger, then another. Not just betrayal, but worse.

"I didn't listen. I thought I knew better. And I believed that if you ever betrayed my trust, I would be able to deal with that situation swiftly and dispassionately. You would have simply disappeared. This is Seattle. No one wonders, no one worries if a street boy vanishes. It happens every day. But—

His expression softened as he remembered. "But you never gave me cause. You surprised me, Jacob. More than that. You have shown yourself to be a rare and precious delicacy. I am as proud of you as if I had given birth to you myself.

"You will recall that last month I had my attorney visit. You were not party to that meeting, but I gave him very specific instructions for your future. One of the things I instructed him to do was redraw my will. No, Jacob, don't panic. I am in no danger of death—certainly not any time soon, and probably not for a much longer time than either of us can imagine. But accidents do happen and I wish to have you provided for in such a case. Should anything untoward happen to me, you will inherit this house and the contents of my various bank accounts. But I promise you that is extremely unlikely. It turns out that my disability, my condition, also makes me very hard to kill. Not impossible, just difficult.

"'But that is not what I need to discuss with you tonight. I have given great thought to our situation and I have come to a decision. It is the right decision. It will be the best thing for both of us. It will not be easy at first, not for you, not for me, but it will be necessary.

"It is time for you to attend the university.

"My attorney has made arrangements with his associates in Boston. They will arrange rooms for you near the university, they will manage an endowment that I will provide so that you will have a dependable income. You will not want for the necessities of life. You will have cash in your pocket, enough so that you can enjoy comfortable meals and wear fashionable suits and present yourself as a fine gentleman wherever you go. You will have a line of credit at the largest bookstore in the city. And your tuition at the university will also be guaranteed for as long as you choose to attend. You will have letters of reference from all of your tutors, so the question of your admission will not be an issue.

"There are no conditions to this endowment. You may take it or leave it, as you choose. No, wait—do not answer yet. I said there are no conditions. But I do have a request. Several requests.

"First, I request that you avoid any actions or behaviors that would bring you to the attention of the police. You must not allow yourself to be tempted to return to your childish habits. I doubt that you will, but I would be terribly disappointed if you did.

"Second, I request that you keep yourself free of disease. You know the ones I mean. I cannot forbid you to enjoy the pleasures of physical intimacy. That would be cruel and inhumane. I ask only that you choose your partners wisely. If you find a partner worthy of your most supreme affections, you will have my blessing. You deserve a lifetime of happiness, it is such a rare commodity. No, Jacob, please let me finish, I know what you're going to say, it is not necessary, and I do not want you bound by an impossible promise, it would only make you unhappy and resentful—

"Third, and this is the most important of my requests—I request that you study ferociously at the university, whatever interests you the most. Philosophy, history, science, economics, medicine, law—any or all of those things would please me. But not religion. There is no profit in that. It is an intellectual dead-end. But study anything else, everything else, and study it with enthusiasm and passion. Make yourself knowledgeable. Make yourself wise. Make yourself an expert in many things that will give you the power to manipulate the circumstances of the world.

"My fourth request is that you write to me regularly—but no more than once a month. I do not want you to feel beholden, and as you know, I am not one for letters, but I would like to keep apprised of your progress in your studies and your observations of the lives around you. From time to time, I may offer my own advice and suggestions to you. You may heed my words or discard them as you wish.

"And that brings me to my fifth request. I request that you stay away from this house and my acquaintance for at least ten years. You may not return before your twenty-seventh birthday. You may return at any time after that—but only if you have not found a permanent partner to share your life. Because under such a circumstance, a return visit would be disruptive to everyone involved.

"If I am not here in this house, and I do not think I will be, despite the many pleasant hours we have shared, I will not be hard to find. My representatives will have a sealed envelope for you, with information how to locate me if and when I move on. It is very likely that I will. With my... condition, I often find it necessary to relocate at least once every decade."

When he finished, I did not speak for a very long time. There was too much to assimilate. Finally, I said, "I will go. I will obey all your conditions—"

"Not conditions. Requests."

"But—"

He touched my cheek. "What is it, Jacob?"

"May I make a request as well?"

He nodded.

"I request that—no, that is not fair. Never mind." I waved it away as if I had not spoken.

Monsieur smiled. "I know what you were going to ask. You were going to ask me not to bring another boy into this house, not to replace you with another. And I know why you stopped yourself as well—because you realized that would have been an unfair thing to ask.

"You don't have to worry, Jacob. It's not in my nature to bring boys into my house, one after the other, and then fall in love with them—and then send them off to university. You have been...a unique adventure. I do not think my heart could stand another such."

I nodded and smiled, feeling better already that he understood me so well. A thought occurred to me. "But Monsieur—without me here, who will take care of you?"

He shook his head. "You needn't worry about that either. The gentlemen of The Community are not without resources. We have acquired a small team of trusted associates who understand us and who tend to our specific daytime needs. I shall arrange matters with them. If necessary, I can close up this house and stay at—well, never mind, you don't need to know about that now. I will be all right."

A week later, I boarded a ship for San Francisco. From there, I traveled east on the newly-completed transcontinental railroad to New York, an amazing city—so amazing I was tempted to abandon my journey to Boston and stay there instead. But after seeing the condition of the young men strolling the streets, I knew I should not succumb to that idea. I headed north and a few days later, completed my enrollment in the university.

Jacob stops talking. Lost in thought, perhaps, remembering a world that no longer exists in memory and barely exists in photographs.

"I think I understand—"

"Yes. He was waiting for me to ripen. He was waiting for me to become a worthy companion. He could have had me any time, but he loved me too much for that. Instead, he wanted me to earn my immortality. He wanted me to become a true partner—interesting enough to justify a life together. That the two of us would always have a wealth of experience and knowledge to share.

"But more than that, he wanted—perhaps even needed—a companion with proficiency. The world was changing faster than The Community could keep up. Monsieur recognized that. Staying current with science and medicine and economics is a necessary survival skill for an immortal. And style as well—think about it. Being out of fashion is dangerous. It makes you conspicuous."

"Ahh." A glance at my watch. "Dawn is coming."

"I know. I can already smell the changes in the air."

"I want to hear the rest of your story."

"Yes, of course you do. You want me to tell you how his letters suddenly ceased, and how I came back to Seattle to discover he had died in a fire—a daytime arson. You want to know about my inheritance and how I found The Community again, and how I finally did get turned, and who the arsonists were and what happened to them afterward, and why I had to leave Seattle.

"And after that, you'll want to hear about my experiences in Europe during The Great War. For a person like myself, a war can be great fun. Ahh, but most of all, you'll want to know what it's like to kill and feed. And you want to know how I choose my...victims. Yes, I suppose that's an accurate word."

Jacob touches my arm. I do not recoil. I do not pull back.

"I'm only immortal. I'm not immoral. I don't feed on innocents. Neither do most of the other gentlemen of The Community. Here's a clue. Have you noticed something about this part of the world? Have you noticed there has been a significant decline in violent crimes? Think about that and wonder."

"One more thing," he says. "A secret—about the monsters, why they happen. Young blood tastes better. More than that, the younger the blood, the more alive it makes us, the more it keeps us useful. So yes, that was the initial attraction of Monsieur. He saw me as a puppy, a tasty snack. And yes—that also explains why so many of the monsters are so quick to create more. They can't help themselves—they don't know the difference between feeding and fucking. And that, my friend, is why the rest of us must work so hard to keep them from happening and kill them when they do." He flashes his teeth. "And they taste good too."

A nervous laugh. And then I realize he isn't joking.

"Oh."

"Yes," he says. "Now you know what's wrong with your stories. All of you."

He stands. I stand quickly to keep up.

"Will I see you again?"

"I don't know. Will you?"

"I, uh—"

He cocks his head curiously. "You what?" Before I can answer, he waves the question away. "Never mind. I know what you were going to ask. You always do, all of you. The answer is no. Not today. And maybe never. Today was just...an interview."

"Maybe never?"

"Maybe—and maybe someday, I'll check back."

"You'll check back?"

"Of course. Right now, I'm just waiting to see how the fruit ripens."

And then, he's gone, disappearing into the last of the darkness, as if he's made of shadow himself.

I expect someday to see Jacob again. I wonder what he'll offer. I wonder if I'll accept.

I toss the pages across the table at the others. "And that, my dear little puppies—*that* is how you tell a vampire story."

Jacob in Boston

The next one steps up, tossing a program book on the table between us. "Make it out to Mike," he says. "Mike with a Y."

"Myke, right." I look up. He's a hulking shape. Part of the cape-and-pimple brigade. Yeah, I know that's judgmental, so what? I didn't hold him down and stuff all those French fries in his mouth. I scrawl, "*To Myke. Beast wishes*," and sign my name.

"I read your story," he says. "It was terrible. You got vampires all wrong."

"Ahh," I nod and smile—my number-three plastic smile. "Thank you for sharing that."

He looks confused for a moment. He was probably expecting an argument. I never argue with fans. I just keep smiling and reply with something like, "Why don't you write your story and show me how it should be done," but this time, we don't even get that far.

Instead, he says, "I read a lot. I read everything. You're not very good."

"Ahh. Well, I'll keep it a secret if you will. I wouldn't want to embarrass my publisher. He'll take it personally."

Frowning, Myke shakes his head. "You're a jerk." He picks up his program book and wanders off to annoy the author next to me, a charming woman who dresses all in black—with red piping. She wears purple and glitter eye-shadow and tells each fan what she sees in his or her aura.

The tables are lined up against the wall and all the authors are sitting in a long row. There's no escape. I don't know why I'm here. I've only sold seven stories, four still haven't been printed, and most of the fans at this convention don't even recognize my name.

I have been told that it is part of the job to establish a presence. If you want to be a successful author, you have to establish a brand identity. You have to build a community around your work. That's the core of your wider audience.

Right now, I'm a community of one.

Two more fans listlessly shove their program books at me. The next few just walk by. I pull out my phone and look at the time. The dark lady next to me puts her hand on my forearm. "Don't do that," she whispers. "It's rude to the fans."

"Oh, yes. Thank you. I wouldn't want to be rude to the fans." I push my phone back into my pocket. Only a few minutes more anyway.

And then I see him—

To no one in particular, "I think I'm done here."

I gather up my pens and the name-card the convention provided. I grab my bag, hoisting it over my shoulder.

He's standing silently in the shadows of the alcove leading to the restrooms, a hint of amusement in his eyes as I approach, but he greets me with a knowing nod and a smile.

"It's been a while. I wrote your story. I didn't think you'd mind."

"I expected you would. Why do you think I told you?"

"Because you were annoyed with all the ignorance—?"

"No."

"Oh?"

"Because I wanted to see if you could understand."

"And—?"

"I'm here, aren't I? I read your story."

A quick glance around the convention hall, the giant room is emptying out. "Do you have time to talk? Have you eaten? We could get a bite—" And then I realize what I've said. "Sorry, that was dumb—"

He holds up a pale hand to stop me from saying anything else. "I can eat. I can drink too. I know a pub. Are you through here?"

"Oh, yeah. I'm through. I don't even know why I came—" I look to him. "Why did you?"

He puts a hand on my upper arm and guides me through the last few stragglers. "Same reason as you," he says softly. "Fresh blood."

"Huh?" I stop and stare at him, pulling away from his touch.

"You. You're fresh blood in this genre," he explains. "They don't know it yet, but you're what they're hungry for." He adds, "Me too. You're what I'm hungry for."

"Jacob—!"

He laughs softly and takes my arm again, affectionately. He leans in and whispers, "No. Not that. I'm hungry for someone who understands. If *that* was all I wanted, I'd have already taken it."

. ﬩ ⬥◆▷◗◆◖◁◆⬥ ﬩ ﹒ ───

In the dark of the pub, Jacob studies me. He sniffs the wine in his glass, then sips it slowly. "Pleasant enough," he admits.

"Your senses are unnaturally heightened?"

"It's part of being a predator. The apex predator."

"Is that how you see yourself?"

"That's how I am. But that's not all I am."

We sit in silence while I consider that.

"Go ahead. What is it you want to ask?"

"You never finished telling me your story. You said you came back to Seattle. You found that Monsieur was gone, his house burned down—"

"The whole block. Almost nothing left standing. Even a month later, the whole area still reeked of smoke and ash."

"I'm sorry. That must have hurt."

"Yes. More than you can understand."

"I think I can guess." He waits for me to speculate. "You said you were an orphan at thirteen. So he was a father to you. And a teacher. A mentor...."

"Go on. What else?"

"Um. A lover?"

Jacob snorts. "Humans. You think everything is about sex. And if that's not enough, you pour romanticism over it like ketchup—" He holds up a hand to stop my objection. "You do. You can't help it. The sexual act is a surrender to the physical nature of your body. You become an animal, frenziedly mating, humping and bumping and pumping at each other, as if you're desperately trying to shut up all the voices yammering in your heads—and then, when you're done, when you've finally achieved a few brief seconds of deafening bliss, you collapse exhausted on top of each other, trying to catch not only your breath, but consciousness as well—what you think is consciousness, the illusion of your self, and that's the sadness you feel, that you have to be human again, instead of the honest animal you were while you were thumping. And then—right there, that's the moment of guilt, maybe not guilt, maybe that's the wrong word, maybe there's no right word for the emotion—the despair of having to abandon the reality of what you just experienced so you can come back to the artificial world of words and manners and rules. All the constructions that keep us from being what we really are. Animals." His words bite, but he doesn't smile. He's sincere. "So you pour your emotional syrup over the whole affair to justify it.

"And you don't?"

"You have no idea what's possible."

"Are you saying there's no such thing as love?"

"Of course not. I'm saying that you don't know what it is. Because most of you die before you can discover it. Most of you are addicted to the illusion of it."

"Are all of you that cynical? Or just you?"

"I'm not being cynical. I'm telling you what I know."

"Oh." I consider it. "You and Monsieur—?"

Jacob's expression flickers away for just a moment, a century and a half, then he returns and meets my eyes. "Monsieur and myself? Was that love? Wrong word. It might have been. If we'd had time. Sex—? Yes, he could have had me if he'd wanted me. I'd been a peg-boy and a street whore. He knew that. Do you know what Seattle was like in those days?"

"A rainy seaport with muddy streets?"

"On a good day, yes." He refills my wine glass. "In those days, Seattle's population was mostly male. Lumberjacks, teamsters, blacksmiths, boat-builders, whalers, fishermen, barkeeps, undertakers, and the men who sold them shovels, horseshoes, and harpoons. It was a pretty rough town. So not a lot of women. But men like sex. Men need sex. A man gets laid, he's a lot less likely to be violent. All those endorphins, you know. They're good for you."

"Yes, I know."

"Sex is an addiction for men. Do you know what an addiction is? It's the pursuit of a memory—the memory of pleasure. You discover sex as an adolescent and you spend the rest of your tumescent life trying to recapture those first moments of wonder and discovery. It becomes an obsession, looking for the right orifice.

"In Seattle, you had your right hand—or your left. Or you could find a friend and pretend you were just helping each other out. Or you could find a fairy—yes, that's what they were called—very effeminate men who would enjoy servicing you. Or you could go to a boy-house and spend a dollar for a peg-boy. Or you could take a street-boy into an alley and hope he wouldn't knife you. Or you could go to a brothel.

"Did you know how much whoring there was in Seattle? A lot? More than that. More than you can imagine. You've never seen anything like it. None of you have. But it was a frontier town—and it was men who settled the frontier first. For years, most of the city's income came from the tax on whores. It was collected monthly. And yeah, even the boy-houses paid. They all did. It was Seattle's most lucrative industry.

"The richest woman in the city was Miss Lou Graham. She ran a very high level brothel. The girls wanted to join her business, because it was a chance at an education. They'd learn how to behave in society and land a really rich husband. They usually married off within two or three years. Do you know how rich she was? She donated more money to start the city's school system than all the rest of the donors combined. You want to think about that. Buildings. Books. Teachers. Maintenance. That's wealth.

"If you were a woman in Seattle, then yes, Miss Graham's house was the fast track to a better life. If you were a boy, no. Not gonna happen. Yeah, it was fun to talk and pretend that we might find a rich patron who would take us off the streets, but no—with all the boys available, why would any man of that nature choose any boy as a permanent companion? You'd have to be a very special boy, wouldn't you? But the street-boys weren't special. We were hungry, dirty, ill-mannered, always looking for an advantage—not the kind of creature you wanted to bring into your house, let alone trust."

"But you and Monsieur—?

"Monsieur knew what I was. He didn't care. He could have taken me any time. And we both knew it. I'm sure he was tempted. Was I scared of him? Yes. That first night and for many nights thereafter. If he didn't want me for sex, then what did he want me for? And on the night I realized what he was, what he *really* was—I should have been horrified, shouldn't I? I should have run screaming from his house. I should have run to the police and told them about the monstrous creature who lived there.

"But I didn't. Because by then it was too late—"

"You'd fallen for him?"

"No. Worse than that. Much worse. I'd become comfortable. I'd gotten used to bathing every day, wearing clean clothes, eating at fine restaurants, reading books—especially the books, I'd never known the world could be so immense, so interesting—we discussed each day's reading over dinner. I liked it—all of it. I was enjoying my life with Monsieur, being his daykeeper.

I didn't care what he was. I wasn't giving up the good life.

"By the time I knew what he was—I also knew what he wasn't. He wasn't any of those things that people said about his kind. I knew that the same way I knew I wasn't any of the things that people said about me or my kind. Monsieur was—" Jacob stops abruptly, remembering. When he returns to the conversation, it's with a sad smile. "He was a better man than any of those who are so quick to judge."

"So you did love him."

Jacob nods. "Perhaps someday you'll understand. Yes and no. I never got the chance to love him as we both wanted. But I loved him in the expectation that one day I would."

I wait for him to continue. He studies my face. "You're having trouble with this, aren't you? It doesn't make sense to you. You're a mayfly. You don't have the luxury of tomorrow. You have to mate tonight. Your mating is desperate, frenzied, rushed—because tonight might be the only chance."

"I think you exaggerate—"

"Only to make a point. What you don't understand is something you won't understand until you experience it."

"Are you offering it to me?"

"No. Not yet. Maybe not ever."

"So why tell me about something I can't understand?"

"Because you're not through writing. This conversation is your next story."

I wait in silence, not answering.

"I'm right, aren't I?"

"Everything is source material to a writer. Walk past his or her keyboard, you're going to end up in the story somewhere. A writer's mind is a black hole, it sucks in everything that gets too close to it."

"If I didn't want you to write about me—about us, The Community—I wouldn't have sought you out."

I want to ask why, but instead I return to the previous question.

"Okay. 'Splain me. How do you love? People like you."

"Slowly," he says. "Very slowly. So slowly you can't see it. Think of a tree. You see it as a static moment. You do not see it as a process. But it is every bit as alive as you. Every moment, it breathes, it feels, it hungers, it tastes the world around it—and it grows. You just can't see it.

"Day after day, you can't see any change, so because you can't see it you assume there isn't anything happening. Only as the seasons pass would you notice the tree responding to its environment, stretching itself toward the sunlight, putting forth leaves to catch the life-giving rays, opening its flowers to attract flying insects—you might notice when it buds and grows fruits for birds and animals to eat, but you wouldn't notice them spreading its seeds in their droppings. But mostly you don't notice anything until finally the leaves turn gold and red and fall to the ground when summer fades. The tree hardens itself against the brutality of winter and you'll notice how bare it is. When it finally awakens again when spring thaws the ground, bursting forth with new leaves, maybe you'll notice that the tree is a little taller, a little thicker, little fuller. And maybe after a few years, after many years you'll notice that it towers over you now, giving you shade against the day and shelter against the storm. But you—trapped in your mayfly existence—you can't notice any of that without time, a lot of time.

"And so it is with us. We have eternity. We don't have to eat every day, we can go dormant for years, lying in our silent retreats—a heartbeat once a second, once a minute, once an hour, once a week. Seemingly dead to any observer who cannot see the processes at work. But from the inside, when you live that slowly, you see the wheels of the universe turning majestically. We see everything differently, we experience the race of the glaciers as a mad rush. We watch the writhing of rivers and the crumbling of mountains. So we move through our lives methodically, patiently, without hurry or stress. Because we know we have time. All the time we want.

"Our relationships? Beyond your comprehension. Beyond all human comprehension. When you have eternity, you take your time to get the moments right. The mating dance is prolonged. I was too young to know this when I lived with Monsieur. I was still a mayfly. Impatient, driven by hormones and adolescence. I ping-ponged back and forth between frustration and despair—and anger as well, sometimes even to the point of madness.

"But every evening, he'd come downstairs in his elegant dressing gown, all graceful and calm and oh, so pleasant. He'd look at me, deeply—he had the most beautiful eyes, pale gray, almost luminous. I couldn't look away. He would look into my face for long, almost painful moments—not commanding, but searching, his gaze shifting almost imperceptibly from one emotion to the next, curiosity, skepticism, concern, affection, wondering, analyzing—I learned to surrender to his eyes, searching them in return, I was looking for understanding. Now, today, I can understand the irony of that moment. I could not find what I was looking for until I was looking from his side."

"You do that now?"

"Everywhere." He smiles knowingly, his eyes fixed on mine for a long thoughtful moment. Finally, he returns to his story. "I cannot say how long we'd spend just looking at each other, but this was the ritual every night. Whatever it was he needed to see, when he was finally satisfied that he'd seen my heart, Monsieur would whisper, 'Very good, Jacob, very good.' Then he'd pour us two glasses of very old wine. In the winter, we'd sit by the fire. In the summer, we'd go out to the garden.

"The evenings were bright, made brighter by the gaslamps. They burned brighter than you think, but they were warm. The mantles inside gave off the most beautiful incandescent glow." Jacob shakes his head, smiling at some remembered moment. "Electricity is not an improvement. It spoils the mood. It just isn't romantic.

"But Monsieur and I, we had the most marvelous evenings. I didn't realize just how wondrous those days were until they were gone. You can't imagine the adventures we had, exploring the landscapes of history and architecture, art and philosophy. And novels too—oh, the novels! Victor Hugo and Charles Dickens and a most marvelous Frenchman named Jules Verne. New books arrived from New York every month.

"Sometimes I would get to the new volumes before he could. When that happened, he'd ask me if I thought a book might be worth his time or not. But more often, he was passing books to me. Sometimes we'd both be reading, other times, we'd sit opposite each other and discuss what we had read. Sometimes he would recommend a specific volume from the shelves, something that he thought would illuminate some point or other. But most of the time, he encouraged me to choose for myself. Our discussions—" Jacob stops himself. He refills our wine glasses. "Sometimes we argued ferociously over some detail, what it really meant. Did I think Monsieur Verne's outlandish submarine adventure was really possible? Or was it too fanciful to be taken serious? I wanted it to be real, I argued it was inevitable. He was skeptical, but he'd already seen the beginnings of the industrial revolution, so he had to admit it might be possible. He just didn't understand how an iron boat could stay afloat underwater. Neither did I, but apparently Monsieur Verne believed it, and that was good enough for me.

"But I know that Monsieur loved the arguments, And so did I. Sometimes they went on for hours as we picked over every bit of evidence, every aspect of an idea. We weren't arguing with each other, thoughtlessly contradicting each other's assertions—no, it was never about who was right, it was about the progression of statements that allowed us to examine an idea in depth—exploring the possibilities, discovering the meanings. The rules for any discussion were simple—you had to be able to justify your assertion with facts and logic. I think that was the very best part of my education. Monsieur trained me to be a thinking man—a good man."

"A good man? But you kill people to eat."

"Yes, sometimes I do kill people. And sometimes I feed on them. Sometimes I have to. Sometimes I want to." He stares across the chasm of years at me. "But today I'm not going to kill."

"I'm not your type?"

"You're still not ripe."

"I suppose I should take that as a rebuke...."

"Take it however you take it."

"So, if I'm not that interesting, then why—"

"I didn't say you're uninteresting. I said you're not finished. Not complete. Not ready."

"What is it you're looking for?"

"If you have to ask—"

"Please don't play games with me. It's arrogant. It's patronizing. If I want to be treated rudely, I can go back to the convention."

"I'm looking for the kind of conversations I used to have with Monsieur. Conversations that challenge, that excite, that astonish. I want to be moved, touched, and inspired. I am what I am—something beyond your ken—but I still have a soul. A hungry soul. I'm looking for someone to argue with."

"Ah. Well that lets me out."

"Why?"

"You have a century and a half head start on me."

"Yes, I do. What do you have?"

"Um. Curiosity."

"That's a good place to start."

"I can't argue with you. I don't have the—"

"Stop that."

"But it's true—"

"If you're going to argue for your limits, you'll make them real. Stop it." He made as if to rise.

"No, please. Don't go. I just—" I took a breath. "You're intimidating."

"Yes, I am."

"I want to know your story."

"That's not enough."

"I want to write it."

"That's still not enough."

"I want to know what it feels like—!"

"That's what I wanted to hear." He waves the empty bottle at a passing waiter. "Another, please?" He turned back to me. "Now, you. Try arguing from the other side. Argue why you should be important to me."

"Um, I can write your story."

Jacob is unimpressed. He glances in the general direction of the convention center. "There are a hundred other writers who can. At least. And there are at least a thousand wannabes who'd suck me off for the chance."

"I can write it better." I hesitate. It sounds arrogant, but I speak it anyway. "Better than all of them."

"Why?"

"Because most of them won't take you serious. I already do."

"Tell me more about that."

"They'll do it for the money. Or the fame. Or the mystique. Or because they're chronovores and starsuckers, wannabes and frauds, all looking for credibility."

"And you're not?"

"Doesn't matter who I am. What matters is the job. I want to get it right. The story has to be told by someone who cares enough to tell it from the inside."

Jacob leans across the table and stares into my eyes. For a moment, I'm taken aback. Disconcerted. Then I realize what he's doing and I surrender. I don't know how long we sit that way. The waiter puts another bottle of wine on the table, but he doesn't interrupt. He must think we're lovers. He must think Jacob is about to propose. Or maybe he thinks it's a staring contest, I don't know. Jacob's eyes are dark, his pupils are deep. And I'm lost in his gaze. I start wondering about the boy he was, what he saw, what he felt? He's that same boy now—but with a century and a half of experience being that boy. There are so many questions I want to ask. He was there when this world was built. He saw it all—

Or did he? Did he throw himself into the center of it? Or did he hide away in some dark corner of the world where he wouldn't be discovered? A place where he could feed at will?

How often did he feed? And how did he choose his...victims?

I suppose I should feel afraid, but I don't. I passed fear a long time ago. Now, all that's left is—

Jacob.

He leans back, breaking the contact. The waiter has filled our glasses again. I hadn't noticed. I grab mine, not for wine, but for retreat. I'm as exhausted as if I've just run a marathon. Not physically exhausted—emotionally. As if we've just had the most intense sexual intimacy possible.

"What was that? What did you do?"

Jacob smiles. "I looked at you. That's how Monsieur used to look at me. Call it the charmfield. The sparkle zone. Whatever. You feel it, yes? We are closer now."

Slowly, I catch my breath. I study him intensely. And realize—there isn't anything he could ask that I would say no to. If he asked me to bare my neck, I would. If he asked me to sleep with him, I would. If he offered me eternity—

I would.

But no. I'm not ready yet. He has to know that. He doesn't want to make a monster.

"So, are you satisfied? Can we continue?"

He spreads his hands wide. "Ask."

I put my glass down, I pop open my laptop, slide it into place. "Tell me. You were at school. Monsieur's letters stopped. You came back to Seattle."

Jacob nods. He steeples his fingers in front of his chin, remembering, considering, choosing where to begin. "I enjoyed the university, much more than I expected to. It was as much an adventure as our regular evening discussions—but this was a much larger exposure than those quiet focused chats. This time, this place, there were all those learned professors, and their aides, the graduate students, and my fellows as well. It was so much more high-spirited and free-wheeling. In some ways, I was the coarse bumpkin from the coast, but I was also an object of some curiosity as well—because I had lived on the frontier, they questioned me incessantly about what I had seen and done. Not just my fellows, but the instructors as well—they wanted to know about Seattle and San Francisco, the train ride east—did I see any Indians? Or buffalo? When they asked about my parents, I hesitated, I couldn't tell them anything of that, of course. Not my past, not Monsieur, not anything.

"But Monsieur had foreseen the curiosity of the others. In the short weeks before my departure east, we created a cover story, close to the truth, but far enough away from the truth to avoid arousing suspicion. To my fellows at the university, I was the frontier orphan. My parents had died, but I had been raised by a devoted uncle who had raised me as his own son, provided me with skilled tutors and readied me for adulthood, finally sending me to Boston to complete my education. It was enough of a story to satisfy them, and after a while, as the pressure of the term set in, most of them lost interest."

• ⊷≔⟨•❍◯⊙•⟩≕⊶ •

I was at university for seven years. I could have stayed longer. I would have stayed longer, if I could. There was so much to learn. I know Monsieur wouldn't have minded if I had stayed forever, soaking it all in. Especially the music.

Let me tell you about the music. Boston in 1876 was a city of grand concerts. It was a golden age. We had Bach and Mozart and Beethoven and Wagner and we were just getting Tchaikovsky's piano concertos and his symphonies too. They were a sensation—oh, the marvelous arguments we had about all that clanging and banging on the keyboard, all the fire and fury of his symphonies. Later on, he even used cannons! What an audacious thing to do. Oh, what fun we had. We didn't have that kind of music in Seattle. Not yet, not then. It was a banquet and I stuffed my ears with it. I had no idea such things were possible.

Monsieur had tutored me well, I knew how to play the piano and the clarinet, I could hold a violin and bow it correctly—but in Boston, I soared. I spent long hours in the night, not just practicing, but exploring the sounds and shapes of the instruments, all the different textures. The flavors of sound!

From time to time, Monsieur would recommend that I seek out one or another of his acquaintances in Boston, but not too often. I met several members of The Community, but I did not spend much time with them. Still, Monsieur wanted me to have knowledge of them in case I found myself in a circumstance where I might need assistance beyond my own means.

They were very much unlike The Community in Seattle, they seemed to have a fine patina about them, like a fine mahogany desk that had been polished until its surface shined as deep as a dark mirror. I had the feeling they regarded me as something of a coarse nuisance, but they were never impolite.

One in particular, Colonel Guignard, did express some curiosity about life on the west coast—I didn't know at first if his title was honorary or fairly earned, at the time I suspected it was honorary. Later I found out that my first impression had been correct. In colonial and antebellum times, the title was given to men of the landed gentry for financing the local militia without actual expectations of command. So Colonel Guignard was that old—at least.

Over dinner, one night, he told me that he had owned property in Virginia and Kentucky, and most recently had enjoyed the cuisine of New Orleans. He did not go into detail, but the way he phrased it, I had no doubt there was a deeper meaning, he wasn't talking of land, nor was he discussing the more common aspects of the groaning board.

The Colonel had retreated north shortly after the rail lines were completed, he did not say why. He had not returned to the south since then and apparently had little desire to do so. He had a curious lack of affection for the region, he said that its culture was a perfumed illusion, a bit of crinoline hiding a degenerate culture. Likewise, he found the northeast stifling, too wrapped up in business and industry.

Being in The Community, Colonel Guignard said, a man must be prepared to move at least once a decade. The west seemed promising and he wanted me to tell of my adventures. I did not feel comfortable revealing the sordid aspects of my boyhood, so I discussed only my time with Monsieur and that seemed to satisfy him.

In return, I asked Colonel Guignard for more information about The Community. He shook his head politely and said that information was reserved to actual members of The Community, but he did understand my curiosity. And my service to Monsieur was well-regarded.

After the first few evenings, we did not meet often, and I got the sense that Colonel Guignard was already preparing for his next move. I felt somewhat relieved about that, as I had by now begun to develop some of the skills necessary for success in the academic world. I began to feel, shall I say it—comfortable. I was an effective student because I enjoyed the journeys of knowledge.

Because of that, or because of my occasional meetings with various gentlemen of the town, acquaintances of Monsieur, my fellows at the university found me distant and removed. I didn't mind. I had spent too many of my formative years on the underside of life, now I was on the brighter side, discovering the joys. I was, perhaps, enraptured by the wealth of ideas and knowledge available to me. I was drunk on the adventure.

As I said, it was the music that first entranced me. You cannot imagine what it was like then. You have everything too easily available, you have all of your favorite recordings at your fingertips, all you have to do is plug in your earbuds and tap the screen. Your technology has spoiled you. By making it all so easy, you have become separated from your own ability to appreciate the efforts of composers in orchestras.

In those days, we had no movies, we had plays. We had no records or radios. So a concert was an event. It was special. It was an opportunity to experience something glorious that was not possible except as a grand cooperative effort. There were concerts every week, performers of all kinds came through the city—to me, it was magic, it was wealth, it was the ultimate expression of the human soul. Music is such pure emotion, I used to sit there with my eyes closed, letting the textures and melodies paint pictures in my imagination—I doubt you will ever understand. Electricity has spoiled you.

But the music led me inexorably, inevitably to a broader appreciate of everything else—painting was next. The impressionists were starting to make their mark in the art world, Monet and Renoir and some strange red-haired wild man in the south of France. The romantic composers were challenging the comfortable forms of the symphony with liquid rhapsodies and melodies that flowed like wine, they were reinventing music—so were the bold and bizarre painters of this new impressionist movement changing the nature of art, exploring the ways that human beings perceived light and color—not trying to recreate the world as it is on their canvases, but the way we experience it. It was a most remarkable time—unequaled for a century. Yes, I can say that. I was there.

I wrote long letters to Monsieur, describing everything. Sometimes I sent him photographs and prints and sheet music, but I wish the phonograph had been invented sooner. I wanted to send him the sound of the orchestra as well.

Monsieur wrote back, once a month. We both wrote the most carefully coded letters, innocuous to any casual reader, but laden with meaning to both myself and him. We referred to our separate companions only by initials. Monsieur would write that D. was thinking of relocating to New York and I would write back saying how much I admired D. and if he moved to New York, I would be happy to visit with him. Sometimes we wrote about the doings of people who did not even exist. K. has begun courting a lovely young heiress. R.'s father had suffered a terrible financial loss and R. might have to leave the university.

Monsieur believed that the public mail had no great degree of privacy. Therefore our exchanges must seem as innocuous as possible. Occasionally, he would recommend a book for me. Occasionally, I would write about what I had read. While he and I both found these exchanges useful, I'm certain they would have been boring to anyone else. But as much as I enjoyed sharing my studies with him, I missed our evening conversations, our discussions in depth.

I told him that, and he told me that he missed my companionship as well. But neither of us dared to be any more expressive than that. Mostly, Monsieur continued to acknowledge my enthusiasm for learning and the insights I shared with him. He always began by telling me how happy it made him to receive my letters and how proud he was of my progress—the evidence of my education was apparent in every sentence. No, not the facts I was learning—but the ability to consider what they represented, what they meant, what they suggested—everything they pointed to. His careful praise was the fuel for my drive, my passion. I realized then how much I was falling in love with him, how much I missed him, how much I wanted to see him again.

Because.

Because I was beginning to feel ready.

It wasn't that I wanted to join The Community as much as I wanted to be worthy of it. I told him so. I didn't use the exact words. I said, "I want to be worthy of you."

And he wrote back, "You are earning your place in history. Of that, there is no question. But first you need complete your education in the areas of business and finance and mathematics. These are skills that will be critical in your future."

I admit, at first I found those studies dry and tiresome, but soon I realized there was the same beauty in numbers that there is in music—and the geometrical ratios were part of our perception of beauty in painting and architecture and sculpture. There's a beautiful understructure of logic to be explored.

From there, I tumbled sideways into studies of physics and astronomy. Newton and Copernicus were the recognized landmarks, but there was so much new work being done, it was hard to keep up. But I wanted to know if an iron submarine could really float. Would heavier-than-air flight ever be possible? These were marvelous questions to consider. It was all about math and physics. Monsieur approved of all these tangents, of course, but he always pointed me back toward the mechanical aspects of survival as well.

I kept up my studies in every area he suggested, I learned how the stock market worked—that was useful too—but I began to wonder about the nature of The Community as well, so I began taking courses in biology.

Oh my, I had not realized there was so much to learn. Gregor Mendel's study of genetics and Charles Darwin's book on *The Origin of Species*. The arguments we had about what this might mean—about race and inheritance and everything. It left me stunned. Who are we? What are we?

It was as if the very ground beneath our feet had abruptly evaporated, leaving us adrift in a chaotic sea of uncertainty.

I must interrupt myself here—I don't know if Monsieur intended it or not, I always felt that he was comfortable with the circumstances of his situation, he did not question it, at least never in my presence— but as I began to research the workings of the human body, the diseases and disorders that afflict us, it became apparent to me that men of The Community were bound together by a commonly-shared affliction, the symptoms of which were not supernatural in nature at all, but might eventually be understandable as a specific physical disorder.

Because I suspected it was most likely a condition of the blood, I directed my studies toward that area—I started with malaria, also an illness of the blood, and worked outward from there. But while I was able to identify the occurrence of similar symptoms in other ailments—like the extreme sensitivity of the skin to daylight that occurs in certain diseases we now call porphyrias, the cutaneous porphyrias which cause blistering or necrotic reactions to sunlight—or the prolonged periods of sleep-like unconsciousness that narcoleptics experience, these symptoms were also found among the porphyrias, including muscle weakness, coma, and even psychosis—but try as I might, I could not find any common factor linking these conditions. The conditions were so rare, there had not been any significant studies.

Frustrated, I realized I had to look elsewhere. Again, I considered the symptoms. Enhanced hearing occurs in those who have lost their sight, as well as a superior sense of smell. Moments of superior strength sometimes occur in periods of extreme emotional stress. And the urge to feed on human flesh—well, that is a mental disorder of the worst sort, beyond the comprehension of rational men. But again, I found no common denominator.

Whatever the cause of Monsieur's condition—and the other men of The Community as well—it was beyond my current ability to discover, certainly not without specimens to examine. In my youthful naivete, I began to believe that here was a new frontier of medical science, and that if I could analyze, explain, and perhaps even cure the condition, I would immediately make a name for myself as a great doctor of medicine.

I requested an evening meeting with Colonel Guignard and broached the subject politely. As carefully as I could phrase it—I presented my concerns to him. Without ever using either of the words *disorder* or *disease*, I told him I had become curious about certain biological processes and conditions, how they occurred and whether or not they could be reversed.

After some back and forth, the Colonel finally understood what I was referring to. He stiffened immediately. Even before he spoke, I saw that he was visibly disconcerted at the idea of subjecting himself to any medical examination, and he did not think any other member of The Community would ever assent to such an invasion.

It was understandable, of course, but it allowed me enough of a glimpse into his thinking to recognize that merely being a member of The Community did not automatically grant wisdom or enlightenment, and possibly not even curiosity. Colonel Guignard, and probably all of the rest as well, had brought their own prejudices and apprehensions with them, even as they joined the company of Nightsiders. It was a small awakening for me, a moment of insight.

But apparently my request had seriously offended Colonel Guignard, and except for a few brief exchanges after that, I saw him no more. Later on, I heard that he had left Boston. I assumed he had headed west, but no one in The Community seemed to know—or they deliberately chose not to share that information with me.

Indeed, after that, my contacts with members of The Community in Boston became less and less frequent, until they became invisible even to me. I wrote to Monsieur of this, saying only that in my innocence, I had somehow offended Colonel Guignard and his acquaintances, and I hoped that it would not reflect badly on him.

When Monsieur wrote back, he told me not to worry myself unduly. Sometimes men of age become fossilized in their thinking, unable to deal well with the changes that occur with the passage of time. I should not let myself be discouraged or dissuaded from my studies. Knowledge isn't just power, it's freedom as well.

Nevertheless, I realized I had reached the limits of the medical knowledge of the time—and what was known about those forced to live nightside would continue to be confabulated with superstition and fear. Perhaps Monsieur and I could discuss this at length at some future time. Or perhaps, if I were ever to join The Community, I would not only experience the changes myself, I would have sufficient medical knowledge to begin a genuine inquiry.

Consequently, with that end in mind I began to study the chemistry of the body's processes—especially the enzymatic processes, so that I would be able to bring a superior insight to my own eventual transformation. It seemed likely that would be the only avenue of understanding available to me.

Let me admit, my professors worried about the intensity I brought to my studies. Yes, they encouraged me, but they worried as well. They'd rarely seen a student so enthused about learning, but to them I seemed to be skipping around from subject to subject without any distinct career goal in mind. I told them that my own education was the only career I desired. They shook their heads and wandered off muttering, but they could find no real cause for concern, nor any recommendation that would have been appropriate. As long as my distant uncle was happy to have me gorging myself at the feast of knowledge, they were happy to keep setting the table and cashing the checks.

I think their primary cause of concern was my seeming failure to connect socially with many of my fellow classmates. I did not live in a house with others, Monsieur's agent in Boston had found me an apartment within walking distance of the campus. I was not the only student with such a living arrangement, but where others often used their private residences for evenings of drunkenness and debauchery, I was most often curled up with a stack of books, breaking away only for the necessities of the body, food and sleep, bath and toilet.

You might find this hard to believe, but I was a virgin until my twenty-third year. No, I don't count my years as a peg-boy or a street-rat. That was survival sex. That wasn't sex as much as it was a way to stay alive. It was a job, something to do, something to endure, but not something to enjoy—yes, there was a physical release, but no emotional fulfillment.

I didn't know that emotional fulfillment was possible in sex. Oh, I'd read the books—all those silly romances that were passed around among the young women, Charlotte Bronte, Jane Austen. They made little sense to me. I also read Henry Fielding, Nathaniel Hawthorne, Edgar Allen Poe, and so many others as well—even the bawdiest of texts, a companion passed me a rare and illegal fiction called *Fanny Hill*, which purported to be the extraordinarily amorous adventures of a young woman, working as a sometime prostitute in 18th century London.

I was curious, yes, but not yet desperate, hoping to understand this mysterious emotion that seemed to captivate the attention of everyone around me. It seemed a bizarre obsession. The closest I had come was my affection for Monsieur, but even that had never been fulfilled.

I had wanted to give myself to him—and now, I believe that if he had taken me the way he himself desired, I would have experienced it as an emotional fulfillment. But no, perhaps not. In later years, I did wonder if perhaps my experiences on the streets of Seattle had stunted my emotional growth, had kept me from developing a true ability to connect to other human beings. I suppose I might someday be an interesting case study for a psychiatrist—but not for a long time, I still regard psychiatry as a questionable field. Too many people who have no idea what they're doing, hammering the facts to make them fit their theories. Never mind, that's a discussion for another time.

I was talking about my friendships—my inability to have any. I wasn't completely alone. I did have acquaintances—a small group of fellows I met with once or twice a week. They had insinuated themselves into my good graces by inviting me to concerts and art exhibitions. In return, I felt obligated to open my apartment to them for weekly evenings of poker and beer. It turned out I was quite good at poker, not too good at beer. But in truth, I suspected my associates appreciated the convenience of the apartment much more than any charm I might have exhibited as a host.

One evening, however, early in the new year of 1881, we had become a little too boisterous in our celebrations, and rather than risk the ire of my neighbors who might have wished to retire at a responsible hour, we adjourned to the streets. But instead of heading to the nearest pub—Boston has never had a shortage of pubs, for that you may thank the Irish—one of my companions, a fellow recently added to the group who I did not know well at all, suggested a visit to a nearby brothel.

I'd never been to a brothel before—not as a customer, only as an employee, a peg-boy. I pondered for a moment what Monsieur might say if he knew. He had encouraged me to explore the pleasures of physical intimacy, but as I had already had my fill of what other men considered physical intimacy it was not an adventure I had any further desire for. Nevertheless, at this point in my life, and not without considerable good-natured and somewhat boisterous prodding from my fellow revelers, and possibly it was the effect of too much liquor as well, I felt somewhat giddy and unrestrained, I decided it was finally time to discover what copulation with a female person might be like. I did not think Monsieur would object. On the contrary, had he been present he would have enthusiastically encouraged me to discover whether the boundaries of my nature were debilitating limits or merely a matter of personal preference.

I will not bore you with the details of our visit. It was an interesting experience, not unsatisfactory, but curiously dispassionate and not something I felt eager to repeat any time soon. The young woman was pleasant enough, she seemed eager to please—whether that was an act or her natural inclination, I had no way of knowing. But afterward, lying on my back, catching my breath, and considering the entire exercise, I had to admit to myself that while I found the female anatomy interesting and physically comfortable, I had remained emotionally detached throughout the entire experience.

To be fair, I did not expect to find love here, nor even the imitation of romance, although the young lady—her name was Rebecca—performed an excellent simulation of desire for me. However, I had learned enough from listening to my various companions and fellows at the university, that any post-coital revelations should demonstrate an aggressive degree of masculine bravado. I chose to affect what I thought was an appropriately lascivious grin while otherwise saying little. My companions took this as a sign of success and when it became apparent I intended to provide no details, they left off questioning.

For the next week or so, my colleagues eagerly discussed the possibilities that might be available in subsequent visits to the establishment, but after one of them realized he had picked up an infestation of crab lice, an unwelcome invasion that would require an extensive boiling of his entire wardrobe and all of his bedding, as well as repeated applications of various petroleum-based distillations to his private areas, tinctures and ointments well-known in the popular lore of collegians—that tempered any discussions of additional outings.

One incredibly stormy evening in February, the only acquaintance to show up for poker and beer was a stocky fellow named Josiah, two years younger than myself, but seemingly much more worldly. He had apprenticed in his grandfather's brokerage during his school years to earn the right to attend the university.

Despite having walked only a short distance, he arrived soaking wet. Fearing for his health—a lesson I had learned well from Monsieur, I made him strip of his sodden clothing and wrapped him in one of my own warm robes, I had several which I wore while reading, that being far more comfortable than street wear.

We waited for the better part of an hour—until it became apparent that our other companions had chosen to skip the evening's game. This was not unexpected. The storm had been gathering ominously all morning and we had previously agreed that if the weather ever became adverse, the game would be postponed—apparently, Josiah did not receive the message.

Because it seemed as if the rain would continue well into the next day, I insisted that Josiah spend the night with me. I did so in all innocence, with little thought to what else might occur. I did not think in those ways then.

My bed was just big enough for the both of us, what you might call queen size today. It was quite cozy. We lay side by side in the darkness, listening to the wind howling outside, the rain pattering against the window, and we chatted amiably about nothing in particular. We chuckled a bit at the foibles of our fellows, reminisced a bit more about our adventures at the brothel, and then fell silent for a bit.

Finally, Josiah said, "It's too bad that we can't go again."

My reply was noncommittal. "I don't want to take the risk. There might be other, less curable, conditions."

"You're right," Josiah said. "Still, I wish there was something...."

There was something in his tone, something to make me wonder where he intended to take the conversation. I said nothing, I waited expectantly.

"Y'know..." He whispered cautiously—as if sharing a dark secret, but still leaving himself room to retreat if rebuffed, "I've heard that sometimes, young men in our situation—with unfulfilled physical needs—sometimes help each other out." When I didn't reply, he added, "Have you heard anything like that?"

I hesitated. I certainly knew quite a bit about the physical needs of men, both young and old. But I sensed that this was a different kind of conversation. I answered slowly. "It's not unknown in Seattle. There are many more men than women. It is a known convenience."

Now, Josiah rolled directly onto his side, facing me. "Have you ever—? I mean, perhaps we could...help each other. If you'd like." Before I could answer, he placed his hand on my chest, then moved it slowly downward, across my belly, and from there to my own surprising desire.

In those days, most men wore long underwear, one-piece flannel undergarments called "union suits." In the winter, it was a necessary protection against the bitter cold. But in the collegian world, the union suit was regarded as an ugly, ill-fitting contrivance. Instead, the style was for young men to wear separated undergarments, usually quite close-fitting. So it was quite easy for Josiah to slip his hand beneath the waistband of my drawers and then beyond. The touch of his fingers against my nakedness sent a shockwave through my body. Until that moment, I had not realized that companions could be physically intimate. In my mind, I had separated the two functions—physical intimacy and affection. In that first moment, I felt as if I was standing on a precipice. I experienced awe and terror and yet an overwhelming desire to proceed. When I finally found the courage to speak, I whispered, "Perhaps this might be easier if we removed our—if we got naked...?"

As if my words had liberated us both, we quickly shrugged out of our separate underclothes. Boldly, Josiah peeled back the covers so that he could see my nakedness and I could see his. I had not been with any man for a decade, not since Monsieur had taken me from the streets, I hadn't forgotten the physical details, but I had never experienced any man like this—as an equal partner in an act of physical intimacy.

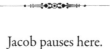

Jacob pauses here.

At some point in the narrative, the waiter had set plates of food before us, the American version of bangers and mash. Now those plates had been emptied and removed. A third bottle of wine sits on the table, still half-full. Jacob reaches for it. "Do you want some more?"

"I'd better not. I'm already way over my limit."

He fills his own glass. "My metabolism is different than yours. Alcohol is a convenient fuel. Where you become intoxicated, I become invigorated."

"Interesting." I don't know what else to say.

"It's another thing your—I'll call them colleagues—your colleagues have all failed to recognize. Most of their tales, pfah!" He pretends to spit. "They make things up. Little horrors to scare little children. They know nothing of the real horror. Neither do you—" He stops himself. "That comes later. Much later."

"You were talking about Josiah."

"Oh, yes. Josiah. He was delicious. No, not like that—" Jacob smiles with the memory. "You go to the movies, don't you? You see how they represent sex? It's all a lie, you know."

"Is it?"

"Have you had sex?"

I nod.

"Male or female?"

"Both."

"Which do you prefer?"

"I think—well, mostly it depends on how much fun the other person is."

"Ahh. I will mark you down as undecided."

"It isn't binary."

"No, it isn't. But one day, if you are particularly unlucky, you may find a permanent partner. And that will be your final choice. Because of the permanence, not necessarily the partner."

I have no answer for that. He has a head start on me. A century and a half head start.

"Have you been to the movies? Have you seen how sex is portrayed in the movies?"

"Yes."

"Have you ever had sex like that—?" His gaze is penetrating.

"I have to admit, no. You're right. The movies are a fantasy."

"No. The movies aren't even that much. They're a shorthand version of a fantasy. A man gets into a car and the car pulls away from the curb. The next shot shows the car arriving somewhere and he gets out. The movie leaves out the hour of the man driving, negotiating his way through traffic, being cut off by rude drivers, cursing to himself, checking his watch to see if he'll arrive on time, stopping for gas, talking on his phone or reading a text, perhaps even looking at the GPS to see if there's a detour around the road closure—no, the movie lies to you and says that he gets in, drives away, arrives, and gets out. You're supposed to pretend you understand there was time and distance involved, but you don't. You experience it as a flicker from here to there without all the intervening circumstances."

"But those aren't important, are they—?"

"Of course, they are. If the drive was uncomfortable, if the traffic was difficult, if another driver nearly caused an accident, the person we're following—he'll be stressed and irritable when he arrives. He won't be in the mood to greet his mistress with affection, he'll go straight to the bar and pour himself a drink while she wonders what's wrong. In the movies, does the hero ever arrive and say, 'Traffic was a bitch! There was a prick in a Porsche who cut me off at the off ramp. I wanted to get out of the car and punch his heart out. But then I thought of you and decided it wasn't worth the effort—' and then they run to the bedroom? No. They just go straight to the next plot point, in a mad rush to the climax. And sex is presented the same way—as a mad rush to the climax. It's a lie."

"And your point is—?"

He laughs. "Very good. My point is that nothing in art, not music, not paintings, not even books—and certainly not movies—ever comes close to the reality, the experiential storm that occurs when the physical and the emotional moments collide."

I have nothing to say to that. I wait for him to go on.

"That's what I'm talking about, the moment—the real moment—when you lose your virginity. In truth, there were moments when I wished I had experienced it with Monsieur, but now I understand why that would have been a mistake. For both of us. It would have been like trying to fill a teacup with a fire hose. The teacup would have shattered. What happened in Boston, between Josiah and myself, that was what Monsieur most wanted in my educational career. He needed me to experience my own humanity before I could become...anything else. He needed me to know."

"And you did?"

He grins. "Most enthusiastically. Many times."

At first, it was mostly fumbling. You may find this difficult to believe, but I did not really know what I was doing. In the past, when men used me, I didn't have to know. I was just a convenient piece of warm meat.

But this—with Josiah—this was the first time I had ever experienced the act as a partnership of interest and intention. So we explored, we touched, we stroked each other, curious about each other's bodies—about the shape and touch and feeling of each other's maleness.

The act of exploration wasn't unfamiliar. Many men had explored my body in the past. Many men had been tender and gentle. Only a few had been rough and brutal—as street boys, we learned how to recognize those men, we warned each other who was trouble. But this was the first time I explored the body of another man, in curiosity and wonder. Josiah had a rough undeniable beauty, a masculine scent and presence. The intensity of the moment was heightened by the combination of conflicting emotions— the overwhelming desire to discover what pleasures might be available to both of us, tempered by the fear of possible discovery and the thrill that we were exploring a territory forbidden by culture and convention—as well as by law.

But we didn't stop. We had passed the point where stopping was possible. We couldn't stop. We had long since crossed that threshold, that Rubicon of desire, the moment that Josiah's fingers slid beneath my waistband. He opened his arms to me and I fell into his embrace. In that moment, we became lovers. I felt his nakedness against me as a revelation. I had never experienced such a sense of immediacy, a partnership of affection.

We finally allowed ourselves a brotherly kiss. The first kiss was uncertain—was this something we should do? The second kiss was exploratory. Was it something we wanted to do? The third kiss—that was the door opening to physical adventure. It was a mutual declaration of 'Yes, let's do this! Let's go all the way.'

We did not know the path to 'all the way'—we had to invent it for ourselves. We did not do everything that first night. In fact, we hardly did much of anything. We held each other close and rocked together on the levers of mutual desire for the longest time—I could have gone all night, it was such a pleasant diversion, yet the more we pushed ourselves together, the greater the tension grew—until finally, Josiah rolled on top of me, grabbing at my shoulders, saying, "I think I can finish this way," and I said, "Go ahead"—a blessing based in enthusiasm, not exhaustion—I wrapped myself around him and rode him from beneath, matching my exertions to his, focusing on his pleasure, concentrating on matching the thrusts of his manhood against my belly—and when he finally throbbed with the first moments of release, my body throbbed in response, so delighted was I with the physical liberation of his spirit that my own spirit released with his, a surprising moment of amazement as we surged together, a delicious unison of purpose. Josiah must have felt the same astonishment for he held me tightly in his arms for a near-painful instant, before we both gasped and collapsed, he on top of me—myself beneath him, savagely exhausted—and we lay there together for the longest time.

And this mutual exhaustion gave us the most wonderful discovery of the evening, the ultimate realization of what two bodies could become when they united in common purpose. As we lay there, intimate yet unmoving, I began to sense the heat of his flesh against mine, the delicious warmth of our mutual connection. And I could feel the beat of his heart synchronized with mine. I could feel the pulsing waves spreading out from our mutual centers, the way the blood coursed through our arteries in rhythmic balance, the two of us beating in time together. The cliché—two hearts beating as one—wasn't a cliché.

This—not the other—this was what Monsieur had wanted me to experience, to know, to understand. I laughed. I laughed at myself. I laughed at the world. I laughed at us and Josiah laughed with me, for no reason at all, except that we were both filled with so much delight, an emotional intoxication that neither of us had ever known before. We laughed in shared amusement because we were the joke we had played on ourselves.

We kissed again, this time from the other side of the act. This time, there was no question of permission. This time, it was the replenishment of connection. Not the coda, the encore. A completion. We didn't stop kissing, we just relaxed into each other's breaths. A moment of bliss so complete there was only the physical being, no thought at all—it was only afterward as my lips brushed against his one more time that I realized just how deeply I had fallen into the experience. I hadn't been there, only the contentment.

We fell asleep that way, wrapped in each other's arms—and we woke again, still in the same position, still holding each other close, when the first hints of dawn began to seep through the curtains. Perhaps the connected rhythms of our lovemaking and our synchronized heartbeats extended even to the syncopation of our slumbers, I can't say, my sleep was dreamless, complete, and in the morning, we both came awake at the same moment, still smiling, almost laughing. We kissed, wrapped ourselves together as if we had never been interrupted by our rests, and continued our passions for several hours more, ultimately achieving another synchronized release, this time with me on top.

I had not known that such things were possible. Not even in all the tales, all the books, all the knowledge that I had so eagerly sought, had I ever found any discussion of the nature of physical passion as deep as what I had just experienced.

Love? No, I don't think it was love—not yet. But, infatuation? Yes, it was infatuation, glorious infatuation! I was enchanted, enthralled, captivated in the moment, awash in amazement that Josiah and I were so perfectly paired in the horizontal dance. I believe he must have felt the same way.

No, this was not simply two male friends "helping each other out." This was the realization of our mutual nature. Though neither of us would ever speak it aloud, it was clearly an open secret between us—that we had discovered, invented, created, some special spark of ecstasy unique to the world. In that moment, I foolishly believed that no one else had ever experienced such a symbiotic passion. I wanted to run out into the streets and yell to the world what we had discovered was possible between two beings—only the realization that no one would understand a word of it unless they had already experienced it themselves kept me from leaping from the bed—that and Josiah's strong arms pulling me back into his embrace. He smelled so good and I was so selfish, I lost myself in him again.

• ⊶≡❬◆❱❁❪◆❫≡❭⊷ •

"This is all...very interesting," I'm searching for the words. Finally, I admit. "Actually, it's unsettling."

"Thank you for being honest."

"I've never heard anyone talk about a sexual experience that way."

"I can understand that."

"You can?"

"Limitations. It's all about limitations. You can't talk about what you haven't experienced. At least, not knowledgeably, not from the inside. I'm sure that Josiah and I haven't been the only human beings to lose themselves in ecstasy that way. But perhaps humans do not yet have the words to write about it. The language is insufficient"

"That's a funny thing to say. The English language has more words in it than any other language."

"That's true—but just the same, there are still a lot of words we don't have. That's why we keep stealing words from other languages. Mostly, we don't have words for things we don't experience. Or don't recognize that we've experienced. If a person has never experienced a specific feeling, he can't recognize any of the meanings the words are intended to evoke."

"That's very...philosophical, I guess."

"General Semantics. Linguistics. I go back to college every few years. Mostly to audit. I've probably qualified for a dozen different degrees. It just wouldn't be practical to apply for them. It's just so much paper anyway. Education isn't about facts, it's about application."

"Too bad they don't teach that in school."

"Yes. Shall I continue?"

"Please. It's just—"

"What?"

"I don't see how all of this applies to the rest of your story."

"You're impatient."

"Okay, yes, I am. You're telling me everything except the part I most want to know."

"The part you most want to know won't make sense without the part that unsettles you. You can't fire the gun in Act Two if you don't put it on the mantle in Act One. Yes, I studied Chekov too. Anton, not Pavel."

I throw up my hands in mock despair. "Point taken. I surrender. I apologize for interrupting."

"You'll find it's worth the wait. After that first night with Josiah, I saw life from a whole other perspective—"

Later, only later, did I realize that it was more than a single threshold that had been crossed, a whole realm had been opened and lay before me. The music I had been studying and playing—I suddenly heard it in a whole new way. It wasn't just a mathematically precise construction, it was also the composer's attempt to capture his emotions and share them, evoking the same passions in the listeners.

It was the part of life I had been missing. Monsieur knew it. That's why he sent me away. He knew I needed to lose my virginity—not the physical, but the emotional. He needed me to understand what it is to be human. Fully human. Otherwise—otherwise, I would have become a monster. And The Community kills monsters. So...it was all for my own protection. I didn't understand that at the time, not until much later.

Josiah and I—we became like honeymooners. I was certain that everyone around us could see the changes in our demeanor, but no one said anything—or they didn't care. The beer and poker evenings, curtailed by the winter, never resumed when spring returned. But Josiah and I spent every weekend together, and sometimes school nights as well. We professed to be study partners, but what we were studying was not to be found in any book, except perhaps the previously-mentioned Fanny Hill—and even that was far more about the physical than the emotional.

For the first few weeks, mostly we fumbled. After our singular adventure at the brothel, we both had some better idea of the male/female conjunction, albeit a somewhat simplistic perception. In our youthful ignorance, it seemed to us that there was only one possible connection between male and female—face to face penetration. Of course, I know now that there are considerable variations, more than either of us had realized at the time, but the act of penetration is still considered one of the most desirable culminations.

The male-male experience, however, exists as a whole other realm of possibilities. For one, the roles are as fluid as the partners' desires. Josiah's curiosity was matched by my own. If either of us touched or stroked, kissed or fondled, penetrated in any specific way, shortly we would reverse our positions so we could each experience the other side of the act. There was no assumption of masculine or feminine roles between us, only the shared experience of two men functioning as equals.

We continued to meet and mate, becoming ever more experienced, ever more knowledgeable about each other's bodies, ever more able to create mutual bouts of pleasure. If I had to pick a time in my life when I was truly happy, beyond anything I had believed I was capable of, I would start with those elusive evenings that Josiah and I created for ourselves.

Let me say here that I am not denigrating the contentment I experienced growing up with Monsieur. That was perhaps the best adolescence any young man could desire. But where Monsieur had focused on the intellectual aspects of my growth, the hours spent with Josiah were an even more necessary emotional expansion.

It did not last, of course. My grades suffered—not severely, but enough. And Josiah's as well, his more than mine. While neither of us were in danger of failing, our seemingly abrupt decline in our academic pursuits brought us both to the attention of the Dean.

I must be fair. The gentleman was not without wisdom. He had held his position for many years, enough time for him to recognize the various enthusiasms of young men. He met with me privately in his study, he wore a severely dark coat and a pleasant expression. He offered me port wine, and we chatted for a short while about various matters peripheral to the subject at hand, but possibly having some bearing on the central issue. Was I happy with my progress at the university? Was my family having financial difficulties? Was I dealing with any personal matters that might be distracting my attention from my studies?

I assured the Dean that my uncle was in fine health, I had no worries there, nor was I worried about the financial situation necessary to sustain my life in Boston. I could not think of any personal matters that were troubling me. On the contrary, I was enjoying my time at the university now more than ever—

It was that last point that caught the Dean's attention. "That may be the problem," he said. "A certain degree of hedonism is to be expected among young men of your age. Most young men outgrow such pursuits quickly, when they realize it is a spiritual dead end—when they discover that the responsibilities of adulthood are much more exciting. There are worlds to conquer out there—the frontier awaits you. There are industries to be created. Men of vision will be needed. Financial wizards will be needed to fuel the engines of exploration and development. Any young man of determination will find no shortage of opportunities—but it does take determination."

"Yes, of course, sir."

"It is my job as Dean to watch out for the well-being of the students. Up until now, your career here has been exemplary, and we have been proud to have you as a student. But lately, you seem to have lost some of your commitment to your classes, and I am concerned with that—*we* are concerned. Not just myself, but your instructors as well."

He cleared his throat, almost embarrassed. "I must admit, when you first came to us, I had some apprehensions that you might have trouble keeping up, but that worry quickly disappeared. Obviously, you were well-prepared for this life, better-prepared than many of your classmates, who I fear have been spoiled in their upbringing. You have always brought an interesting set of insights to your classwork, no doubt, an expression of your upbringing. Your uncle is to be complimented for the tutelage he provided." Another embarrassed clearing of his throat. "Given the superior demonstration of ability that you have displayed, any abrupt change in your efforts has to be seen as a sign of some personal distraction. I am not unfamiliar with the kinds of distractions that young men fall prey to. And..." This time a cough, "...I am here to provide you with appropriate guidance."

"Yes, sir. Thank you, sir. I appreciate your consideration. But let me assure you again that I am fine."

"No, you are not!" he snapped. His expression hardened. "Several of your instructors have discussed your demeanor with me—that you seem to have lost your drive, that your attention has become unfocused, that you seem preoccupied with affairs beyond the campus.

"At first, I thought there might be a young woman involved. Or several. That is not unusual. But most of our young men have learned the skills of keeping their romantic lives separate from their educational careers. You, apparently, have not."

"There are no—there is no woman," I said. A mistake.

"Yes, we know that now."

Oh. I felt a sudden cold tightening of my stomach, a surge of panic.

"Sometimes—" He stopped. He started again. "It is not uncommon. There is no need for shame. Sometimes it happens that young men of a certain nature fall into unhealthy friendships. It is very often a result of the pressures of the work and nothing to worry about. Most young men quickly outgrow such pursuits once they have experienced the superior companionship of appropriate young women. I feel certain that—"

"I *have* been with a woman—" I blurted the words. I should have said nothing. But I felt a sudden need to defend myself.

"Yes. Of course. We did hear of that excursion as well." He no longer looked embarrassed. Now he became stern. "The university is not without its own resources. Be that as it may—" He dusted imaginary crumbs off his dark trousers. "I am not unsympathetic. I do not say this to be harsh. But perhaps you are spending too much of your time with an inappropriate companion. It could lead you into a life of—well, let me be circumspect, there is no need to be vulgar—suffice it that certain unnatural pursuits offer no real profit and a great deal of distress." He paused. "Yes, I know that some people believe the poetry of Walt Whitman is an acceptable refutation, I am not among them."

He softened his tone now, leaning forward. For a moment, I thought he would put a hand on my knee. For a moment, he reminded me of the men of Monsieur's Community, too wise to be trusted, because there were goals they were not speaking.

"I ask you to trust my judgment in this matter," said the Dean. "I have had years of experience counseling young men, enough that I have some familiarity with how this—this aberration may proceed. I can tell with considerable authority that this is a path that will do you little good in life. I strongly suggest that you take steps to widen your circle of acquaintances and develop a broader range of interests. Otherwise, I fear your momentary excesses may continue to affect your ability to focus on your education. And—" He paused meaningfully. "—It could affect your future at the university."

"You use the word 'suggest,'" I said. "Perhaps you mean something else? Like 'demand'—?"

"You may interpret my counsel as you wish. As you are responsible for your own behaviors, you will also be accountable for the consequences. The university does not wish to lose you. I would be personally disappointed to see you go, but this is a choice that you will have to make in your life."

"I see, thank you, sir, for your time." I rose to go. I did not offer to shake his hand, nor did he offer to shake mine. It would have been irrelevant in any case, I was already shaken enough.

While the Dean had never said so directly, he had made himself quite clear. He knew that Josiah and I had been sharing a bed. He wanted us to stop. If we did not—

I would not see Josiah until Friday afternoon. Until then, I fell into such a state, I couldn't have described it. The turmoil in my mind was a storm of unpleasant emotions. I could almost hear voices arguing back and forth—not the least, my own—but also Monsieur's, Josiah's, the Dean's, and even the possible sniggering remarks of acquaintances who had shared many boisterous evenings of cards in my rooms, but otherwise meant little to me. I feared the public shame, I felt unreasonable guilt—I raged with anger as well, how dare any of them judge what they had never experienced! And overwhelming all of that, the dread that I would never see my dear Josiah again or be able to lie with him, wrapped in his arms and tasting his delicious kisses.

My mind churned with possibilities. We could run away together. We could flee to Seattle. Monsieur would take us in, he would welcome my return. Josiah and I could be together safely—all of us. We could protect Monsieur in the daylight, he would provide us safety in the night.

But—

What I did not know, not at that time, was that Josiah had also been called into the Dean's office. It was not the first time he had been apprehended.

Josiah had been my first. I had believed—he had let me believe—that I was also his first. Such was not the case. Apparently, Josiah had a known history of "unhealthy friendships," as the Dean referred to them. I was only the latest.

As I had never demonstrated any previous inclination toward this manner of affection, the Dean had decided that a careful conversation on appropriate morals and manners for a young man, when weighed against the future opportunities that would no longer be available to men of such a nature, would be sufficient to restore me to the path of excellence I had previously been following. He had interpreted my noncommittal replies as acquiescence. Indeed, my blurted assertion that I had been with a woman, albeit it a prostitute, had further served to convince him that I was not a pervert, only overcome by the circumstances—the combination of the pent-up physical needs of the male body and the persistent attentions of a seductive predator.

What I did not know—not then—was that Josiah's previous relationships were well known to the Dean and other members of the faculty. Josiah had been told, more than once, and in no uncertain terms, that had it not been for his parents' wealth and their lavish gifts to the university, he would have been expelled on any of his previous offenses— and Josiah had sincerely promised that he would refrain from initiating any more "unholy relationships" with underclassmen.

Obviously, Josiah had not kept his word—and the continuing decline of his family's finances since the Panic of 1873 and the long depression that followed had weakened the university's obligation to pretend that Josiah's behavior was only an affectation, a phase, and not an indicator of some deeper and much less reconcilable flaw in his character. By the time I found out that Josiah had been dismissed from the university, he was already on a train back to New York.

I did not know what to feel.

Betrayed? Certainly. But by whom? By the Dean? By Josiah? By my own nature? My turmoil was now magnified beyond my ability to endure. I considered rushing down to the train station—I would purchase a ticket and follow Josiah to New York. We could rent rooms in Greenwich Village. No one would bother us there. We could be together again. We could build a life together.

But at the same time—the logical part of my mind was reminding me of Monsieur's own words. "Decisions made while raging are always the wrong decision. Passion overwhelms reason. Take no action at all until you have carefully considered the consequences. What may be most satisfying to your emotions will likely be the least productive to your future."

At the time he had given me that advice—on the day of our parting—

it had sounded like nothing more than a dreary reprise of Laertes' advice to Polonius. That was my fault. Monsieur and I had both come to the conclusion that Laertes was a doddering old fool, self-righteous, puffed-up, and oblivious to the realities around him. But more than that, as eager as I was to travel, to have the great adventure of finding what lay beyond the wall of mountains to the east, then crossing the vast sea of grass that filled the center of the continent, and discovering the frenetic worlds of modern civilization, as eager as I was—I still raged with grief and despair at having to leave the only safety I had ever known. The fear of being separated from Monsieur had so permeated my every waking moment that I felt betrayed by his adamant insistence that I must leave. I heard his words, but I was already so overwhelmed with emotion that I could not hear the wisdom within them.

But now, even as I was felled by my own feelings of rage and despair, the chasm between desire and loss—even as I wanted to succumb to the heat of those passions, I knew I should not. All those years as Monsieur's daykeeper, protecting his chambers against the daylight—that discipline now served me well.

Monsieur had trained me to consider every circumstance. All those long evening discussions, poking, prodding, analyzing and dissecting the various bodies of thought laid out before us—I had eventually developed some small skills of my own. Now, having flung myself back and forth in restless confusion, and finding no respite in my emotions, I was exhausted. As I lay collapsed across my unmade bed—a bed that still smelled of Josiah's presence and our passionate exercises together—even as my physical and emotional components were both so completely depleted that I felt powerless and drained, my thoughts continued to churn unchallenged, only now instead of rehearsing my upsets one more time, the analytical part of my mind began to examine the specific elements of my situation, looking for meanings I might have missed while embraced in desire.

If what I had learned was true, that Josiah did indeed have a history of male seduction, then I was only one more conquest. I had to recognize, and I did so with some annoyance, that Josiah had been using me. Indeed, he had used me well.

I do not mean to say that he did not care. On the contrary. Josiah had cared for me as completely as I had cared for him. But for him, it was only an affection of the moment—not a commitment of his emotions. Myself, not having the same experience with sexual relations, had nothing to measure my feelings against. I could make no comparisons. I had simply been overwhelmed.

But if Josiah had been using me, then I had been using him as well—I had satisfied myself in his arms, allowed myself to succumb to the warmth of his physical and emotional companionship. I had taken my own comfort in the affair.

This thought did not bring me any degree of solace. If anything, it only increased my distress. What could I do now? Where would I find any equivalent joy? Was there another person available to me who could understand? I was even more bereft than before.

Monsieur would understand. I knew that. We shared the same nature. He had said as much, more than once. Indeed, that was part of the reason he needed me to leave Seattle—so that I might mature into my own soul and not be dependent on him.

Having resolved that Monsieur's counsel would be the best course of action, I sat down immediately at my desk and prepared my writing instruments. I began to compose a long letter, carefully worded of course, describing my emotional torment.

I did not discuss the details, Monsieur had been quite clear that the mail was not to be trusted with confidential matters. Once a word is committed to paper, it remains forever available. Whatever secrets might be shared become the knowledge of anyone obtaining access to that page. So I wrote in the same coded sentences we had shared for so many previous exchanges. "I feel I have suffered a grievous loss. I have written to you previously of my friendship with J. We had grown quite close, but now he has left the university and I am distraught. I have already begun to miss his companionship in the evenings. We shared many affable moments and our friendship became so complete that on occasion, when the weather outside was too bitter for him to return to his own rooms, he shared my bed. It is not uncommon for students to bundle up, but in this situation, the closeness provided ample opportunities for the most intense of all conversations, with no subject off limits. We explored all manner of ideas, both intellectual and spiritual, even to the most profound questions on the nature of human affection and relationships. I fear that I will never again have any companion with whom I feel such a profound connection. I have thought that with the passage of time, my distress would fade, but as of this writing I still feel no ease."

I sent that letter off by the fastest possible post, knowing that it would be at least three weeks before I would see a reply. I wished then that I owned some fantastic bird that could fly all night, so that my letter could be in his hands the very next day. But I knew that no human agency would ever provide such instantaneous communication. I would have to endure until the arrival of his reply.

As distressed as I was, I focused myself on my studies for the next three weeks, and to all outward appearances, I had resumed my previous demeanor. I must have been convincing, for the Dean stopped me in the hall one day and congratulated me for heeding the wisdom of his counsel. I offered little more than a polite expression of gratitude—simulated, not actual. "I appreciate that you set aside the time in your schedule for me." He took that as an acknowledgment of his superior wisdom, clapped me on the shoulder in what he must have thought was a manly fashion, and proceeded on his way. By then, I had learned well of his agency in Josiah's dismissal from the university, and I'm certain he knew that I knew, but we pretended cordiality and agreement of purpose anyway.

I continued with my studies and despite the usual flurries of sophomoric gossip, both to my face and behind my back, I said nothing more to anyone about what had happened between myself and Josiah. My goal was simply to persevere and after a few more days, when there was no new information to be chewed over in the dining halls, the subject fell into disfavor, forgotten in the rush of new mysteries to ponder. The continuing and somewhat more outrageous maladventures of the university's varsity football squad quickly became the new center of interest. Perhaps I should also acknowledge that there were quite a few men on campus who desired to keep that particular set of speculations from expanding to any detailed examination of their own friendships. They were quite adept at shifting the conversation away, much to my own veiled amusement. I was beginning to sense that I was not alone in my attractions.

Monsieur's reply did not arrive as quickly as I had expected, which left me both puzzled and troubled. He had never delayed his reply before. The Postal Service had been advertising their impressive record for transcontinental delivery, so I had no reason to suspect his reply was hindered in transit.

I was already feeling some considerable unease when the Dean called me to his office again. I wondered what he could possibly want. It could not be about my affair with Josiah. That matter was ended. And I doubted that the Dean needed to compliment me further on my academic progress.

He had already done so and the man was not known for having an effusive manner.

On the matter of Josiah, despite my first fevered urges, I had not pursued him. Because I believed courtesy demanded it, I had allowed myself one deliberately polite note, sent care of his family, in which I expressed the hope that he would do well in New York. He had not written back and I felt no desire to pursue the matter. Perhaps his family had not passed my letter on to him, perhaps he had chosen not to respond. Perhaps his expulsion had colored his experience of companionship. Perhaps his memories of our times together were not as happy as my own.

I had no way of knowing the details and it would have been unwise to seek out any explanation as that would have required additional communications—and very likely the attention of the Dean again. Whatever the circumstance, the whole affair was ended, if not by his choice, if not by the university's choice, then certainly by mine. This was not a relationship it would be safe to continue.

In the weeks of waiting to hear from Monsieur, I deliberated with myself at some length, long hours restlessly examining my own circumstances. I even made lists, considering all the options in front of me—then, frustrated, I would tear up the lists and burn the scraps of paper in the fireplace. Eventually, however, I came back to the understanding that the best possible course for myself would be to return to the course that Monsieur had set me on. It was the only worthwhile path.

If I were to be of benefit to anyone, especially myself, I would have to put this whole squalid business aside and concentrate again on becoming the kind of man that Monsieur would regard as a worthy colleague. Nevertheless, I still longed for Monsieur's counsel and reassurances.

When I arrived at the Dean's office, he seemed unduly compassionate. Also present was Monsieur's east coast agent, a Mr. Panshin. He was tall and bony and sallow, and he had a humorless demeanor. I did not know him well, I had met with him only a few times, on the infrequent occasions he needed me to sign one set of papers or another, but he also managed my financial affairs, making sure that the regular transfers of funds from Monsieur were deposited into the appropriate accounts—so seeing him in the Dean's office gave me a start. It was my first apprehension that whatever I was about to hear was much more serious than anything I might have previously thought.

The Dean directed me to a comfortable chair, upholstered in dark red leather, and then asked a little too solicitously if there was anything I would like. Water perhaps? A glass of wine? I sensed immediately that something was very wrong.

Mister Panshin spoke. His voice was dreary. "I'm afraid I have some rather distressing news." He withdrew a letter from his coat pocket. I did not recognize either the stationery or the handwriting. "It's from your uncle's agents in Seattle. There's been a—" He hesitated. "—I'm sorry, Jacob. Your uncle is dead."

I heard the words, but they had no meaning.

"Did you hear me, lad? Your uncle has passed away—"

And then, yes, I did finally realize—I came out of my chair as if shot from a cannon. "By your leave, sir! There must be some mistake! Monsieur— he cannot die! He's—" I stopped myself before I said more. "No. I will not believe it. It cannot be true—"

The Dean stepped over to me. He put his hand on my shoulder and pushed me back down to the chair. And now my body did start shaking, the emotions flooded in, the cold fire of panic surging up from my gut, clenching my chest, tightening my throat, I must have screamed—

Next I knew, I was on the floor, on my back, an aide fanning air into my face with a sheaf of papers, the Dean hovering above, the university doctor listening to my heart with a stethoscope, frowning. My heart, my head, my whole body was pounding. I felt pinned against a brick wall of impossibility. No, no, no! Monsieur! No, there must be some mistake—

The doctor lifted my head, supported me for a moment, gave me a draught of some foul-tasting liquid to drink, perhaps it had alcohol in it, possibly something else. Laudanum? Probably. It was bitter. All those alkaloids. I spat out as much as I could. Monsieur had warned me of things that taint the blood. "Water—" I gasped. The doctor took the glass away, returned with another, this time filled with water. This time, I drank to empty the glass. It didn't help, but—

The next day, I was on a train headed west.

Jacob puts his wineglass down. "Shall we have desert?"

I shake my head. "I don't do sugar."

"Smart. Sugar's a poison you know. It does bad things to the blood. The average person, he'll eat more sugar in a year than the whole city of Seattle would have. In that time."

"You're making that up."

"I'm estimating."

"Well, sugar wasn't readily available then."

"And now it is. And you're all addicted to it. You're all overweight and sick. I don't mind the overweight. I do mind the sickness. It affects the taste." He picks up his wineglass again, swirls the last of the darkness around before drinking it. Jacob looks across to me. "There are other flavors, you know. Salt. Savory. Sour. Tart. Not everything needs sprinkles."

"You have a different sense of taste than most people."

"I have an *enhanced* sense of taste, yes. And smell as well."

"Yes, you've said that."

"Unless I remind you, you'll forget."

"You want me to be curious, don't you?"

"You already are. Admit it. You want to know what I've experienced."

"If I didn't, we wouldn't be sitting here." A glance. "—And the staff wouldn't be standing around, waiting for us to leave—" I nod toward the distant waiter.

Jacob signals the man. He holds up a hundred dollar bill. "This should cover it. Keep the change."

The waiter is gracious in his thanks. Jacob and I stand and head for the door. We're the last customers in the pub. As the door closes behind us, I feel Jacob's hand on the small of my back. He slides it up toward my neck. I should feel fear, but I don't. I feel pleasure instead.

I turn to Jacob on the night-lit sidewalk, stare into his beautiful dark eyes. "Tell me the truth—"

"Of course."

"Are you trying to seduce me?"

His smile is faint, almost enigmatic. "On the contrary."

"Huh?"

"It is you who are trying to seduce me."

"No, I'm—"

"Yes, you are." He puts his hand on my shoulder. "Think about it—the whole process of seduction, who's really controlling it?"

"Uh, isn't it obvious—?"

"No. You people misunderstand seduction. It's another way you don't know how to have a relationship. Seduction is a courtship dance. The male puffs up his feathers, dances and postures, does everything he can to attract the female's attention. If she's interested, she stays. If not, she leaves. The seduction doesn't happen unless and until the object of desire wants it to happen. It's the same in every species—from elephants to honey bees. The drones chase the queens, not the other way around. They're all driven by pheromones, instinct, whatever—but it's a universal fact, the female chooses her mate, not the other way around. As much as a man wants to believe he's running the show, it's the woman who's controlling every moment. It's the same with male-male."

"I don't know about that—"

"Yes, you do. You can't lie to me, remember."

"Okay, okay. Maybe, I do, but what you're saying—about male-male seduction—it's not the same."

"Yes, it is. You want me to chase you, but you aren't ready to be caught."

I have to think about that for a moment. I glance away, shake my head as if to clear it, glance back. "Okay—that might be so for ordinary men. But you have powers—don't you? I mean, you haven't talked about it, but you've implied as much. Couldn't you just take me? Or anyone you wanted?"

"That would be rape." His hand is tight on my shoulder. "Rape isn't sex. It's assault. It's about power. And frustration. And rage. The rapist takes something that isn't freely given. It's the theft of intimacy—no, not even that, it's a violent imitation of intimacy."

Something in his eyes. Something in the way he says it. "You've been raped—?"

"I thought I made that clear. Street-boys, especially the smaller ones, are always vulnerable."

"I'm sorry."

"I'm over it. Now. But it was a lesson quickly learned. Choose your clients carefully. And always have an escape route. And have an alternate income to fall back on, too. And—"

"And...?"

"Plan your revenge carefully."

"Revenge?"

"I think I'll wait till next time to share that. It's late, and I do want dessert. We'll continue this again. Later."

"When?"

"When it's time."

He lets go of my shoulder and vanishes into the shadows.

Jacob in Seattle

I'm sitting on the dais—I'm on a panel, alongside three other writers, all of them better known and far more successful, so I don't need to say a lot, just an occasional grunt of agreement. But it's not a loss, I've made a few scratchings on my notepad. I've learned to listen because I learn more from listening than talking. And I don't like to talk because I haven't yet learned how to avoid stumbling into arguments.

The moderator has just said, "Okay, we'll throw it open to the audience now. Are there any questions?" and immediately I have to control my expression because the unkempt guy in the third row, the one whose reactions were out of control for most of the panel, the one who does not understand that the word "question" refers to a specific form of communication, a request for information or clarification, has now stood up to postulate his own assertions about the nature of horror fiction, and in particular how to write a vampire story—and while he doesn't specifically single me out, I get it that he's a traditionalist, vampires should be creatures of horror, therefore he's adamantly opposed to the deconstruction of the trope into tawdry exercises of homoerotic angst, as typified by certain recent authors. "Vampires should be sucking necks, not—"

And by this point, I have no doubt that he's talking about my stories, I'm even more amazed he knows the word *tawdry*. I cover my face with my palm so the rest of the audience won't see how hard I'm rolling my eyes. I can see the bottom of my brain.

Fortunately, before I can seize the microphone and explain to this self-important, self-inflated, self-righteous member of the cape-and-pimple crowd that I write for me, not him—hey, I didn't hold him down and stuff all those greasy French fries in his face—the moderator has cut him off. "Is there a question mark at the end of this sentence?"

"Umm, no—this is a comment."

"Thank you, but we're only taking questions now."

"Umm, I was just offering my opinion. Don't I have the right to my opinion—?"

And that's when one of the other authors grabs the mike and says, "Of course you have the right to an opinion. And after you publish a vampire story or two, we'll be happy to have you up here on the panel to offer it."

This is greeted with a smattering of laughter and even some applause.

The man sits down. He takes his vampires too seriously. But then again, so do I. But then again—I have reason to. There's one sitting quietly in the back row, smiling at me like an old friend.

Well, I guess—yes.

Jacob wears a familiar black hoodie, this one says Boston on the front, no accident, I have to smile at that. His eyes are bright and his face is ruddy, as if he has been freshly out in the sun. I doubt that's the case, nevertheless he glows in that quiet way he has. I search for the word in my mind. I'm always searching for the right word. Mordant? Piquant? None of those.

The panel ends, a small crowd gathers around the other authors, a couple of ladies who appear to be in danger of overflowing their leather bustierres—autocorrect wants to call those devices bestiaries, which fascinates me and leads me to consider what names I would give the beasts contained within—never mind, the women thrust their magazines into my face, asking/demanding autographs. They've read my stories, they like my gay vampires. One of them pushes forward and says, almost conspiratorially, "But let me explain to you what you vampire writers don't understand about male homosexuality—"

"Excuse me, I have—a friend to meet." I gnaw off a leg and escape.

I'm pretty sure I have more experience with male homosexuality than she does, but I'm not about to share that information with her—that's a discussion I'll only have with another man and only when we both have our clothes off.

Jacob is waiting for me at the back of the room. I hug him affectionately. He looks at me oddly. "What's that for?"

"I missed you."

He's unimpressed. "You mortals—you are so desperate in your affections."

"At least we have affections."

"I have a different perspective." He studies me for a moment. "You are maturing nicely."

"Thank you. It's been a while."

"Yes." He takes my arm, like a beau. "Shall we adjourn to a place where there is less commotion?"

"I'd like that, yes." I forget about the party invitations at the convention.

As we head toward the door, he lets go of my elbow and takes me by the hand instead. At first, I'm startled, but then I realize, he's showing off. And holding his hand, I realize I'm showing off as well—flaunting even.

Behind me, how do I see this?—and yet, I sense it clearly—the bustierre women are noticing and murmuring. And possibly several of the nine-to-a-room crowd as well. I realize I don't care. They don't matter. Jacob does.

I glance to him. "Your charmfield is on."

"I fed well last night. I'm satisfied. I'm even...happy. I have resolved something." He smiles, not broadly, but enough to reveal his sharp white teeth. He squeezes my hand—a small signal of connection.

A thought occurs to me.

"What?" he asks, even before I can speak it.

"How many other protégés do you have?"

A slight hesitation. "You're the only one, now."

"Now?"

He leans his head toward mine and says, "Don't ask questions you don't want the answer to."

I reply with silence. There's a sudden knot of cold fire twisting in my gut.

"What?" he demands.

"I hadn't realized how dangerous your acquaintance could be."

"My friendship, my affection, isn't dangerous—" he says quietly. "My anger is."

"I hope I never make you angry."

"I hope so too. I have begun to have feelings for you."

"Well, that's an admission—"

"It should be obvious. If I did not have some interest, if you did not hold some attraction for me, I wouldn't seek you out, would I?"

We are outside the hotel, waiting for a taxi. I let go of his hand and face him. "Then I have to ask. What attraction do I have for you? Am I just another interesting plaything in your long journey through time? Or am I something else?"

"I haven't decided yet," he says.

The taxi pulls up and he gestures for me to enter first. Jacob gives the driver an address. We sit quietly for a moment, then Jacob slides his hand over mine and the silence takes on a new tension.

For some reason, I'm thinking about kissing him. I don't, but I think about it. What stops me is the uncertainty. I don't know how he might react. Would he be offended? Would he think I was being forward? Would that anger him?

Or would he return the affection? For the first time, I am seriously wondering what it would be like to be in bed with him, and which of us would be on top, or would we take turns?

It's the charmfield, the sparkle zone. He can't help it. Neither can I. I hold his hand tightly in mine. He smiles at me. I realize I'm smiling too.

Finally, I ask, "You can't tone it down, can you?"

"No, not really. Not this soon after..."

We arrive at a tree-shaded intersection, only a single street-light interrupts the darkness. Jacob pays the driver. He takes my hand again and we walk a block and a half to an older apartment building. "Is this where you—?"

"Shh."

Once inside, he says, "Don't touch anything. And don't go in the bedroom." He nods toward a closed door.

"Why not? What's in—? Oh." Realization dawns. "This isn't your—"

"No, it was his."

I'm confused. "Why did you bring me here? This is a—" I stop myself before I finish the sentence. —Crime scene.

"Yes, I brought you here. On purpose," Jacob says. "You need to understand what it is you're playing with. For you, this has been...some kind of..."

I can't take my eyes off the door. "It's not a game—"

"No, it is not." Jacob turns to me. "That's the point. You still live in your little world of words, your trails of thought across the page. You are no different than all the other poseurs and wannabes, dabblers and dilettantes. You have no special talent. No—" He holds up a hand to stop me from protesting. "The only thing you do have is a willingness to listen—maybe even a willingness to learn. But that's not enough. You also need to recognize what we are talking about here—it's not a fiction, it's not a fantasy, it's—"

He strides to the closed door of the bedroom. "What it is, is behind this door. Here, do you want to see the bloodstained reality?"

"I'll take your word for it—"

"That's the point!" He advances on me angrily, putting his face close to mine, and for the first time, I feel the stirrings of fear. "Yes, you'll take my word for it—because you don't want to know the reality. You're happy to reduce it to a fiction, a fantasy, a thought experiment—because you don't want to deal with the truth. You can't deal with it, can you?

"If even once, you were to face the reality of what's in that room, you would have to deal with your own complicity in the matter. You are my accomplice in this. You want to make me understandable. Sympathetic. But the reality remains—I kill people. I feed on their flesh. Sometimes I do it out of hunger and sometimes I do it for the sheer pleasure of feeding, the same way you sink your teeth into a piece of steak, never once thinking about the steer that had to give up his life so that you could have that piece of his shoulder. Well, here—when I feed, someone dies. A life ends. A body is left sprawled in the echoes of agony on a blood-soaked sheet. This one—"

Jacob walks away from me, agitated—more energized than I have ever seen him, I begin to get a sense of it, he's full of blood, full of youthful energy—full of his own emotions as well, the chief among them being rage.

He points to the door again. "This one—he had talent, real talent, far more than you with your pitiful scribblings, your feeble transcriptions. He had a future. He could have been important. He was passionate. But—" Jacob stops in mid-sentence and I realize that he's angry at himself, angry at the door that had to be closed—not this one, but the metaphorical door to possibility, the chance that was lost.

"But...?"

Jacob looks across the room, his eyes fiery. "But he had a conscience."

"Oh."

"I don't know if that's a good thing or a bad thing for a writer," Jacob says. "But it's a bad thing for a vampire."

He glares across at me, an accusation.

I want to look away—but I won't.

"You—" he says. "Do you have a conscience?"

No one has ever asked me that before. "I—I don't know. I don't think I've ever been tested for one."

Jacob speaks softer, his rage has subsided. Now his anger only smolders. "I offered him...an opportunity." After a pause, he explains, "He turned it down."

"I'm sorry."

"So am I. He gave me no choice."

I have to ask. "If he had accepted, would we still be—friends?"

"Acquaintances," Jacob corrects. "We are acquaintances. You cannot have friendship with a vampire. You should never assume that relationship."

"All right, fine. But answer the question. If that one in there—if he had said yes, what about me? Us?"

Jacob crosses to me. His expression changes. He trails his fingertips slowly down my cheek, he traces the line of my jaw. Seductively, he asks, "What do you think?" He's close enough to kiss.

Is this what he wants? Is this what I want? Jacob wanted me to confront reality tonight. All right, I will. "I think—maybe, we should stop being acquaintances." There's a double meaning in that sentence, but—he takes the first one.

Jacob pulls back, grinning. "If that's what you want, *mon petit fromage*. But...don't you want to hear the rest of my story?"

Well, crap. He had me there.

I mean, who wouldn't want to know?

We leave the apartment, still not touching anything. Jacob wipes the doorknobs, both inside and out. We head up the street toward a distant glimmer of light, an all-night coffee shop, a mom-and-pop operation on one end of a block of old stores that had not yet been replaced by franchises. Most of the signs have faded, almost to unreadability.

Jacob orders coffee, which he barely touches. I poke at a late-night offering of bacon and eggs.

"So if that's not your apartment, do you have a permanent place—?"

"I have places." He explains, "It's inconvenient to have a permanent residence. After too many years, people begin to wonder why you aren't aging. Jokes about a dreadful picture in the attic are only funny for a short while."

Jacob stirs his coffee slowly, pretending to be interested in it, but I know him well enough by now to know that he never does anything without deliberate intention.

He looks into me abruptly, a sudden piercing stare. "So where were we?"

"Seattle. You were on your way back. You heard the terrible news from Mr. Guignard. You were on the next train west."

"Yes, of course. It was a very stressful journey. Trains were so much slower in those days, with frequent stops for water and coal. And the whole time, my head was filled with terrible imaginings. My circumstances became even more stressful after I arrived."

Of course, I went straight to Monsieur's house.

I stood there alone on the street, staring at the blackened ruins. The remains of only two walls barely stood, there was nothing left of the stately home where I had spent so many pleasant hours.

And, even more horrific, despite the dampness of the air, the never-ending rain of the region, the air around the ruins still reeked of burnt timber. Even the sheltering trees had been reduced to charred stumps.

I felt such anguish, I really cannot describe it. The solid ground beneath my feet had suddenly turned into a landscape of ash. I must have let out a terrible wail of despair, I know I sank to my knees in anguish, because the next thing I knew, the driver of the horse-drawn cab was standing beside me, his hand on my shoulder. "Are ye all right, laddie?"

Of course, I wasn't all right, but—the thing about men, in those days as now, you always say, "Yes, yes, I'm fine. I'll be fine. Just give me a minute." I held up a hand to hold him away from me.

"It was a fine old house here, it was," the cabbie offered.

"You knew it?" I pulled myself to my feet, wiping at my nose with my handkerchief.

"Hard not to, being on this street and all—you have to pass it whether you're coming up the hill or going across. Always wondered who owned it, it being such a silent place these past few years. Shuttered and boarded for a long time too."

"Shuttered and boarded, you say?"

"Aye. There were lights upstairs once in a while, so the place wasn't deserted, wasn't abandoned, but—who knows? This is a strange and dangerous town, it still is. Always will be."

I turned to him, as if seeing him for the first time. "Are you suggesting the fire was deliberately set?"

He shrugged. "I've no particular knowledge, laddie, but that's the talk. Somebody must have wanted the land. It wouldn't be the first time, y'know—" The cabbie glanced at me, at my bag. "Listen, laddie. If ye haven't a place to stay, I can recommend the Seaman's Inn down by the market. Not too much of a strain on your purse. Weekly rates. And the cleanest bedbugs in town, they say. And if you're of a mind for that sort of thing, not too far from the fairies' walk."

"They still do that—?"

"Aye. This town is cursed with a terrible lack of women. Unless you count Miss Lou Graham's place. Quite a few men go there for entertainment."

"Lou Graham is still here?"

"Aye, she's an institution, she is. Never been there myself, but my customers talk. They say she runs the best house in the northwest. Wouldn't know about that, though...."

I climbed back into the cab and let him deliver me to the Seaman's Inn. He gave me his card, his name was Mr. Marley Matthews, and offered his services for hire on a daily rate. I promised that I would seek him out at his regular stand as soon as I was up and about. I would have much to do tomorrow.

The sun was already low in the west, it was too late in the day to attempt a visit to Monsieur's agents in town. That would be my first priority. Then I'd have to find more permanent lodging, perhaps Monsieur's agents could recommend something. And of course, I had to locate the other men of The Community, but those inquiries would have to be as discreet as possible.

I intended to begin my own investigation. I was certain the men of The Community would know much more of what had happened than anyone else. I had little idea what I expected to learn, but I remained possessed of a dreadful certainty that I did not yet know the whole story. Monsieur had always been too careful, too deliberate.

That evening, restless and unable to sleep, I took a walk around the surrounding blocks. The market still stood unchanged. The wharfs still smelled of fish and tar. The sea rattled with foam and the last bits of winter ice.

There was much that was familiar, but even more that had changed. For example, there were new gas lamps lining the avenues—so the commerce that had depended on the secrecy of the evening had shifted toward darker domains.

Nevertheless, I was approached several times by street boys. Knowing many of their tricks, having invented a few myself, I kept my wallet safely buttoned into an inside pocket of my vest. Even the most skilled of pickpockets would not have been able to extract it—particularly because of the silver chain attached to it.

And while it was not what I was looking for, two or three of the boys offered their services for the evening, I politely declined—but one of them reminded me too much of my younger self. He was called Georgie-boy and someday he would be a stocky fellow, enough to remind me of my lost Josiah.

If Georgie-boy had ever been given any other name, he didn't know, he'd never been called anything but Georgie-boy. And he wasn't sure how old he was, I assumed he was about thirteen or fourteen—that from his looks and by what he was able to remember of his early days. He remembered when the schooner *Montana* was built and when she sank in the violent storm that swept huge waves ashore and flooded the streets, he remembered the water coming up to his chest and someone pulling him out. I remembered that storm too, occurring three years before I left for Boston. So he was thirteen, maybe fourteen.

I asked Georgie-boy to join me for a cup of chowder. Perhaps he assumed I was taking his measure, a bit of courteous foreplay before the inevitable invitation to my bed in exchange for a dollar, but no—I was only interested in hearing him talk of the life of the street. I promised to make it worth his while.

I had to reassure him that I was not a cop, nor an agent of any other kind of legal agency—apparently, he had escaped from a rather severe orphanage—but he was thin and hungry and a little too desperate for warmth, and not just the kind of warmth you find by a roaring fire. Like all of the boys, I'm certain he was hoping to find a long-term patron, someone to rescue him from the harsh conditions he presently endured.

He led me to a nearby hole in the wall eatery that catered to the working men of the neighborhood, not the cleanest establishment I'd ever attended, but certainly one of the heartiest. Over fresh sourdough bread and a huge bowl of steaming fish chowder, the two of us talked at length, man and boy. I did not realize it at the time, but I was beginning an acquaintanceship that echoed my own history with Monsieur.

I told Georgie-boy that I had been away from the city for a long time, more than seven years, I was curious about the changes that had occurred in my absence. I did not tell him any specifics of my past, he did not seem interested in any case, nor did I pose any direct questions about his own past. Instead, I let him natter on about what he had seen and what he had heard. He had a sharp look about him and the wit of one who had long-since learned to survive on the streets. Eventually, I managed to work the conversation around to the darker gossips of the city. It might have been idle curiosity on the part of anyone else, but for me it was an opportunity to revisit my own past and be grateful again for the escape that Monsieur had provided.

Georgie-boy revealed that conditions were much the same as I had known them, if not worse. Boys came and went. Some disappeared mysteriously. The boys tried to watch out for each other, but it wasn't easy. From time to time, the word would go around, watch out. Pinky went off with a tall pale man, he was never seen again. Littlefoot never came back either. Be careful of party invitations, Collin was assaulted, he came back bleeding from a bite on the neck. Georgie-boy spat, some of the boys were superstitious, he wasn't—but there were bad things happening, bad people out there.

I couldn't offer much reassurance. Monsieur had once admitted that there were men in The Community who satisfied their hunger on the street boys. Young blood not only tasted better, Monsieur revealed, it also had a profound rejuvenating effect, it was one of the ways the members of The Community stayed so youthful-looking.

I said nothing of what I knew. If I had, the boy would have thought me mad. And perhaps I was living in a delusion. From time to time, the thought had occurred to me that perhaps Monsieur, and in fact the entire Community, were merely men who liked to pretend a supernatural identity, that unable to deal directly with their natures, their attraction to other men, they sublimated their sexual urges into an exquisitely detailed, bizarre fantasy life. I had no real evidence—other than Monsieur's assertions—that The Community was what Monsieur claimed it to be.

Georgie-boy had correctly perceived that I was newly arrived in Seattle and that I would shortly need to find a more permanent placement than the Seaman's Inn. He said he knew of a place, not too far, where a flat had recently become available. He would take me there, if I was interested— and then, very hesitantly, he asked if in return, I might let him sometimes escape the cold and the wet of Seattle's worst nights.

I said that I would certainly consider that option, but first I would have to see the flat. I admit, that it seemed too convenient an opportunity, but the economy of Seattle had not changed so much since my days on the street. Like my friendly cabbie who I am certain must have received kickbacks from Miss Lou Graham or from the Seaman's Inn, even Georgie-

Boy was always available to accept a finder's fee as well.

I felt bad for him—even in the depths of my own despair, I still had enough human feeling to recognize that others still existed in more dire circumstances, living in the darkness beyond the gas lamps, a darkness that the politer elements of society ignored, except when looking for their own illicit pleasures. I'd seen—I'd even serviced—the men who wore silk undergarments, the ones whose wealth had removed them so far from the lives of the working men and women that they believed themselves not just a class apart, but even a whole species apart. But on their knees or their bellies or their backs, they grunted just the same. I had no respect for that hypocrisy, not there and not anywhere else. My time in Boston had only honed my distaste for the pretense of gentility. I was too aware of its underside.

I gave Georgie-boy a handful of loose change, told him to find a warm bed for the night—he suggested that for a few coppers they would turn a blind eye if I took him back to the Seaman's Inn, and for a moment I was tempted—not for the favors of his body, which might have been pleasurable enough—but out of concern for his well-being. In the end, propriety stopped me. Pleading exhaustion from my travels, I declined.

Monsieur had taught me nothing if not propriety, a set of inhibitions I would occasionally have cause to regret. But on this night, I still had too much on my mind to think of my own carnal pleasures. Another time, perhaps—

Despite myself, I interrupt. "The boy was thirteen. Or fourteen—"

Jacob holds up a hand for silence. "Times were different then. And the boys were desperate."

"Don't try to justify it—"

"I'm not. I'm telling you that times were different then. Men and boys took comfort from each other. Age was not the issue. The boys were hungry. The customers were tender in their affections, more than you realize, much more than the shocked look on your face reveals. There was no 'age of consent' then, there was only convenience. That's a blue-nosed fiction—"

I put my fork down, horrified.

Jacob looks at me, pityingly. "Call it survival sex, if that will assuage your offended sensibilities. It's what the boys did because it was all there was for them to do—a service they provided for the men who wanted even the barest pretense of affection in a violent city. This culture, today, your culture—" He waves his hand as if indicting the entire continent. "— How dare you assume that the pretentious standards of this century are so superior that you are fit to judge the morals and manners of any other time or place. Your culture is rife with hypocrisy and lies. You pretend to nobility of purpose, but you are arrogant fools. You pretend that you are enlightened, that you are living the superior lives because you have electricity and technology and hamburgers—while you rape the very soul of the Earth in your greed. Trust me on this, I have seen so much more of life than you, more life than any of you mayfly-beings, and if I have not yet seen all the different ways that the worst of human ways belie the best of human words, I have seen enough to know that a bit of tender affection, regardless of the age of the participants, is far superior to the emotional and spiritual violence that you poor pathetic mayflies inflict upon each other in your desperate efforts to have your lives be about something before they wink out of existence.

"Your culture—and yes, you are a servant of it, you repeat its conversations, lending them the authority of your conviction—a conviction without evidence—your culture, like every culture before it, believes it has found the right way to exist, and all others are merely exotic experiments. Do you honestly believe that sensuality does not exist until one is old enough to obtain a driver's license? And only then, is an erection a permissible event? And only if it is applied in appropriate positions? And only certain people are allowed to do certain things and only in certain ways, because any way other than that is perverse? Idiots—you're all idiots. An erection is an erection. It doesn't concern itself with philosophy or theology, ideology or even legality, it cares nothing of the inhibitions of the culture, it simply wants a good time. Any boy who has reached puberty, who marvels in front of the mirror at the feelings his engorged organ inspires in him—he will be just as curious, just as eager, and just as carnal at that age as he will be a few years later, that age at which you assume the exercise of his erection with another is now an acceptable passion—"

"Jacob, I was fourteen once too, but I didn't, I never—I mean, it would have been wrong."

"No!" Jacob says, his voice quiet but insistent. "You didn't because you didn't have the opportunity—because that's the way that circumstances were constructed around you and eventually you came to believe that the way things are is the way they have to be. You live comfortably inside your self-constructed box of limits.

"No—this isn't about what's right or wrong—and even to debate it in that context is bizarre." Jacob leans suddenly across the table and grabs my hand. In a whisper so low, I can barely make out the words, he says, "You have no trouble believing that I have killed a man tonight. You didn't even have the courage to look at the body, nevertheless you accepted that violence as a necessary part of my existence—and in that, you have made yourself a moral accomplice to that murder. But now that I admit that I might have once had the desire, let alone acted on that desire to invite a fourteen year old boy to my bed—a street-hustler who knew all too well what he was doing, and who was not only willing, but hungry for my favors—that horrifies you? What kind of hypocrite are you that you can condone an act of selfish and bloody violence while condemning the sharing of affection, merely because of your own squalid and barbaric assumptions about the age of one of the participants? Is there some arbitrarily decided magic day when sex suddenly becomes legal—and the day before that, it's a crime? Do you get how insane your thinking is?"

"Jacob—" I start to protest, but he cuts me off sharply.

"No, just no. Look at yourself, look hard. If I had been something different that night, if I had fed on him, you would have been less offended. If I had been the kind of creature that I have since become, and if I had turned him that night into the same kind of creature I am now, you would be less offended than you are at this moment. You would be curious about his subsequent adventures—you would want to know all the details of how he sucked away the lives of his customers, those who you believe preyed on him and the others. *That* you would have condoned, wouldn't you? Because it suits your beliefs and biases, it satisfies your prejudices. But I tell you this now, as hard as it is for you to believe, and as hard as life on the streets might have been, it was not one desperate rape after another—" He stops himself. "All right, yes—sometimes boys were brutalized, sometimes worse. I won't deny it was a hard life. But it was not *only* like that. Or even always like that. There was also a kind of freedom—"

Jacob lowers his voice, his tone. "You need to understand that it was a different time, a different place, a very different way of thinking and believing and behaving. Men and boys—they did what they did, because it was all that they knew. We did not think of age as either a limit or a definition of our ability to desire. Besides—" And now he allows himself the hint of a smile. "—We were already living outside the boundaries of propriety. We found each other where the fairies walked. That's what they called men like us. Polite society pretended we didn't exist, or if they did notice us, it was with a deliberate pose of condemnation and distaste. So why should any of us have cared what polite society thought? We took what little comfort we could from each other. And who are you, who is anyone, to sit in judgment? You weren't there."

"You're right. I wasn't there."

Jacob studies me. "But still, you judge."

I shrug. "I can't help it. I wasn't there—I can't understand."

"I don't care if you understand or not. I'm not asking for understanding, Nor am I asking for acceptance. And I'm certainly not seeking your approval. I'm simply telling you what happened—and why. And now that you've issued the obligatory disclaimer of responsibility, do you want me to continue—or are we through for the night?"

"Through for the night? Or through, period?"

"Yes—*that* you understand." He finally lets go of my hand.

I lean back, sagging against the red leather cushion of the booth.

"What?" he says.

"Jacob—" I begin slowly. "I want to know about you, about The Community. About how you live and survive. What you think and feel, what you experience. I want to know what it is to be the way you are. I'm certainly as curious as you were when you studied all those medical texts at university. But—"

"But what?"

"But so far, you haven't told me any of that. You haven't told me how you were turned, who turned you, and why? All you've shared with me is your sexual history—and as fascinating as some of it is, if that's what I wanted to know, hell—I might as well go read that flatulent stuff those two ladies in the bestiaries write. When do I get to hear about the stuff that I don't know—?"

Jacob laughs. "Sometimes you can be such an idiot. All those silly convention panels, all those articles and essays and yammering blogs about the essential sexuality of the vampire mythos, blah blah blah—you think they're projecting their own desires onto this? No—not at all. They're responding to what's already there.

"The blood and the violence—that's about the power, but that's just what's visible on the surface. It's what's underneath that, that's the real attraction. It's about sensuality—not sex, not as you understand it, but the sheer physical excitement of being. You cannot imagine what it is to have your senses heightened to such a degree that even the faintest scent of a rose is an overwhelming experience, delicious beyond belief.

"That's why we avoid the daylight, why we retreat to our coffins—we need to isolate ourselves from the avalanche of experiences, the tumult of existence, we need that break from sensation the same way your body needs sleep. We need those periods of dormancy just to assimilate the incredible experiences of our waking lives.

"You—" Jacob points across the table, almost but not quite touching my chest. "You wonder why I seek you out? It's simple. You smell good. You smell delicious. You tempt me. And yes, I have considered what a feast you would be, more now than ever—but I enjoy our conversations too much. I like telling you my story, watching your expressions, hearing your heartbeat increase with excitement, sniffing the changes in your sweat as you become aroused or afraid—you are a veritable smorgasbord of flavors. If you were me, you'd understand. But you're not me, you're not one of us, you will probably never be one of us—unless I change my mind and think that immortality might be more comfortable with you as a companion, but you're not there yet, nowhere near there, so unripe as to still seem shallow, but the desire within you, that hunger—I can smell it and it is intoxicating, so we continue in our odd uneven way, bouncing from coffee shop to coffee shop, what a strange and unremarkable relationship we are, wouldn't you agree?"

My silence is my reply.

Jacob laughs at me. "Yes, I like the way you smell. That's all this is—all this has ever been."

Seattle in daylight is gray. It's damp, except when it's wet. If the sun is visible, it's because the clouds are uneven. The northern reaches of the Pacific Ocean are the birthplace of great storms, rolling east across the sea to collide against the looming mountain ranges, the impassible barriers of the western edge of the continent.

This morning, the air was crisp and cool, almost invigorating, and I looked forward to tackling the challenges ahead of me. When I stepped out the front door of the Seaman's Inn, there was Georgie-boy waiting for me, arms folded, leaning against a lamp post. He wore an oversized gray sweater he must have inherited from a departing sailor, and a self-satisfied smile.

I must have looked surprised, for he said, "You didn't expect me, did you?"

I nodded. "I had my doubts. I'm pleased to see that you're dependable. The rooms you spoke of, they're still available?"

"Indeed they are," he said, drawing himself up. "As soon as the sun was up, I was there to make sure. Old lady Grogan wasn't happy to have me banging on her door—not until I told her I had a man coming. A man from a good situation, I told her. She didn't believe me, she never does, but you are a good man, aren't you, sir?" Georgie-boy took me by the hand and started pulling me down the street. "Come along now, please. Let me show you."

The streets were wet, there were puddles everywhere, and where the paving was uneven or nonexistent, there were great stretches of mud, spanned by wooden boards. I picked my way carefully, realizing only then how much I had been spoiled by the cobblestoned roads of Boston. But it was a short journey and we soon arrived at a two-story building that might have looked more at home on one of the hills of San Francisco, with its narrow bay windows. It was old, but not yet ramshackle. The Seattle weather gave even the freshest paint a heavy scouring—it appeared that this house had been repainted regularly, if not annually. That was a good sign.

Georgie-boy pounded on the door, which was quickly opened. Mrs. Grogan had been waiting, perhaps a little too eagerly. She had gray hair piled high in a series of decreasing buns which made her look like she was wearing a small wedding cake on her head. As odd an affectation as that might have seemed, it was also a good sign. A fussy woman often keeps a very clean establishment. Georgie-boy stayed only for a few moments, to make sure that we were getting along well, and then ran off on some errand of his own. I suspected that he was embarrassed—that he feared Mrs. Grogan would assume I was one of his clients. By removing himself quickly, perhaps he thought he would keep the thought from forming in her mind.

The room proved suitable and the weekly rent was low enough to be questionable. It was on the second floor, in the front, with a good view of the street below and the harbor beyond. Mrs. Grogan herself was desperately amiable, the rooms had been vacant for nearly a month, and while she did not need the immediate income, Mr. Grogan had left her well-enough situated, she didn't like living alone in such a large empty house. Well, almost alone—she had a younger sister who lived with her, but her sister was ailing and not always the best of company. No, Mrs. Grogan needed someone responsible—also someone who could bring in wood for the fire—and while she didn't mind occasionally paying Georgie-boy or one of his friends to manage such an errand, she preferred to have someone of a more trustworthy nature. Although, she did admit, Georgie-boy was one of her favorites and she never minded giving him a hot meal on a cold night. She'd never had any children of her own and so…

I realized halfway through this discourse that Mrs. Grogan was a lonely woman, eager to have someone to talk to, preferably one who listened more than spoke. She had so much to say and there were so few people who had the time to stop in for tea—

And then, she said something I found odd at the time, but on later reflection, revealed the essential goodness in her heart. She said, "Seattle has its share of ruffians, I'm not renting the room because I need the money, but because I want a man in the house. A good man. A gentleman. So I won't object if you have the occasional visitor, but only if he's a gentleman as well. And if you should have him stay the night, then let me know in time so I can prepare an extra breakfast for the two of you.

"And one more thing—" She laid her hand on my arm. "Georgie-boy is such a dear. Please watch out for him when you can. From time to time, I've found him sleeping under my porch to get out of the rain. He doesn't know I know, he's got a makeshift bed under there. It's a rough life he's in, and I don't like him going off alone with dangerous men, so if you ever feel like taking him to your bed…well, it would be one less worry for me, knowing he's with a true gentleman and not one of those rough-hewn sailors. Mind you, a lady like myself isn't supposed to know about such things, but this is Seattle and I wasn't always a lady—truth be told, I met Mr. Grogan when I was working for Miss Graham. She took good care of her girls, she did. The men appreciated it too.

"Mr. Grogan took a fancy to me right from the start, and of all the men who visited, I have to say I found him both tender and charming. He treated me well, he did. Sometimes we just sat and talked. He told me of his fears as well as his dreams, and I would hold him to my breast and let him suckle like a babe. I rather enjoyed that and I think he liked that even more than all the other things a man is expected to do with a woman—but after several months of regular visits, he confessed he couldn't afford to keep coming so regular, and at the same time he couldn't stand the thought of me in another man's arms, so he offered me a home of my own, even a room of my own if I was so inclined. I was smart enough to recognize a quick and comfortable retirement, so I said yes and I set out to keep him so happy that he would never again wander off to Miss Graham's. I believe I succeeded in that. The few years we had together, before the accident that took him from me—those years were the happiest of both of our lives. The only regret I have was that I couldn't give him a son. He understood, he never held it against me, and instead we made up for it by helping as many of the street-boys as we could, when we could. They were our family, they still are.

"Mr. Grogan made his money in timber and he was not blind to the ways of the world, neither am I. Understand me now, I'll have no truck with harshness of any kind. The Good Lord didn't put us here to be cruel to one another. A smile is the most valuable thing you can give and it costs you nothing. Would you like some more tea, dear?"

At last, when I was finally able extricate myself from the conversation, I felt much more comfortable with my new circumstances. It was time to set out on the rest of the day's errands.

I found Mr. Marley Matthews at his regular cab stand, it was a convenient short walk from Mrs. Grogan's, as well as from the Seaman's Inn—which may have been the reason he recommended the Inn at all, so that he would have a customer for his drive back.

Nevertheless, I was glad to see a friendly face and gave him the address of the lawyers who had managed Monsieur's affairs in town. I did not ask Mr. Matthews to wait for me, I had no idea how long my business would take. Instead, I sent him to pick up my trunks from the railway station and deliver them to the upstairs rooms at Mrs. Grogan's. Matthews grinned in that overly-familiar way that cabbies sometimes do, he said he knew Mrs. Grogan well—I got the feeling he may have known her even before Mr. Grogan. But he assured me not to worry, he would pick up my luggage immediately, it would be no trouble at all.

Monsieur's representatives had their offices discreetly tucked away at the back of a rather large building, one that had been divided and subdivided so many times that whatever the original architect had intended, that design was now completely obscured.

I knocked, there was no answer, but the door was unlocked. I had never been here before, but I had met on several occasions the senior partner, a Mister Durant, a dour-faced gentleman given to generously dyspeptic mutterings about the nature of life in general and the way that circumstances continually scraped away all possibilities of joy.

The door opened to an anteroom—a young male secretary stood up on my entrance. I announced myself, I did not expect Mister Durant to still be alive, so I asked to see whoever was in charge. The secretary excused himself for a moment, then came back to usher me into the darker recesses of the office. There, on a dais, behind an oversized desk, Mister Durant sat, making notes on a yellow legal pad. I was taken aback, surprised to find him still alive, still as spry as I remembered, and still muttering quietly to himself.

He didn't recognize me, of course. Not at first. The last time he had seen me had been seven years previous, on the occasion of my departure for Boston. But now, as he settled his glasses on his nose, and as he repeated my name to himself, his memory awakened and his face lit up. He rose immediately and came around the desk, stepping down from the platform on which it sat, all the time smiling as graciously as he could manage. It must have taken some effort on his part, his features had fossilized over time into a rather severe visage. But he shook my hand and led me to a chair, gently pushing me down into it. "Young Master Jacob, of course, of course. You arrived last evening? We've been expecting you ever since the sad news—I'm sorry that you've had to journey all this way on such a terrible occasion. Please sit, sit. Can I get you anything?" Without waiting for my answer, he called to the secretary, "Russell, be a dear boy and bring us two brandies."

Mister Durant parked himself opposite me in a matching chair. "Of course, we were all dreadfully shocked at the news of your uncle's sudden passing. I cannot begin to tell you how deeply we feel the loss here in these offices—but our grief is very likely only the barest shadow of your own. You have our most profound condolences."

"Yes, thank you. I do appreciate your concern. This is a very difficult time for me."

"Much of life is difficult," Mister Durant agreed. "We do our best to ease the worst of it. Not always easy, not always easy. But we make our way as we must."

Russell brought in a tray with two brandy snifters. He poured a generous finger of the liquor into each. I was beginning to suspect that Mister Durant's sudden affability came from someplace deeper than just the mutual loss we shared. I decided to wait and see where he intended to lead the conversation.

"Tell me," he began. "How was your time in the east. Were you comfortable in Boston? Were you doing well in your studies? I assume you will be returning for the next term? Or will you be staying here in Seattle?"

"I haven't decided yet. This is all very upsetting. I'll need some time to sort my feelings out. And without Monsieur's guidance and support, I am at a loss. I confess, I have no idea at all what prospects I might have in the world."

"You're not alone in that, Master Jacob. None of us have any idea what the future might hold for us. Disaster is always available even to the best of us, awaiting only the opportunity of a single careless misstep. Yes—" He stopped himself, lost in thought for a moment, then resumed reluctantly, "Fortunately—I say this with no small amount of satisfaction, you are more fortunate than most—your patron was well aware of the essential hostility of circumstance and fate. Better than most men, I'd hazard. He left very detailed instructions on all matters, and his last will and testament were quite specific. We've taken the liberty of filing all the appropriate papers, we did not know how long your journey would take, but you should have no worries about your future—"

I noticed then what he had not addressed. "Mister Durant, I'm grateful for your efforts, as well as your concern for my well-being. I appreciate your reassurances, but first—please tell me, where is Monsieur buried? I would like to visit his grave before I speak of anything else."

Durant fell uncomfortably silent.

"Sir—?"

"It distresses me greatly to have to tell you this. We believe his body was consumed by the fire."

"You believe—?"

"The authorities searched the rubble quite thoroughly, they did not find any remains."

"Then perhaps he may have been away somewhere—"

"That was our hope as well—that perhaps he had been away, but no—none of his acquaintances, none that we know of, had entertained him that evening. He has been missing ever since the fire, there is little other conclusion. I suppose it is possible the fire crews did not search deep enough. Perhaps the basement—? But then why would the Master have been in the basement?"

Why indeed—? I could think of one reason, but I was not prepared to discuss it. Monsieur had kept a coffin in the basement, a place of deep retreat during thunderstorms. He did not fear lightning or thunder, but the flashes of brightness, and the crashing explosions of sound were extremely painful to his heightened sight and hearing. On one such occasion, as he made his way downstairs, Monsieur had paused to say, "Roderick Usher was a fool. A coffin is well-insulated, it's quiet, it's dark, it's restful. It would be even more so, buried in the ground—but that would limit my access, wouldn't it?" He spoke with quiet wit, but he was serious as well.

That coffin in the basement—I could not ask about it, but I was determined to investigate. "May I ask, was there a storm the night of the fire?"

"This is Seattle, Master Jacob. There are always storms."

So there was hope—a feeble hope, but nonetheless perhaps a straw to grasp. Perhaps Monsieur still lay beneath the rubble, the charred timbers blocking his escape. He would not die, he would simply enter a deeper state of dormancy, what a doctor would have termed a state of suspended animation. So there was hope. But I dared not speak it here.

Mister Durant was still talking, he said, "We did hold a prayer vigil for him, of course, but we have not scheduled a memorial service. We were waiting for you—to see what your wishes might be."

"A memorial service? Yes, please. As soon as possible. Schedule it in the evening so that all his closest friends may attend."

Durant put down his brandy glass, picked up a convenient yellow legal pad from a nearby table and began making notes. "Yes, yes, of course. Do you have any preferences?" He shouted to his clerk, "Russell, bring me that file, please?"

Russell hurried in, "It's on your desk, sir. I put it there this morning." He retrieved it and passed it to Durant, it was a very thick folder, full of papers of all kinds. Durant shuffled through them impatiently. "Hm, yes, let's start at the beginning. I will need your signature, granting me power of attorney—unless you have someone else in mind?" He looked up expectantly.

"No, sir. Nobody knows my uncle's affairs as well as you do."

"Ah, good. Yes. If you'll sign here and here and here, we will be able to complete the task of putting all of these affairs in order as quickly as possible."

After I passed the signed forms back, Durant looked at me sharply, his eyes magnified by the lenses of his eyewear. "There is something you need to know, Master Jacob, and I hope you will take this in the proper spirit—I

would like to offer you the continued services of this firm, we would like to
continue managing your affairs."

"I don't see why not. You've done well for my uncle, all these years."

"I do like to think we have, yes. And I appreciate your continued trust.
But I need you to understand the gravity of your situation."

"Sir?"

"Unless another claimant comes forward, and I do not expect that to
happen, you are the only heir. I have been compiling a list of your uncle's
properties and investments, it's quite extensive. You are going to be a very
wealthy young man. Quite. Indeed. Yes. Your patron was very wise with his
investments. All that wealth—if you'll pardon my candor—it could make
you a target for some very unscrupulous people. I must urge caution on
your part."

"Of course." At that moment, I was not thinking of money, and I had
no idea how much we were talking about. I assumed perhaps a few thousand
dollars, maybe a bit more, plus the value of the house—perhaps there had
been some insurance.

"Meanwhile, if you need money now, I can set up an account that you
can draw upon, I'll just need your signature for the bank—"

I won't go into all the details, but Mister Durant was correct, my
inheritance was substantial. I had known that Monsieur was well-off, but
I had not known the full extent of his holdings. Indeed, it was some time
before I knew the full extent of my fortune.

I would have traded it all in an instant.

◆ ╌╌✦•❍●❍•✦╌╌ ◆

"He left you everything—?"

"At first, I thought so. Later on, I wasn't so sure." Jacob waves his coffee
cup at the waitress. She hurries over to refill it.

"There's a lot I haven't told you. And apparently, you haven't given
much thought to it either—maybe it's a grownup thing."

"What is?"

"Having a life. All the minutiae that needs to be managed. Groceries,
for example. That's a daily challenge. We don't subsist on blood alone,
there's not enough sustenance in a pint or even a gallon. It's one meal, that's
it. And it's only when the hunger overcomes us. So yes, groceries. Think
about it. If it's painful to go out during the day, you need to find stores and

eateries that are open after sunset.

"Or how about a place to live? Rent a room somewhere? How long until the landlord gets suspicious of the daysleeper? Own your own home? That's a better alternative. You have privacy. But then there's all that upkeep—someone has to mow the lawn, bring in the newspaper, collect the mail, and so on. And then there's the long-term maintenance, repainting the exterior every few years, repairing the plumbing or the electricity—and then there's the taxes, they have to be paid.

"And that brings me to the essential problem. Money. If you cannot work during the day, what can you do that pays the bills? Night watchman job perhaps?" Jacob smiles. "That's what you—all of you—have missed. Continue to miss. You think in terms of Castle Dracula, this huge abandoned ruin, where the undead rest in their silent coffins during the day but arise each evening to prowl the countryside until forced back into hiding at the first glimmering hints of dawn—and yet Count Dracula is still able to serve Jonathan Harker an edible meal of meat and bread and wine. Who prepared it? Can you imagine Drac in the kitchen baking fresh bread? I can—because I like fresh bread. But it kind of undermines the horror of the situation, doesn't it? More fools, you—you like the kind of horror that drools blood or startles you like a cat jumping out of the dark. You don't stop to consider the deeper, darker horrors of existence, do you?"

I spread my hands in a gesture of literary helplessness. "You're right. We don't know. I don't know. That's why I'm here—"

"No," says Jacob. "That's only part of why you're here. The *other* part—you're hungry for the power you believe I have. That's the fascination. That—and the sex, of course. Not the sensuality, because you still don't understand the sensuality—you hear the word and you think of sex, that feeble pistoning you use to escape your own life for a moment or two."

Jacob pauses to refresh himself. He raises the mug and smiles. "Coffee—my second favorite drink." Putting the mug down again, he continues, "In this world, someone like Monsieur, or someone like me—we can't stay in any one place too long. If there were an instruction book, one of the most important rules would say, 'Always be prepared to move quickly.' Because all you need is one nosy neighbor to ruin everything.

"Seven years—that's the longest one should ever stay in one place. Think about it. Sooner or later, someone's going to get curious about why you're not aging." Jacob pauses, considers. "Maybe that's not as firm a rule anymore as it was a century ago. The way you people move about, it's like your whole civilization is liquid. You're never satisfied with where you are or what you're doing. You're always chasing the next shiny thing. You move from job to job, leaping from one to the next before you've mastered the previous. Apartments as well—you don't like this neighborhood, you want to live in that one instead. And if you're offered an opportunity in a new city, you're packing your suitcase before you've even checked the weather. I've seen neighborhoods turn over their entire populations in less time than it takes to corrupt a politician.

"Nevertheless—seven years is the longest someone like me should ever stay in one place. Seven years. Fewer is better. You don't want people asking questions. You want to be ephemeral, unnoticeable, untraceable. It's getting harder now—what with birth certificates and driver's licenses, fingerprinting and DNA, Social Security numbers, credit cards, bank accounts, security cameras—especially security cameras! Yes, I do show up in mirrors and yes, you can photograph me. That's what an immortal has to deal with. I miss the days when cash was enough. Staying untrackable in a technological world? It's a challenge. It's not impossible, not yet, but it's getting harder. And yes—your television shows suggest that it's simply a matter of finding that guy who can forge a passport, except finding that guy isn't all that simple, is it? You know who's good at creating false identities? The CIA, the Witness Protection Program, and that other agency that doesn't have a name. They're good at it. Not people like me."

Something was troubling me. I hold up a hand to interrupt. "Wait a minute. You said that seven years is the most you should stay in one place. But...you lived with Monsieur for what? Five years? He had to have been there for a few years before you met him, so there's at least seven right there. And then he stayed in his house for another seven while you were in Boston—"

Jacob nods. "Yes. I didn't know then what I know now. Monsieur had stayed much too long in the Seattle house. I didn't realize until much later, but he did that mostly for me. It was a dangerous thing to do. He had fallen for me, you know—that was even more dangerous for him, a man in this kind of existence.

"There's more—" Jacob hesitates. "The lawyer, Durant, he was very meticulous. He had kept exhaustive records. He showed me that he had filled two file cabinets and had been working on a third when the fire took Monsieur from me.

"Later on, after I had satisfied myself that Monsieur's coffin had not survived the fire, I became obsessed with those files. I wanted to find out everything about him that I could—as if somehow that would restore the comfort of his spirit to me and bring me closer to the man he was.

"I asked Durant if I could examine those files. Of course, he made them available to me. Those cabinets revealed the depth of Monsieur's existence. They opened up adventures of discovery and revelation. At one time, Monsieur had owned properties in nine different cities, Portland, San Francisco, Sacramento, Denver, St. Louis, Atlanta, Charlotte, Philadelphia, and New Orleans. He'd sold three of them before he took me from the street. The more I traced his history, as detailed in those files, the more I realized he had been repositioning his assets continually, the way one might arrange and rearrange chess pieces on a board to examine various defensive positions.

"But then, I noticed, there was a moment when the pattern of his moves had shifted. No longer reorganizing for convenience, he had begun aggressively liquidating his Seattle assets—beginning almost immediately the day I left for Boston. That startled me, but I pressed on. Monsieur had sold all but two of the remaining houses—most of them for cash. He'd sold off a sizable piece of his investments as well.

"Most curiously, he'd sold his library as well, all of it—large parcels were shipped to buyers all over the country. The paintings, the piano, the rare sculptures, everything. He didn't do it all of a sudden and never so much at one time as to arouse anyone's suspicions, but when I looked at the entire process from what I assumed would have been his perspective, he wasn't liquidating his wealth as much as he was relocating it. The money—? A great deal of it had been invested in bonds, most of which would be approaching their maturation date in the next few years. But a good portion of it had also been funneled into distant investments. There were stock certificates granting shares of ownership in several banking establishments.

"As near as I could tell, Monsieur was shifting his resources to at least three, possibly more than that, new identities. Poring through those dusty papers, I began to get a clearer sense of the meticulous care that Monsieur had taken to ensure his survival. Durant had kept everything from the first day that Monsieur had engaged his services from an address in Chicago— that was even before Monsieur arrived in Seattle and first purchased the house in which I later grew up.

"Monsieur wrote long letters to Durant, at least once a month, several pages at a time, each one specifically detailing where and how Monsieur wanted his funds moved around. It was quite a story, and I'm sure that in this current era, the equivalent machinations would be of great interest to the tax collectors.

"Monsieur had money coming in from several untraceable sources—his previous identities, I suspected—and he was already in the process of creating new identities and moving resources into their accounts. It was a continuing process for him. The identity in Seattle—? I'm certain he kept that one alive as long as he did specifically for me. He didn't need it, but he needed me. At least—that's what I want to believe."

"But it cost him his life. He was killed in the fire, wasn't he?"

"Was he?"

⊹ ⊱•●◐◷◖•⊰ ⊹

I could have bought a new house, I could have built a house to replace the one that was burnt—but I had no desire to do so. Instead, I hired a crew to remove the rubble from the lot where Monsieur's elegant mansion had stood. I instructed them to proceed carefully, searching for any evidence of a body—

If Monsieur had set the fire himself, and if he had truly wanted to convince the authorities in Seattle of his death, he would have left a body to be discovered charred in the ashes. It would not have been difficult. There was no shortage of men prowling the streets who would not have been missed—even more so, there were many whose sudden absence would certainly benefit the lives of others. Abusers, cutthroats, thieves—all the violent and corrupt who preyed upon those they presumed weaker than themselves.

At one time, I might have assumed that those who preyed were predators, deserving to be removed, and that those they preyed upon were generally good, undeserving of the assault—but now I know otherwise. Too many of those who have been victimized have invited the predations by behaving as victims. A cruel thought? Yes, but when you look at the world through the eyes of a predator, you begin to recognize that we are all predators. Or prey. And it is always a choice. Even the weakest have their own ways of preying on the strengths of those around them.

If it disturbs you to hear that, you can imagine my distress at realizing it. Never mind—I'm getting ahead of myself.

There was no body in the ruins, no coffin either—though I did not call attention to that absence. In the end, when the crews had completed their sad work and hauled away the last of the still stinking timbers, there was nothing left but a black scar on the ground, a scorched reminder, an ugly memory.

On the last day of the work, while I stood surveying the echoes of my life, I was approached by a short fat man in a hound's-tooth checkered coat. His card identified him as a real estate agent. He wondered if I was considering selling the land, he had several prospective buyers who had expressed interest—

I told that little man that I had not yet decided what I intended to do with the property and strode away, angry—not angry at him, not angry at myself, but angry at Monsieur. If he had not died in the fire, then he had abandoned me—and that was a far far greater loss for me to deal with than the possibility of his death.

I could not fathom why he would suddenly choose to erase himself from my life—or had that been his plan from the beginning? And it had taken him seven years to complete it?

Or—even more distressing—had it been something I had done?

My last letter to Monsieur had been a confession of my grief over losing my relationship with Josiah. I had believed that we had established a mutual devotion akin to the love the poets extolled, but it turned out that I had apparently been deluding myself—I had been infatuated, more in love with the idea of being in love than actually achieving that state— circumstances revealed Josiah to be a predator in his own way, a predator who used physical affection as his deadly bite.

I had been left in a state of emotional turmoil. In my desperation, I had written a long letter to Monsieur—in retrospect, considering it now, perhaps I had not been as discreet in my narrative as I should have been.

Monsieur had cautioned me—as much as we wanted to believe that the mails were secure, we should never depend on that assumption. There were always those whose integrity in the matter was less than they professed. And, to be quite blunt about it, men of our nature were easily preyed upon by blackmailers. He knew. He had dispatched a couple of them himself. Just before moving immediately into a new identity.

Had my letter to Monsieur been opened and read by someone other than the intended recipient? The thought troubled me, growing at the back of my mind like an abscess—because if that letter had raised suspicions around Monsieur, it would have made me even more vulnerable and exposed. But if so, as yet, no one had approached me. And considering my newfound wealth, I would be an ideal target for a blackmailer.

Realizing that, I knew that I needed to protect myself immediately. I also recognized that if anyone knew where Monsieur had gone, it would be the other members of The Community in Seattle. So, although I had begun spending my days rattling through the files in Durant's office, ignoring the annoyance of Russell the secretary, whose territory I had invaded, I spent my evenings prowling the various dark attractions that The Community favored.

I assumed that I would have no problem reconnecting with Monsieur's associates, but these are men who spend most of their existence making themselves invisible, unnoticeable, impossible to find. If they do not want to be found, they will not be—you are unlikely to stumble upon them by accident, and even if you do know where to look, you have to know exactly what you're looking for—I had that advantage.

But if you do not want to be found, you do not put yourself where anyone can find you. In short order, I realized that for all intents and purposes, The Community in Seattle had disappeared. It was as if they no longer existed.

Nevertheless, young men still disappeared from the streets on a regular basis—transients, seamen, and thugs as well—so I knew they had to be here. They just didn't want me to find them.

All of which suggested that whatever sin I had committed, however much I had hurt or offended Monsieur, my crime had been a crime against all the members of The Community and therefore all the members of The Community would be shunning me. Despite my knowledge, despite my years of service, I was now excluded from their company.

In my grief and loneliness, I allowed Georgie-boy to share my rooms—and my bed. Mrs. Grogan clucked approvingly. And while your mind might go immediately to the carnal aspects of that relationship, let me assure you there was little of that—not because he was not desirable, he was quite that way, but because I had little desire left in me at all.

Whether or not Georgie-boy understood my detachment, he accepted it. Having a warm bed and regular meals was a significant improvement over a makeshift bed under a cold porch, especially during a Seattle winter. Perhaps you will assume that I was taking advantage of him—you could just as easily make the case that he was taking advantage of me. Or perhaps we both used each other for a moment of warmth and comfort against a cold uncaring existence.

At some point, I resolved to be his mentor, teaching him how to be a gentleman the same way Monsieur had taught me. Perhaps we could find an apartment together, a place where he could have a room of his own, I could send him to school, or bring in tutors, and we would share books and music in the evening. We would discuss our daily adventures in front of a comfortable fire. We would have that life.

Or we could travel for a bit. I told him I did not plan on staying in Seattle forever. There was a whole wide world to explore and I had the means to do so. It would be pleasant to have a companion, what did he think?

I shared all of this with Georgie-boy, more than once. He listened with feigned interest, he seemed mostly unenthused. I realized that everything I described—all of this—these were alien experiences to him, he had no referents. I might just as well have been talking to him about a trip to the moon in one of Mr. Verne's capsules shot from a giant gun. But he said, "If that's what you would like—" and I realized that he was speaking the standard answer of a street-boy to a patron. Was that how Georgie-boy regarded me? A strange realization began to grow inside me—you cannot purchase affection, only the illusion of it. As much as I had known that in my own desperate time on the street, it was strange to experience it now from the other side.

It saddened me. It made me realize just how much of my life had been built on illusion. Indeed, if there was any reality at all, it was the harshness of the streets. Georgie-boy was a daily reminder of that. From time to time, he would ask me when I planned to leave the city and I knew his questions were not about me as much as they were about himself and his own eventual fate. I could have left at any time, there was nothing really keeping me here—only my own commitment to discover what had really happened with Monsieur. So I deflected his questions, saying only that I could not leave until I concluded my business, and I reassured him each time, telling him that I still had too much to do. I hadn't solved the problem—

I knew there had to be a way that the members of The Community stayed in contact with each other, I just did not know what it was. I tried placing advertisements in the local newspapers.

We did not have the advantage of an internet. In those days, we used the ads in the personals column as our social media. It could sometimes be very delicious reading, and occasionally a source of some very salacious gossip.

My own ads were usually discreet, but later quite direct:

"Newly returned to Seattle, would like to reconnect with the friends of my uncle."

"Still looking for the community of immortal souls."

"I have lost my mentor, I do not know why."

"Please do not hide from me, I am desperate."

"Am I not entitled to know why?"

I'm certain that my personal ads must have produced some amusement among the members of The Community who saw them, and possibly some discussion as well, but if any were predisposed to contact me, perhaps their fellows dissuaded them.

There was no response at all—not from The Community at least. I did receive a few odd inquiries that were easily dismissed as coming from cranks or eccentrics. One or two suggested that Jesus would offer me comfort, another simply condemned me to burn in hell for all eternity. There was one inquiry from a young man who, in his own discreet way, inquired whether or not I was possessed of a certain attraction, he did not specify the nature of that attraction and I had little interest in pursuing the matter.

Logically, I should have ended the matter there. I had wealth—enough to sustain me for a long and comfortable life. I could travel if I wished, I could do almost anything I wanted. Monsieur and The Community had sent me a message. "You are not one of us, you will not be one of us. Go away and create a life without us."

Except that once you know of the existence of a community of immortal men, a community in which all the senses are enhanced and desire is no longer a commodity, but a flavor, then life without access to that experience is a frustrating prison, one in which the only adventure left is to watch yourself grow older and weaker with every passing day.

I imagined myself at the bottom of a dark well, I was climbing a ladder—a seemingly endless climb—but at the top was the irresistible radiance of life, only to find the access barred, an iron grate had been installed across the opening. I could feel the warmth of a distant possibility, a realm that had once beckoned, but I could no longer reach it.

Finally, one afternoon, as I was finishing the last of my readings in lawyer Durant's files, realizing there was little more to learn—also realizing that there was little in these pages that would point me toward the other members of The Community, I worked up my courage and asked Mr.

Durant if I might have a moment with him.

I began by thanking him for his generosity, for helping me decode the various documents and papers in his files, allowing me a glimpse into Monsieur's history. Seeing the various ways he moved and planned revealed the underlying patterns of his thinking. It was the tangible expression of his soul.

By now, Durant had developed a measure of affection for me—I assumed it was genuine, in those days the practice of law had not yet been completely corrupted, although the process was well under way by the end of that century—but still, Durant's generosity seemed authentic enough that I felt it appropriate to broach a darker subject.

Nevertheless, I couched my words carefully. I said, "From time to time, Monsieur would attend evening gatherings with other gentlemen like himself, gentlemen of similar interests. Did you ever meet any of them or have any business with them?"

Mister Durant demurred. "I'm not sure who you mean. Your uncle had business and social connections all over the city—indeed, beyond the city as well, as you have seen in his papers."

"Yes, but—" I hesitated, unsure how to proceed. "—But sometimes I believe he may have spent some time with men who shared some of the same physical infirmities that he did. You know he had an extreme sensitivity to sunlight—"

"Ahh," said Durant. "Yes. I'm aware of that which you speak. Your uncle preferred to meet with me only after dusk. If we had business that had to be conducted during the day, I would attend him at his home—in a severely curtained room. He was never at his best while the sun was up. What a terrible oppression that must have been. It was as if he could feel the glare of it through the timbers of the building."

"Perhaps he could. Living with him as long as I did, I was very aware of his condition, his need for darkness—and silence—during the day. When I was in Boston, I studied medicine and discovered that it is not an unknown condition for a man to have his biological cycles so disordered—reversed, if you will—that he is forced to live a nocturnal existence. I assumed that my uncle must have—well, might have—found some comfort or solace in the company of others who shared the same existence. I apologize if there are confidences to which you have been sworn, but if not then I'm curious if you might put me in touch with any of those men. Perhaps one of them might be able to share some insight into my patron's final days."

"Ahh," said Durant, his favorite expression when he didn't want to commit to anything. He considered for a moment, his expression darkening toward a frown. "At the moment, I cannot think of any who might fit that description, and even if I did, any guarantees of lawyer-client confidentiality might preclude my sharing that information."

"Nevetheless," I said. "Perhaps there must be information that is not protected by privilege. There is something I need to know. I ask only a single audience with any of Monsieur's acquaintances—"

"Yes, nevertheless—" he agreed. "That is not an unreasonable request. I will certainly keep your request in mind."

He pulled out his pocket watch to check the time, snapped it open, frowned, closed it, returned it to his pocket, his signal that he intended to end this audience. "I must tell you, Jacob, that I have very little personal contact with clients. The affairs of this office are such that once the initial relationship is established, there is little need to meet. This is what most of my clients want, and I have found it much more efficient to conduct the majority of business communications through messengers and the mail. It makes no sense to drag people across the city just to exchange a few signatures—and having documents on file provides an excellent record of all instructions, as you have seen. Thus, I need only a single secretary and a small staff, several of whom work out of their own homes and set their own hours for completing their assignments.

"Additionally, I must inform you that I have begun preparing for my own retirement, possibly next year or perhaps the year after that. But I have already begun the process of passing clients on to other firms who will better suit their needs. But please, don't feel that I am in a hurry to abandon you. I had great affection for your uncle, I have the same affection for you, and I will be pleased to remain at your service for as long you need, for as long as you find my efforts satisfactory. All of these files, of course, belong to you, and you may claim them at any time. Indeed, I would welcome the additional space in my chambers."

While he spoke, I felt reassured. Later on, as I made my way through muddy streets and allies, back to Mrs. Grogan's, I began to wonder if perhaps he had been gently inviting me to find another attorney.

More important, he had easily dodged the question of acquaintanceship with any other members of The Community—at the moment, he could not think of any—that was not the same as saying he did not know of any. The precise phrasing of "I cannot think" can just as easily mean "I cannot allow myself to think about this, right now." Either way, it meant that Mr. Durant would not be an avenue of communication with any member of The Community. Not for me anyway. But it now seemed very likely that he was informing someone in The Community of my situation, specifically my inquiries.

My thoughts were in turmoil, all the way back to my rooms. If The Community had turned its back on me—why? What crime had I committed in their eyes? Had it been my unfortunate request in Boston to Colonel Guignard? The idea that the men of The Community might be worthy of medical study? The Colonel had cut off our relationship after that—understandable under the circumstances. I had been naïve and the request, despite my every attempt at courtesy, must have offended him.

But Monsieur had reassured me that despite Colonel Guignard's withdrawal from my life, despite my enthusiasm and youthful naivete, despite my foolishness, my sin had not been mortal. And yet—I wondered now if perhaps Monsieur had not been fully honest with me in that regard. Perhaps I had offended The Community more than I realized and perhaps Monsieur had glossed over the matter to spare my own feelings.

But then—why had Monsieur suddenly disappeared from Seattle? Had my letter about my affair with Josiah caused him some kind of upset? I could not imagine how—in our days before the university, I had shared much more intimate details of my life on the streets. Monsieur knew my past, he knew what I had done and why. But—the thought occurred to me—Josiah was the first time I had acknowledged an emotional intimacy. Had he felt betrayed by that revelation? I couldn't see how. Monsieur had quietly encouraged me to explore my passions in Boston—just be discreet.

But if I had angered Monsieur, then why had he named me his sole heir? Yes, his papers suggested that what I had inherited was only a small part of a much larger fortune—one that had seemingly evaporated through a series of strange investments, transfers, and unsecured loans. Nevertheless, Monsieur had left me a considerable inheritance. Was that his parting gift? His way of saying, "Here's cab fare, now begone."

But why? If he was angry with me, wouldn't he have said something? And if I had really aroused his rage, then why didn't he simply slice open my jugular with a sharpened fingernail and drain my blood? Or perhaps another member of The Community would have been happy to perform that service—

None of this made sense to me. And as I walked back to Mrs. Grogan's, I became more and more agitated, an anger rose inside me at how unfair this situation was. Even after living with Monsieur for seven years, corresponding with him for another seven, apparently there was still too much I didn't understand.

But a peculiar thing happened as I turned the last corner—a break in the clouds revealed the westering sun. Beams of gold came slanting down like the finger of God, and caught me suddenly, dazzling me out of my angry reverie. And as I stood, momentarily caught in the glow of sunset, it was as if destiny itself had punched me in the chest and said, "Wake up, Jacob. Wake up."

And I did. At first, I blinked in confusion. What had just happened? Oh, it was only the sunset, the glorious spread of colors across a yellow sky, the blanket of clouds illuminated in shades of rose and violet. So beautiful I stopped to stare in awe. So marvelous, it filled me with joy and sadness, both at the same time. The sheer glory of the sight was a revelation—the regret came from my identification to The Community. This was a sight that they would never see. They couldn't leave their basements, their attics, their bedchambers to appreciate the magnificent splendor of the sprawling sky.

And that was the realization—the epiphany that stopped me in my tracks. It wasn't just the momentary warmth of the sunset that caught my heart, it was the grandeur that it represented—the headier vision of a life filled with brightness.

I blinked and blinked again. I had to ask myself—why was I wasting my time on these creatures that scuttled through darkness? They were no longer human, they had given up their humanity, so why was I pursuing a memory? What relationship was truly possible with any of these callow, selfish men? They needed daykeepers, yes—but they did not need and clearly did not want to spend much time in the world of mortal men.

I stood there on the street corner, cabs splashing past me, seamen bustling past, the stink of salt and fish and tar all around me—I stood there puzzling in wonderment—mostly at myself. Why had I invested so much of my recent energies on this search? What did I expect to gain? What did any of these creatures have that I might want?

I began laughing. A couple of passing sailors looked at me oddly, but I ignored them. The joke was on me—I had been so comfortable at Monsieur's feet, I had believed myself exalted. No, I had failed to see that I had been nothing more than a convenience for him—an illusion of companionship and affection, a kept boy. I had never been his family, I had never been anything more than hired help. At best, I was his plaything, a toy, a pet.

I don't know how long I stood on that corner, it must have been a long time because a passing officer asked me if I was all right, if I needed help. I dismissed him with a shake of my head. "I'm fine," I reassured him. "I'm fine. I have been lost in thought, but now I have found the way out." The officer nodded, tipped his hat, and moved on.

It was obvious to me now, The Community had nothing I wanted— they had a shadowed existence, they hid from daylight, they had no affections for anyone but themselves, they were strange and lonely, affected with a peculiar bitterness—a longing for what they had lost, a normal life.

This insight was a profound one. I felt suddenly liberated. It was as if I had stepped out of a gloomy tunnel into fresh air and daylight, and now, holding a lantern high and casting a bit of illumination back into where I had been, I saw only the sadness of that world. There was no joy in it. So why would anyone want such an existence? Why had I ever wanted it? Seen in the light of my sudden awakening, the men of The Community no longer seemed worthy of my attentions, they were neither admirable nor honorable.

No, I was done with The Community. Done. I would conclude my affairs as quickly as possible and I would leave Seattle. Where would I go? It didn't matter. Anywhere but here—

Durant could set me up with someone to manage my affairs in almost any city. As kindly as he professed to be, I suspected he knew more than he was saying, it might be wise to separate myself from his control.

Mrs. Grogan, of course, would miss me. But as much as I appreciated her attentions, my affection for her was not strong enough to anchor me to Seattle.

Georgie-boy, however—

I wanted to rush home immediately to share my newfound liberation with him, and more than that—the adventures that now lay before us. I would not leave and abandon him back to the streets. He had become too much a part of my soul.

I would take him with me—that brought me up short. What if he didn't want to come? My first assumption had been that of course, he would want to continue as my companion—but then I had to ask myself, exactly what would he assume that I was offering. What would our new relationship be? Would I be some kind of uncle to him? Or something else? His patron? His bedmate? Did he imagine himself a kept boy? Or had he come to regard me as something more than an easy meal and bed?

This might prove to be a difficult conversation. Georgie-boy had little experience of the world. The street, yes—the world, no. He would not fully comprehend the choice I would be offering. And given his occupation, he would very likely assume the offer was based solely on carnal desires. I doubted that he realized yet that I felt something more than that.

But that was something to consider as well—what feelings did I have for Georgie-boy? Was I deluding myself again? The same way I had deluded myself about my relationship with Monsieur? And again with Josiah? Did I even know my own feelings anymore?

I promised myself that I would have to make every effort to be fair to Georgie-boy and not impose my own wishes on him through sheer force of either purse or personality. He must be the captain of his own soul.

The sunset was already fading to shades of blue and purple when I resumed my journey home. I was full of resolve, I was even elated at the prospect of leaving Seattle once and for all and starting a new life, somewhere that was solely my choice and free of all encumbrances of the past. Perhaps I would travel, I could go to Europe or the South Seas. Or anywhere. I could retrace Darwin's voyages and see all the strange creatures he'd written about. Australia perhaps, what a marvelous journey that might be. Or India—land of elephants and tea, all the strange spices. Perhaps far Cathay. Africa—the undiscovered continent? Too many choices, too many. It would take a lifetime to circumnavigate the globe—but perhaps that's what I should do.

When I arrived at home, Mrs. Grogan prepared a light supper for me, the inevitable fish stew and sourdough bread. I expected Georgie-boy to be there to join us as well, but Mrs. Grogan said that he had gone off with a client and she did not expect him back any time soon. She *tsk*ed disapprovingly. "I thought he would have given up that life. He's a good boy, he is. I just wish—" She stopped herself. "Well—I had hoped better for him, and I'll say no more."

For Mrs. Grogan to announce that she would say no more, was simply an overture to the much longer recital of everything she wasn't going to say. She went on for some time, revealing an extensive knowledge of the city, life on the streets, and the kind of clientele that Georgie-boy was most likely to encounter, how much she disapproved of them, and how much she still hoped that I might serve as a proper example of how to have a better life, enough to inspire the lad to give up his tawdry escapades and seek out some kind of real education. This went on until the last of the pie was finished, and the third cup of tea had gone cold in front of me.

I could have excused myself at any time, but I was waiting for an opportunity to tell Mrs. Grogan that I intended to leave Seattle at the earliest opportunity. Indeed, I planned to spend the morrow finalizing affairs with Mr. Durant, all with an eye to ending my relationship with his firm as soon as possible. I would have him contact the bank and arrange letters of credit so I could set up accounts in San Francisco or any other city. Eventually, I would have to find a new attorney, I would ask Durant for recommendations, certainly he would have associates elsewhere in the country, but while I would note his recommendations with interest, I had no intention of hiring any of them, as I no longer felt I could trust his confidentiality.

I hadn't decided yet what to do with the property on which Monsieur's house had stood, I would have to ask Durant's advice on that. I did not want to wait in Seattle through the interminable processes of offer and counter-offer, deposit, and escrow. Perhaps I would allow the land to lie fallow against the day of a possible return.

Then there was also the matter of booking passage on a steamboat south, was I booking passage for one or for two? Whether or not Georgie-boy would accompany me was a decision that would have to be postponed until his return. I expected it would be a short conversation—either an enthusiastic yes, or a grumpy refusal. But until I spoke with Georgie-boy, I would not discuss any plans with Mrs. Grogan.

Georgie-boy did not return before I turned in for the night. I took myself to a bed both cold and empty. It made me realize how comfortable I had become with his warmth beside me—and how much I would miss it if he did not accompany me.

I awoke in the morning, still feeling liberated. The past was gone, soon to be buried. All I had to do was arrange a few details and I could leave this city and all its turgid memories forever. But I arose alone, Georgie-boy had not returned, had not joined me in slumber, and I felt unusually annoyed by that. I made my toilet, skipped Mrs. Grogan's offer of breakfast, and walked out into the brisk Seattle morning. The inevitable bank of clouds had already rolled in, making the day grayer than usual.

I considered which way to go.

Should I walk over to the corner where the horse-drawn cabs waited for customers? Mr. Marley Matthews would greet me warmly, tipping his hat and holding the door for me. He'd share all the latest gossip of the city as well.

Or should I head down toward the wharf, where the fairies walked, to see if I could find Georgie-boy? He was probably loitering with his fellow street-rats, probably outside one of their usual hangouts, a cheap fish stand, sharing a beer or a cigarette. While it wasn't the best time of day to look for patrons, it was their time to be with their own.

I decided to head to the boardwalk. Perhaps one of the other boys would know where I could find Georgie. From half a block away, I could see a gathering crowd. Something about the look of the scene—

I quickened my step, I started to run—

The street boys were gathered on the opposite corner. Their expressions were dark, unreadable. I didn't see my Georgie among them. An officer stood between them and the body in the street. He didn't have to keep the boys away, they weren't going to come any closer. Without knowing, I knew. My heart clenched.

The body was covered by someone's coat. The coroner's wagon was just pulling up, I pushed through the few onlookers and went directly to the— the shape, praying the whole time it wouldn't be him.

"Sir, you mustn't—"

"I'm his—uncle!" I shouted, shoving past the officer, and grabbed—

"You shouldn't—"

"I have to see—"

—and pulled the coat back.

The look on dead Georgie's face was—not describable. His eyes were wide, his mouth was open, a silent O of horror, but what caught my attention was the splash of crimson at his neck. Someone—or something— had ripped his throat open, a great gaping bite. I staggered, fell backward, an involuntary grunt of shock escaping my lips. Someone grabbed me from behind to keep me from falling, probably the officer I'd shouldered aside.

"You shouldn't have looked, sir. You just shouldn't have. Now you'll have the sight stuck in your head forever." The officer replaced the coat over Georgie's face, helped me to my feet, took me by the arm and turned me away. I forced myself stare up at the windows of the building opposite. Curious faces looked down at the scene. I felt like I was choking.

"When—?"

"Sometime in the night. The boys there—they found the body."

I glanced across the street to the rest of the street boys. Georgie's brothers in grime.

"You knew this boy, sir?" The officer's tone were suspicious.

"I—I—no, I didn't know him. I thought I did. I—I was mistaken. I'm sorry—" I shook free of his grip. "I'm sorry—I'll leave you to your investigation."

"Nothing really to investigate, sir. Nothing really. This happens all the time, only not so bloody. Not much we can do about it, no witnesses, y'know—"

I nodded, covering my expression with my handkerchief and made as if to walk away, circling a bit and eventually coming around to where the other street boys huddled together in their own mix of anger, shock, and grieving.

"Hey!" said one of them, a wiry dark-haired boy. "I know you. You're his—"

I held up a hand to stop him from finishing the sentence. "Shh." I fumbled in my pocket, pulled out a wad of bills, quietly passed them around. "Did any of you see anything? Do you know anything?"

They all shook their heads, but they took the bills anyway, I didn't care. The dark-haired boy said, "It was one of the dark men, it's always one of the dark men. We try to be careful, but—"

"Yes, the dark men—"

I handed him the rest of the bills in my hand. "Take care of yourselves, please, all of you—" and stumbled away, a wash of furious emotions raging through me.

Why Georgie-boy? Why not me?! If they were that angry with me—? My thoughts were in turmoil. None of it made sense.

It was one of the dark men. Of that, there was no question. Indeed, it could have been Monsieur himself. Maybe he'd been toying with me all those years—and finally felt so guilty he had to send me away. Maybe it was one of the others, angered at my continuing curiosity or my efforts to contact them—enraged because I refused to leave them alone. But whatever the reason, there was no doubt in my mind that Georgie had been killed because of me.

A message. A warning.

We've run out of patience. Now go!

I walked back to Mrs. Grogan's slowly. She saw the look on my face and knew, even before I spoke—but then I said the words and she collapsed into my arms.

After a few hours of silent rage, I left my rooms and went to the Seaman's Church to arrange the funeral. The priest was reluctant to bury Georgie in a Christian cemetery—

I thrust a handful of bills into his hand. "The boy deserves it, he does! You will not deny him this—"

"He's not a proper Christian! He was a—" The man couldn't get the worlds out.

"Is that what you think? That you have the right to judge? You'll bury him proper—"

"No, you listen to me. You cannot come storming in here to demand—

"—or I'll have every street boy in Seattle claiming you've paid them with church money for your adventures in sodomy—"

It was not an idle threat. Georgie had shared some of his adventures with me, he enjoyed sharing the most salacious gossip. It had been entertaining at the time, I had never imagined I would find it so useful. "Now you take this money and you send this poor boy's soul to Christ—or I'll send you to Hell myself, you bloody hypocrite!"

The priest blanched, his face going so pale I thought he might pass out, but he nodded quickly, nervously agreeing to everything I demanded just to get me out of his office.

The service was a simple one—the organist played one or two appropriate hymns and the priest set a few prayers. Mrs. Grogan and I sat on one side of the church—Mr. Marley Matthews had driven us to the church, now he came in and joined us. "I knew the boy," he said. "Not well, but I'd seen him around. If you don't mind, I'd like to pay my respects too." He sat down next to me.

On the other side of the aisle, nearly a dozen street boys, all ages, sat quietly and respectfully. There wasn't much of a eulogy. The priest really didn't know what to say, and none of us in the pews wanted to share anything either.

At the graveside, a few more prayers were said, and the coffin was lowered into the ground. I had already arranged for a stone to be set. It wouldn't be ready for another week or two, I wasn't going to wait. But I gave the boys my card, and told them they could reach me through Durant if the stone was not properly arranged.

Mr. Matthews' horse and cab were waiting patiently at the street. He offered to drive Mrs. Grogan and myself back to her house, no charge of course, he said. Just as we were starting to board, the wiry dark-haired boy came up to me. "Sir—?"

"Yes?" I followed him a few steps away from the cab.

"Me and the others, we just wanted to say thank you for what you done, arranging the funeral and all. Georgie was a good'un and he deserved better, but I just wanted to tell you—he really liked you, a lot. He said—"

"Yes?"

"He said that you was talking about going away somewheres. All permanent like. And he was going to ask you, if you'd take him with. He really did like you—and not just 'cause you was his—you know, patron-like."

My throat was suddenly tight, I found it hard to speak, but I got the words out anyway. "Thank you," I said. "Thank you for telling me. I'm glad you did." I reached into my pocket, pulled out some more bills. "Take care of the other boys. Keep them away from the dark men. Get out of Seattle if you can—" I wanted to tell him more, but no—I couldn't.

I hurried back to the cab and climbed in next to Mrs. Grogan, who sat quietly wiping her nose. "That was a nice thing you did," she said. "Trying to take care of the boys like that. But I'm afraid they'll just spend it on cigarettes and beer, like they always do. They don't think about tomorrow, none of them. If they did—well, never mind." And she started sobbing again. I pulled her into a sideways hug and we rode the rest of the way in silence.

That afternoon I finished the last of my packing, the next morning I was on the lumber train south to San Francisco.

My last personal ad appeared in the following day's paper: "Wherever you are, I will find you—and I will repay you."

"Hmm."

We're standing on the dark street, well away from the street-lamp.

"Yes, I hear the puzzlement in your voice."

"You've raised more questions than you've answered."

Jacob nods.

"Did you find them? Did you kill them?"

He grins. His teeth gleam. His eyes shine. His skin seems translucent, like porcelain, pale in the wan light of the moon. "Do you know how hard it is to kill a vampire?"

"No, I don't."

"Very," he says. "First you have to find him—and you're only going to find him if he wants to be found. And if he wants you to find him, it's because you've annoyed him, and—" Jacob shrugs.

"But you found them?"

Jacob studies me for a moment. "What do you think?"

"I think...you must have. Or you wouldn't be here now."

"There's too much that you still don't understand."

"You're right. Because after all that, after everything they did to you, even after you decided to have nothing more to do with them—"

A flicker of a smile. "Like I said, there's too much that you still don't understand."

"Okay," I let it drop. He'll explain when he explains. Or he won't. I'm beginning to understand—he's waiting for me to figure it out for myself.

"Well, anyway—I'm sorry for your loss."

Jacob sneers. His expression is ugly. "I hate that phrase. It's what you people say when you're pretending to care. It's a hollow meaningless courtesy. It only pretends compassion. Listen to the words—it says, 'I'm sorry you're feeling shitty.' It doesn't say, 'I share your pain.' That's what compassion means. I share your pain. You've grown up in a culture that runs away from pain, hides from it, makes it a bad thing and drugs it out of existence. Most of you aren't worth killing—"

"That's a strange thing for you to say. You just told me how The Community killed Georgie-boy—"

"You still don't get it, do you!"

"What—? I thought you—"

"It wasn't a warning! It was an initiation! They wanted to see what I would do next! They needed to know if I was ready!"

And with that, he disappeared into the night.

Jacob in San Francisco

This time, we're at a banquet. The Horror Writers of America are having a convention. They're handing out awards. There's a lot of talk about vampires. I'm sitting with one, nobody notices—our table is off to one side, and we're not beneath the strongest lights, so while it's not shadowy gloom, we're not in the brightest glare either.

Jacob cannot hide his amusement.

"Hey, these are good people," I whisper.

"Yes, that's what's so funny."

Tonight, Jacob is dressed all in black. His fingernails are painted shiny black. His eyes are outlined in black and his hair stands away from his head like a black toilet brush. His skin is as pale as paper. He doesn't need makeup for that. He hasn't been out in the sun for years. He looks like an ominous Edward Scissorhands. He is the perfect parody of a goth vampire—no one would suspect him of being the real thing.

We whisper together, sharing a unique perspective on the evening's program—until the woman next to me asks if we're boyfriends.

I blush. "It's complicated."

Jacob laughs.

Later, we adjourn to my room in the hotel. We leave the lights off. I wonder if Jacob is planning to seduce me. He hasn't told me much about vampire sex. Do vampires even have sex? I imagine they must. He's hinted at it a few times. I wonder how it will happen—*if* it will happen.

I open a bottle of wine, pour two glasses. Jacob takes one. He looks at me, laughs again. "Would you prefer I do the Lugosi thing? 'I never drink...wine.'" He sips, smiles, nods, speaks in his normal voice. "Not bad. I've had worse."

He parks himself opposite me, he doesn't sprawl—he sits with an easy grace. Relaxed. "How have you been?"

"I'm having a career."

"You're not in your Writers' Group anymore."

"No, I'm not." I shrug, as much a denial as an explanation. "You can't go jogging with an anvil."

"Elucidate?"

"I wasn't getting the kind of feedback I needed. I was getting psychoanalysis instead. From amateurs. Not fun. I don't think they understood what I'm trying to do. They told me I was writing the wrong kind of story, that I was trying to work out my sexual issues—and readers don't want to read that."

"Are you?"

"It's your story I've been telling, not mine."

"Fair enough."

A moment of silence while he studies me. I study him. His expression is thoughtful.

Abruptly, he stands, goes to the window. I follow. We both look out at the lights of the city. Some people think a city at night is pretty. I'm not one of them. I find myself wondering what's going on in all those little lighted windows, and what's going on in all the ones that aren't lit.

Jacob speaks first. "So, tell me...what are you trying to do?"

"I'm trying to understand—" I stop. "The thing is, I can't really understand what I haven't experienced—I don't know how to write it from the inside."

"Are you asking to be turned—?"

"No—no, I'm not." The words come out too quickly. "Well, maybe, someday—but I'd have to—I don't know—I mean, from this side, I don't know if I should—and from the other side, there's no way back, is there—you never found a cure—so it's a one-way trip—and if I were turned, would I still want to write, I don't know that I'd want to give up my career—"

Jacob nods, smiles, laughs, enjoys himself at my expense. He holds up a hand to stop me. "Shh, relax. It's not going to happen. At least, not tonight. And you already know why."

"I do—?"

"Your little speech just now—"

"Oh. Yeah. Right." I laughed with him, unembarrassed.

We sit for a while. Finally, I say, "Something that I've been thinking about—"

"Yes?"

"There was nothing behind the door, was there?"

"Why do you say that?"

"I listened to the news, I checked the newspapers, I went to the news sites, I googled—there were no reports of a death. There was no discovery of a bloodless body, its throat ripped out—that would have been a front page story. There wasn't even a missing person report, nothing. So, you might have showed me a door—but there was nothing behind it."

"Does it matter? You believed there was. You wanted to believe I was capable of a horrendous murder. You were on eggshells the rest of the night."

"So you lied to me. Why?"

"You don't know that I lied. You didn't open the door, so you don't know what was behind it. But right then you so believed there was something behind it, you were afraid to open it. Now because you didn't see anything, you believe there wasn't. But this isn't about what was there. It's about what you want to believe. Why do you want to believe I lied?"

"I don't—I don't know what I want to believe. Oh hell, Jacob. Sometimes I think this is all a great big put-on, that you're just another delusional fan who's taken himself too seriously—that you've created this whole vampire persona as a way of—of being something more than just another escapee from the cape-and-pimple crowd."

"You really think that?"

"Well, why the hell shouldn't I? How much proof have you ever given me that anything you've said is real? I mean, it's a great story and all—I've made a lot of money off you. Hooray for me, but it's still your story, not mine—and you think I'm not lying awake nights wondering if I'm a real writer at all, or just someone who got conned into transcribing your homoerotic fantasies about sleeping with little boys and then ripping their throats out—"

Jacob moves fast. His hand is on my throat, his mouth on my neck, his teeth pressing into my skin, just a little bit more and he could rip into my jugular. He's astonishingly strong, I can't move, I hold my breath—

And then, instead of biting, he licks my neck—languorously. Very slow and sensuous, he traces the line of my jugular with his tongue, and I am suddenly so aroused, my erection is trying to twist itself out of my underwear. It's painful.

Jacob releases me, steps back with an expression that is both angry and amused. "I could prove it to you in a minute." He turns away, back to the table, picks up the wine bottle and refills his glass. "But I don't want to kill you. Not yet, anyway. But Jesus Fucking Christ on a bicycle—sometimes you really piss me off." He salutes me with the wine glass. "What do you want to believe in now?"

"I'll believe the evidence."

"How very twenty-first century of you." He drinks, refills his glass, refills mine, brings it across to me. "Here."

We return to our chairs. Hotel chairs. Well-padded, but still not really comfortable. Upholstered with that stiff dirt-maroon material that doubles as sandpaper. The bottle of wine sits forgotten on the table beside.

We stare at each other, he's studying, evaluating—my thoughts are churning. I'm always two steps behind. But then, if he's for real, he's had a century and a half head-start. With age comes enough experience to recognize patterns on the first move, not the last.

"So...it was a test. The door."

"Everything's a test. Yes."

"Did I pass?"

"No." He says it without judgment. "But then again—neither did I."

"Huh?"

"I told you about my Georgie-boy, how I found him dead on the street, his throat ripped out—sometime before dawn. That was my initiation test. The Community wanted to see how I would react to his death. Actually, any death would have done. Mrs. Grogan. Mr. Matthews. But Georgie was easiest, the most convenient. And the closest to me. So—he was the obvious choice."

I stare at Jacob. Unnerved.

"I thought you loved him."

"I thought I did too."

"But—?"

"But that was then. Before I became *this*...."

I have nothing to say. I'm trying to wrap my head around his meaning.

"You don't get it, do you?"

"Um, 'splain me...?"

"He was food. Nothing more. When I was still mortal, he was something to satisfy my emotional hunger. So I was wrapped up in him. But after I became *this*, I came to understand both hunger and emotions in a whole other way. The apex predator always has a higher perspective. Hunger is a need. It must be satisfied or you die. Emotions are merely feelings, a physical reaction to pleasure or pain. You feel your emotions here in your chest or your gut. Emotions are visceral. On the mortal plane, your level—they're rooted in survival. Your emotions function as warning lights, red or green or yellow. Over here, emotions are flavors to be savored or not, as the mood strikes. Because I have a different relationship with survival than you do."

"Oh."

Jacob stretches out an arm sideways, plucks the half-empty bottle off the table, refills his glass, and replaces the bottle, never once looking at it. "You are out of touch with your own existence. I am not. I know who I am. You do not know who you are—*what* you are."

"Okay, 'splain me some more."

"You are a predator. So am I. You kill to eat. So do I. The only difference is what we put on the plate. I'm the apex predator. You're a killer. So am I. But you—in your infatuation with all those silly mythologies you wallow in, you've made me and others like me into some kind of romantic heroes. No, we're not—we never have been. Have you ever stopped once to consider, what kind of person becomes a vampire? What kind of person *wants* to be a vampire? Someone who has no problem killing. Someone whose conscience has gone so far into remission, it's evaporated—his appendix has more function." He sets his empty glass down on the table. "You still have a problem with death—your refusal to open the door. And when Georgie-boy died, the way I reacted—yes, that was me showing The Community, I wasn't ready either."

He leans forward. "See, here's the ugly truth about who I am, who we all are—we're monsters. We're serial killers. We're ghouls. We're cannibals. We're the worst thing a human being can be. But you're still fascinated by us. Why? Because we have the charmfield, the sparkle zone, the charisma— because we can kill, we have power, and human beings, mortals like yourself, are so hungry for power, you'll do anything for it—you'll lie, cheat, and steal, you'll betray each other—and some of you will kill for it. And some of the best of your killers become apex predators. That's who we are."

"Sociopaths? Psychopaths?"

"Don't get them confused. Do you know the difference between a sociopath and a psychopath?"

"No."

"Psychopaths get caught."

"Oh."

"A successful vampire is a cunning sociopath. He's charming, he manipulates, he takes what he wants, and he doesn't care about what you want. A psychopath—he's not charming, he's just a monster. Even the men of The Community are appalled by that behavior. It's...well, it's just bad manners.

Jacob considers his empty glass, decides not to refill it, places it on the table, returns his attention to me. "Yes, we have had a few people fail to cope with their own transformation. They become psychopaths, they get drunk on power, they turn into monsters, killing at will. It's the imbalance of hormones. But the way you people portray us, you think we're all psychopaths. No—you don't see the real Community. You only see the ones who—well, most of the time, we find them and take care of them before you even know they exist. Most of the time, we clean up after them too. A missing person report is better for us than a bloodless body in a dumpster. But that's the point, *mon petit fromage*—I am not your friend. Vampires don't have friends. We are all sociopaths. We have to be sociopaths or we're going to die a very ugly death—"

"Hunger—"?"

"Not exactly. Not hunger, not as you know it, but a kind of hunger much more painful and debilitating than anything you can imagine, worse than anything a mortal can experience, because it goes on and on and on, without end. It's a sensual grind as well as a physical one. No, until you're willing to kill—you can't be transformed."

I put my own glass on the table. I hadn't realized I was still holding it until I looked down at my hands. They're shaking.

"And that's the point—you don't just become a vampire. You have to be trained. And first, The Community has to see that you're trainable. What is your relationship with death? Does it fascinate you? Does it intrigue you? Does it draw you into its embrace? Are you willing to be its agent? Are you willing to kill to eat? That's an easy one. Are you willing to kill to defend yourself? Another easy one. But are you willing to kill simply because you enjoy killing? Ahh, that's the crucial difference—are you enough of a sociopath to succeed as a vampire? What The Community doesn't need is another self-inflated idiot calling attention to himself. The self-appointed Master of Darkness usually dies quickly. That's at least one thing your movies get right. That psychopaths make lousy vampires. The rest is bullshit—"

"Wow. I hadn't realized."

"No, you haven't—and neither have any of your colleagues, at least none of the ones I've followed. That's why you're all so laughable—all puffed up with self-importance, and how many of you have actually taken the time to consider the physics, the economics, the psychology, the morality—yes, morality—and the simple raw experience of this existence? What a bunch of claptrap. What do you think a vampire does? Do you think I just sleep in a coffin all day and only come out to drink blood? Why would anyone want that kind of existence? It's booorrrring."

"I don't think you're being fair to—"

"Are they being fair to me? To my...associates? They make us out to be monsters. Or worse, teenage fantasies."

"Well, you have to admit—"

"No, I don't. I don't have to admit anything. At best, you're a snack. And I don't play with my food. Yes, I am a monster—but I'm not the kind of monster you believe. I'm not any kind of monster you know."

I have no words. Shrug. "You're right. I've got nothing. You've deconstructed the mythology."

"The mythology?" Jacob snorts. "I haven't even touched the mythology." He reaches for his glass, refills it. He sips. "I eat, I sleep, I drink—" He gestures with the wine. "And once a month, I get my period—"

"The full moon?"

"Oh, hell no. Where did you get that idea? More of those silly horror movies? You've got to stop wallowing in that bullshit. No—not the full moon. That's the worst time of the month for hunting. It's too bright, bright enough to see shadows. The prey can see every flicker of movement. No—the dark of the moon. Much much better. The darkest of darks. All the different colors of black. When the darkness gets so deep I'm invisible, that's when I feed—"

"You can see in the dark?"

"Better than you can in the day." Jacob smiles, his sharp teeth gleam. "Do you know that sometimes I watch you at night? Sometimes you go out for a walk. Sometimes I track you—"

"I—I—really?"

"Yes."

"Why?"

"It's fun. I like watching you. You're so serious, so intense, you're cute."

"That's because I'm thinking. I like to work at night, it's easier, everything is quiet and I'm alone. Sometimes I take a walk because that helps me sort out my ideas." A thought occurs to me. "Do you follow me a lot?"

"No. Only when I'm so bored I can't stand it."

"Should I be worried—?"

"No. You should say thank you."

"Uh—why?"

"Two months ago—I wasn't the only one watching you walk."

"Oh?"

"I didn't like his intentions. You belong to me, not him. He smelled bad, he tasted worse. I spat him out and left him in a dumpster."

"Hm."

"Yes, you're thinking back. You've been tracking unsolved murders, haven't you? Trying to figure out which ones are mine. Or anyone's."

"Well, yes. I'm trying to figure out how to find a vampire. You couldn't do it in Seattle."

"I told you before, you don't find vampires unless they want to be found. And if they let you find them, you're probably in deep doodoo."

"But you found them—The Community."

"Yes. Eventually. And if I thought finding a vampire was hard, killing one is even harder."

The train to Sacramento took most of two days. It was a slow, bumpy, uncomfortable ride. It was a lumber train, carrying wood from the Washington forests, but it also had two baggage cars carrying bushels of fresh apples, live crabs and lobsters in sea-water filled barrels, salmon on ice that had been driven down from the mountains, some silks and spices and tea that had arrived from China or Japan, I wasn't sure, and one car for passengers, most of whom worked on the railroad or for one of the line's major shippers. The meals served enroute were simple, but hearty. I had no cause to complain.

Mostly, I sat alone at the far end of the car, scribbling my thoughts in a notebook, trying to organize myself for my new life. I started with what I knew to be real. The Community was real. The Community had killed Georgie-boy.

That suggested several possibilities, any or all of which I had to accept as real. The Community was watching me closely—how, I couldn't be sure, but certainly if they had known about my relationship with Georgie-boy, then I had to have been under their observation.

That also suggested that lawyer Durant had been keeping them posted on my inquiries as well. I couldn't prove that, but if someone had visited him shortly after dark on that last evening, and if he had shared our last conversation—the one where I had asked him to put me in touch with any of Monsieur's associates—then that gave that visitor enough time to seek out Georgie and dispatch him so violently.

I had told Durant that I was leaving Seattle on a steamship heading south, that I would debark in San Francisco, and that I would write to him as soon as I had settled in. I even went so far as to have Russell, his secretary, rush out and book passage for me.

Mr. Matthews, the cabbie dropped me off at the pier, and we parted as if we were old friends. As soon as he had driven away, I loaded my trunks into another cab and went straight to the train station. I paid for my passage on the lumber train in cash.

I wasn't certain that I had not been observed, but at the time I had some small suspicion that the men of The Community in Seattle might have been satisfied just to see the last of me.

On the other hand, my last personal ad had been a declaration of war. I had published it in the personals column, they couldn't have missed it. "Wherever you are, I will find you—and I will repay you."

In retrospect, that was probably a mistake. It had marked me as their enemy, and they would certainly have little hesitation in giving me the same violent death as they had done for poor Georgie.

I needed to make myself as hard to find as they were. That would require some thought. It meant I could not stay in any one place very long, maybe only two or three nights at a time. Hotels, inns, boarding houses might suffice—the problem there was that those places often kept records. I would have to find establishments where cash was an acceptable substitute for credential. Most of those would be places of dubious repute.

But—whatever I did, if I fell into any kind of a pattern, that would also be a trap. I would have to keep shifting my behaviors.

That sparked a thought. The men of The Community were cunning and they were patient. They acted on their timetable—no one else's. They studied patterns—I knew this from my time with Monsieur, and again as

I had pored through the records that Durant had stored in his office—records I had claimed, packed, and shipped to a receiving agent on the other side of the continent, with sealed instructions to forward them to a second, and from there to a trustworthy third who upon opening his sealed instructions, would place the files in a secure storage facility—one of the same facilities that banks and some government offices used for their outdated records. Upon completion of this task, he would publish a coded personal ad in a specific national newspaper. The code would tell me—and only me—what city my files had been sent to and where I would find them.

I didn't think the files had any real value, I had gleaned some information from them, but most of what I had discovered was how well Monsieur had learned to hide himself through a variety of barely legal financial maneuvers. I assumed that other members of The Community were equally skilled at evading detection. It was a finely honed survival skill. I was a neophyte up against masters. There was little point in continuing that avenue of research.

Perhaps at some point in the future, when I had gained more experience, I might have a second or third look—or I might have someone with more experience go through the various papers, someone I could trust not to report back to The Community. There might be something else in those files to discover—something I had missed the first time through. I doubted it, but I couldn't rule out the possibility.

But an idea had occurred to me. While in Boston, I had been comfortable in an apartment of my own. Acquaintances from the university had made my rooms a convenient gathering place away from the campus—a place for drinking, smoking, cards, and occasional lascivious exercises. One of the young gentlemen had come from a family of well-established locksmiths. They provided safes and security vaults for banks, jewelry stores, government offices, and various other establishments that needed to store valuables.

My acquaintance had remarked that no lock, no safe, no bank vault was invulnerable to attack. Nothing is unbreakable given enough time and effort. The physical universe doesn't have absolutes. A vault isn't about safety, it's about deterrence.

The security of the vault is not the vault itself, but the time and energy it would take to break in. If it costs more to break in than the value inside, then it's not worth a robber's time. "It's a question of who's willing to spend the most—you building your vault, or the burglar who wants what's inside.

Your job isn't to construct a system that can't be broken, there's no such thing. Your job is to construct a system so far beyond the capabilities of an invader that it discourages all attempts."

As the train jerked along through the dark forests of Oregon, his remarks bubbled up in my memory. I had no security, but I could make all attempts at observation and detection more trouble than they were worth.

Toward that end, I had to demonstrate—I laughed out loud at the realization—behavior so irrational there was no obvious pattern.

Or—

Another thought also occurred to me. I could allow myself to be observed sinking into a life so degenerate that I no longer represented a threat to The Community. That might work too.

Or—

I could simply get on a steamer and sail off to some far horizon, someplace where I would have no power at all to effect any danger to The Community.

Or—

I could retreat to a mountain cabin so remote and difficult to achieve that it would take several days for anyone to reach me. No member of The Community could risk being exposed to that much sunlight. Or maybe a desert location. That would be even more unapproachable. But I wasn't exactly excited about the idea of living in so much isolation.

Perhaps—

I could build or purchase a big house, a mansion, something alone on a hill, and then fortify it, put up a moat, walls, fences, bring in vicious dogs, hire guards, and become—

That one stopped me. That was exactly what a member of The Community might do—retreat behind an unimpeachable barricade.

If I wanted to find a vampire—maybe that's what I should be looking for.

Hmm.

I scribbled all these thoughts in my journal so I wouldn't forget them. I kept that book close to me, in an inside pocket, triple-buttoned—and connected by a metal chain as well. It was more valuable than my wallet.

My mind kept churning.

Hmm, Maybe I could set myself up in a house anyway, someplace not too obvious, but just enough—and use that as a decoy while I hid out somewhere else.

Or—

If I lived on a boat, I could sail out each night, up the river to somewhere in the back of the Sacramento Delta where there aren't any roads, and only come back to shore after sunrise. That might be one way to stay out of the reach of The Community.

At least, I had options now.

I arrived in Sacramento late in the day, which was not an ideal time. I left my trunks at the baggage claim and walked around the corner, up two blocks, left, two blocks over, one block back, then waited in a doorway to see that I hadn't been followed. Satisfied, I headed toward the business district, and checked into the first hotel I saw, a somewhat shabby building, but I had resolved to live beneath my means and adopt the general demeanor of a man who was living from meal to meal, job to job. I would soon be dressing the part, wearing workman's dungarees and cap. I didn't know if a disguise would hide me from a determined Community, but it could provide some small advantage. As cunning as they were, there was always the possibility that they would not think to search for me outside the pattern of life I had lived in Seattle—a slim possibility to be sure, but I had resolved to learn all the different ways to be invisible in the hopes that the combined efforts would provide a greater degree of protection.

Maybe. Maybe not.

I had to recognize that that my departure from Seattle had not been immune to detection. It was possible some private agent, some daysider had been assigned to watch my actions, just like Durant, and that person might have tracked me to the train, might have then reported back to The Community that I had not left by steamboat. It was equally possible that someone in Seattle had telegraphed someone in Sacramento, had told them to watch out for me. And it was possible that someone reporting to The Community here, and eventually to The Community in Seattle, had seen me debark.

But even if that were the case—and I couldn't discount it entirely—all that it might prove was that yes, The Community had frightened me so badly that I was fleeing like a terrified dog, running and hiding and doing everything I could imagine to keep them from finding me. And that part was true anyway. They had terrified me.

As for the rest—well, I had the beginnings of a plan.

I knew I couldn't outthink them. Not yet. The Community believed me to be naïve—too naïve to be a threat.

Well, yes I was.

But that didn't mean I couldn't learn. And if there was one thing I had learned from Monsieur—and again in Boston—it was that I was more than just a good student. I had what could only be called an obsessive desire to master any subject that interested me. More than once, I had immersed myself so deeply in a specific study that it alarmed my professors. While at first they had considered me an excellent student, they soon began to fear that I was possessed of some manic compulsion, plowing through one book or journal after another, as if caught up in a desperate search for the ultimate level of truth, the last elusive fact that would unlock all the mysteries still unsolved.

And that was true too.

It was the mystery of The Community that I wanted to solve. All the mysteries of The Community. Yes, I wanted the secret of life everlasting, but not at the price that Monsieur had paid, living life in permanent shadow—so yes, I wanted to find a cure for his condition so he could return to the daylight. I believed then—and still believed even after the betrayal of his disappearance—that on some level, he desired a mortal relationship. Perhaps even some of the other men of The Community regretted what they had become, and perhaps they too secretly hoped that one day there might be a cure.

Somewhere in my fevered thinking, I realized that I had no way to know if The Community was watching me or not. So whatever I did, however I behaved—I could never assume I was acting in secrecy. That led me to a rather amusing realization. If I acted as if I thought I was hiding, The Community would assume that I believed I had fooled them. If I knew that I was not fooling them at all, I would have my secrecy in plain sight.

So I would behave like one insane, scrambling from place to place, running and hiding—

And at the same time, I could commit a number of acts so bizarre—seemingly rational in the context of my terror—but so jumbled and outrageous as to confuse anyone trying to discern a pattern, especially The Community.

It was the conversation with the locksmith scion. I had no real protection—but I could have deterrence. I could make my behavior so scrambled that The Community would deem it not worth the effort to figure out if any of my actions might represent a serious threat to them.

I won't bore you with the details. Assume that I spent a lot of time in coaches, on trolleys, on boats, on trains, or simply walking bizarre patterns. I also changed my habits—my manner of dress and speaking, the meals I took, and especially how I managed my finances. I was never without an escape plan, never without access to a go-bag.

Occasionally, on some outing or other, I might have accidentally met and spent a few moments chatting with someone who might have worked as an attorney, or as a private investigator, or once even a representative of the Pinkerton Agency. It could have been on a ferry boat in the San Francisco harbor, or on the Skunk Train in northern California, or maybe just grappling together in the back room of a bawdy house, pretending to be lovers. Information and cash might have been exchanged, as well as signals for how to meet again in other discreet circumstances—never the same circumstances twice.

To confuse any pursuers, I made sure that I met with other men as well, sometimes buying strangers a meal or sharing a bed in a hotel. Sometimes cash was exchanged for these dalliances as well—clumsily, in case anyone was watching. Sometimes I gave these strangers envelopes to be dropped into the mail at their convenience. Someone intercepting one of those posts would have found only a few cryptic sentences—possibly a code of some kind—or just as often a jumbled collection of words meaning nothing at all.

If I was being observed—and I had to assume I was—then somebody somewhere might be considering if it was really worth the effort to discern the details of everything I was attempting.

Actually, I wasn't attempting much. I had chosen Sacramento because it was the capital of the California territory. Legal documents of all kinds would be filed there. Working through two or three intermediaries, I had agents looking for all kinds of information—most of what they pored through was unnecessary for my research, but I didn't want to alert anyone who might be watching for someone conducting certain specific searches.

Think of it this way—if you don't want someone to know you're looking for a particular spoon, you go rummaging through the knives, the forks, the teacups, the dinner plates, the spoons, the napkins, the sugar bowl, and pretend to be happy when you come up with the silver gravy bowl, all the while remembering exactly where you noticed that particular spoon in passing.

At some point, I realized that I was beginning to think a little bit like the men of The Community. This was how they had to live their lives every day—furtive, discreet, and leaving false trails everywhere. If they had wanted to train me to be one of them, they couldn't have found a better way to inspire my commitment.

I was angry and frustrated with Monsieur. I was furious with whoever had killed Georgie-boy. And whatever outward appearance I might have conveyed by my seemingly scattered behaviors—even if men of The Community were dismissing me as given to irrationality, they would not and could not ever assume that I had forgotten what they had done.

If you are an immortal, you play the long game—and you assume that revenge of any kind is inevitable. As long as I was alive, I had to be seen as a threat to them—no matter what I might be doing, no matter how difficult it might be for them to discover what I was *really* up to.

But Sacramento was only a decoy. I made frequent trips to Oakland, Berkeley, and San Francisco—because while Sacramento was full of lawyers and legislators, the cities surrounding the bay were the real heart of the California territory. Almost all the commerce of the state came through that port, especially San Francisco.

The city had traffic. It had travelers. It had vagrants and street boys and seamen. It wouldn't notice if a few disappeared during the darkest nights of the month.

I was certain that there would be houses in this city—mansions—that were mostly dark and shuttered during the day, dimly lit at night, filled with gatherings of dark secretive men. The safest place to hide is in the middle of a crowd. Perhaps one of these narrow homes, comfortably inconspicuous in the middle of a long block of similar homes, housed a darker secret than just another businessman and his family.

• ⊷≡•◑➁◖•⟫≡⊶ •

"And you found one, right?"

"Oh, hell no."

"Huh?"

"I was looking in the wrong places. I was looking where I thought a Nightsider would hide. I was still thinking like me—not them. And...I was thinking that they all lived like Monsieur. They didn't. They couldn't. They wouldn't. But—" Jacob smiles. "It wasn't a useless exercise. Because while I was learning how to be furtive, I was also learning how to think like someone who couldn't stand exposure. Because, I couldn't either—"

I nod. Yes.

Jacob continues. "I was going out at night, prowling the same places they might prowl in search of victims. I waited until the darkest nights, the foggiest nights, the nights they would most likely be hunting. I hid in the shadows, like they would, and watched the streets and alleys, hour after hour, hoping to catch a glimpse of a single predatory figure.

"To protect myself from attack, I wore a stiff metal collar around my neck, I wore heavy leather armor under my clothing as well. And a heavy dark cloak over everything. I must have looked like a bit like one of them—or just a confused black bear. After three or four nights of that, I stopped. If they caught me, they could have killed me despite my precautions. The fact that I was still alive suggested they didn't want to kill me. Perhaps they found me amusing.

"It's possible I might have seen one or two. It's possible I might have seen one or two and not recognized them for what they were. And it's just as possible they knew I was there and stayed well out of sight. Even if I had spotted one, I wasn't sure what I could do—I didn't dare accost one of them. They had strength and speed far beyond anything I could muster. They could outthink me, I had to believe that. And if I tried to follow one of them back to his lair—he would have eluded me quickly.

"I had not yet figured out how to open up a conversation with one of them—it was my hope that upon sensing me in the shadows, one of them would come to me—"

"And—"

Jacob shrugs. "And we could talk, perhaps—? But it didn't happen."

"So, how did you—"

"I'm getting to that. One night, as dawn was creeping across the east side of the bay, I went to a shabby hotel near the wharf, a place I had deliberately visited more than once, and rented a room. It was a spur-of-the-moment decision, brought on by exhaustion. I just didn't have the energy at that moment to go through my usual pattern of evasions. I found my room, upstairs in the rear of the building, and didn't even undress. I collapsed onto the bed, staring up at a ceiling which had seen much better days, and sighed aloud, 'I need a daykeeper—' And that was the realization that flooded through me like the sudden shock of a swallow of hard liquor, and even after the shock fades, it still leaves a resident glow. That's what I was feeling. I hadn't been looking in the wrong places. I'd been looking for the wrong thing—"

"You needed to look for a daykeeper...?"

"Precisely! Vampires think like vampires. Daykeepers think like daykeepers. And I knew how to think like that. Monsieur had taught me that much."

"Do you think they might have been aware of that too?"

"They should have been, shouldn't they? Except remember what I said. Nightsiders are sociopaths. All of us. It's part of the condition. There's no alternative—because you have to kill to feed. And you have to feed or you'll die horribly, writhing in horrible agonies of hunger and despair—and it will take a long long time. Immortals don't die easily or quickly. So even if you're not, you learn how to be a sociopath. Very quickly.

"A sociopath is a charming narcissist. He's never wrong, not in his own eyes. He's a narcissist so self-involved he trusts no one. He uses people until he uses them up. He's willing to lie, cheat, and steal to get what he wants. He can't have compassion. He doesn't have empathy. It gets in the way. He has to win, no matter what, whatever it takes—because winning is survival. Losing is death.

"So," Jacob continues, "The daykeeper is merely a piece of ambulatory furniture, a tool, an object, something to be manipulated and used. Not something with feelings, something to be discarded when it wears out, replaced with another. So, the likelihood that the Nightsiders would think to protect their daykeepers...? Well, perhaps a few of them might have demonstrated some attachment to a particularly useful individual, but...it's like dogs—they die, you replace them. You miss the one that died, you play with the one that replaces it and you get on with the lie you call your life. Any questions?"

"I have a whole bunch of questions, let me get my notebook—"

"Not yet," Jacob says. "Later, perhaps. Or perhaps not. I meant questions about daykeepers."

"I knew what you meant. I'm learning. Maybe too slow for you, but—"

"Actually, you're learning quite fast. For a short-timer." Jacob allows himself a chuckle, a dark sound deep in his throat. "I live on a different time scale than you."

"You're training me, aren't you?"

"Oh, that's not the half of it—"

"But you are—"

"Perhaps, perhaps not. You still have a vestigial conscience."

A sudden thought. "What's the other half?"

"I intend to blow that whole stupid vampire meme out of the water, once and for all. I want the human race to know who the real monsters are."

"Um, who? You—or us?"

Jacob grins. "What do you think?" His teeth are unnaturally white. Eventually, I'll ask how does he do that? I'd think after a hundred and fifty years, a person's teeth would not only be worn down, but very dark as well. Yellow. Or black. Or was this another part of the...the condition—?

"I think..." I say this slowly. "I think they won't care. Based on the little I've seen, people enjoy their fantasies and their horrors too much to give them up. It's easier than facing reality."

"I hadn't figured you for a philosopher, but all right—that counts as an insight."

"Thanks. So—you had an epiphany. About the daykeepers."

"Not an epiphany. A realization. But it was enough."

⁕ ⊷╾╼⬦●▶◐◀●⬦╾╼⬌ ⁕

It took a while, several months in fact. By now, I had shifted most of my attention to San Francisco, and even though I continued to perform extensive evasive maneuvers, I was now spending most of my time circling the bay. I had gotten what I needed from Sacramento, most of it was useless, but it had given me a good sense of the size of the problem in front of me. And it had given me some appreciation of the various ways that property was used across the city. There were large areas that I could safely ignore. There were other areas that required closer investigation—to be blunt, areas within easy walking distance of the best feeding grounds.

Yes, it was possible that the Nightsiders in this city might have their own carriages so they could live at some remove from the darker neighborhoods—but my experience of The Community was that they protected their privacy so ferociously that the fewer humans who knew of them at all, the better. So I developed a justifiable suspicion of certain streets and properties.

Now that I was shifting the focus of my search to the daykeepers, I felt I would have much better results. I passed new instructions to the detectives I had hired, adjusting the guidelines of the search. Continue looking for housing circumstances where the central occupant remains mostly unknown—but now pay particular attention to the caretaker situations as well. Look for male caretakers of a certain nature. Do not approach, just pass me the information and I'll sort it based on additional criteria that are beyond your need to know.

Packets of information were handed to me through various subterfuges—hidden within a folio of etchings at the public library, an envelope left behind on the ferry, a bag on the train, a few papers folded into a newspaper on the counter of the diner, even a mail drop at distant post office. Never the same way twice.

Looking through the reports—again, this took several months—I suspected several possible candidates, but three stood out. They were all within the same neighborhood, two on the same block, the third around the corner. That was suspicious enough to warrant further investigation.

I had one of my hired investigators rent an upstairs room that would provide an excellent view of both houses on the block as well as a nearby row of small shops. I moved in under cover of darkness.

I also had him arrange deliveries of meals, mail, and packages, so I would never have need to leave the room—and risk being seen. When my new landlord inquired of my agent about the strange privacies that his new tenant desired—the landlord was not to approach the room or the tenant under any circumstances, all communications must go through the rental agency—my representative paid him triple the rent and hinted that it was for his own good that he not know any details about his new tenant. Just don't believe any of the curious tales that might soon be circulating.

Having a bit of fun, he even gave the landlord a long list of bizarre stories not to believe, all of them deliberately designed to discourage further inquiry. Whatever the neighborhood gossips suspected, the landlord was instructed to deny everything—that I was a reclusive eccentric, that I was severely ill, slowly wasting away from some exotic failure of the liver, that I was one of those melancholic souls who wished to avoid other human beings, that I was a deeply troubled author working on a very personal memoir, that I was recovering from the traumas of the Indian wars where I had seen companions savagely butchered and had even participated in a few butcheries myself, that I was a foreigner and did not speak much English, that I was hiding from a jealous lover, that I was under quarantine by my doctor because of some still unnamable condition, that I had been wounded in battle leaving me terribly disfigured—I had to wear a wooden mask, and didn't want to shock passersby with my hideous appearance— or in fact, the easiest story to believe, and possibly the most accurate, was simply that I was incurably insane and my secured residence in this room was a place where I could be safely kept away from others for my own good. And theirs as well.

Of course, all that secrecy made me an object of immediate curiosity in the neighborhood anyway, the exact opposite of what I wanted. But again, I had to assume that I was still in fact under The Community's watchful eyes, and that all of these extreme efforts were simply more evidence of my terrified obsession.

When the landlord's daughter brought me my meals, I answered the door with a veil over my face and possibly holding a gun behind my back. At least, I made her think that. Every time I spoke, I spoke with deliberate gruffness, as if I was annoyed not just at the interruption, but at the mere existence of anyone intruding on my privacy. Of course, I instructed her in the strictest terms that she must not tell anyone about anything she might see in my room—I told her that it could put her in danger. No, there was nothing illegal going on in here, she did not need to involve the police, but yes, she did need to be cautious, even afraid. I did not tell her so, but I could not allow her to be my friend. I had already seen what The Community would do to anyone they suspected of being my friend.

Of course, there was nothing to see in the room anyway, I kept everything draped in black, every piece of furniture, the chair, the bed, the table, the dresser, everything. I had black velvet curtains across the windows. This sometimes made the room stifling during the day, so even with the curtains drawn I kept the windows half open for what limited circulation I could arrange.

During the day, I sat on a high chair, way back in the shadows, shielded as much by the curtains as I could manage, and studied the street below through a variety of telescopes and binoculars. I kept everything draped in black, of course. Anyone trying to peer into my windows would have seen only gloom and indeterminate shapes.

At night, however, with all the lamps out—with myself carefully draped in black, I could sit much closer to the window and watch the unfolding tableaus on the street below.

Night and day, I made extensive notes. I grew to recognize the shopkeepers and their families, their regular customers, even many of the passersby—wives buying bread and cheese and onions, and fish or sausage for the evening meal, husbands on their way home from work, children off to lessons—

My notebooks grew thick. I made charts of what I observed, charts about individuals, notations about each house and who lived there, who visited, and the hours they kept. But I paid special attention to who entered and exited the two most suspect addresses, and who they spoke to on the street.

Surprising myself, it was not as hard as I thought to identify the two men who were probably daykeepers. It wasn't just their places of residence, it was their manner of behavior—they were openly secretive. I'll explain.

During the day, they performed the usual tasks of shopping and commerce. But they did so in a subdued manner. While I could not hear any of their words at this remove, I watched the way they moved, the way they stood, the curt manner with which they conducted their business at each of the various stalls. I recognized the unscented candles, soaps and oils they selected—items that would not overwhelm the delicate senses of their masters. I watched not only what foodstuffs they purchased, but the quantities as well. I noted each day's purchases in my diary. I was well aware of the specific dietary needs of a Nightsider—and how in the days following the darkest nights, these men purchased less than usual.

More telling, the only lengthy conversations they engaged in were with each other—and these conversations were always well away from anyone else's hearing.

At night, after the street had fallen quiet, occasionally a dark figure would emerge from one or the other of the suspect dwellings. Sometimes a horse-drawn cab would pull up in front of one of the doorways, blocking my view—I was never certain if someone was leaving or arriving.

Three months stretched into four—and I was finally certain. I had three newspapers brought up with my meals every day. I read them carefully for any notices of mysterious deaths or disappearances. While there was never a one-to-one correlation with the moonless nights of the month, there were enough occasional stories to give me pause—and they tended to match up with the daykeepers making fewer purchases of meat, often enough to give me pause.

Only one question remained in my mind. Were the Nightsiders in those homes aware of my existence? If they were, then they were tolerating me. If they weren't aware, then why were they being so careless?

But either way, what was my next move?

I spent long hours considering the daykeepers.

One was in his fifties, perhaps even older than that, he moved slowly and methodically about his business. The other was younger, possibly in his twenties. Any other young man of his age would have had a spring to his step, but even on the brightest of days, this fellow seemed cloudy. I wondered if I had looked like that when I had lived with Monsieur.

In my mind, I called this man Wellington. No reason. He just looked like a Wellington to me. On Saturdays, he left the house early, carrying a large shopping basket on his arm. He skipped the local stalls and headed toward Market Street instead. He was usually gone for two or three hours. That should be more than enough time.

Because Friday had been the second night of a full moon. I did not expect the Nightsider inside to be recently fed. He was probably conserving his strength for the upcoming darkness, nearly two weeks away.

Getting into the house was not a problem. I had learned a few tricks from my locksmith acquaintance, including how to obtain a master key. Once inside, it was immediately obvious to me that this house had been outfitted for a member of The Community. Heavy drapes covered all the windows.

This was not a house with a basement—houses on the west coast were not yet built to stand for a century or longer. Most of the houses in the bay area were simple frame structures. They seemed flimsy in comparison to the brick buildings of Boston. I had no doubt that a fire could sweep through this city like an enraged demon. As soon as I concluded my business here, I intended to move on—

The stairs creaked as I climbed them. I hoped that the occupant upstairs would assume that my footsteps were Wellington's—but it was probably a shallow hope. I was depending on this Nightsider being in a sleep so deep, he would be unable to waken. Monsieur had hinted that such was possible—

Inside the master bedroom—a bedroom so dark it could have been the inside of a coffin—there was a large canopied bed. A tall thin figure, dressed all in black, lay motionless on top of the covers. He was of indeterminate age. His features were pale, like Monsieur's, his hair a curious shade of silver, his expression calm, restful.

Perhaps it was overly dramatic of me, but I had a stake and a mallet. As I placed the stake in the center of his chest—

His eyes opened and his hand reached out and grabbed my forearm. "I don't think so," he said. And then, "Tell me why I shouldn't kill you."

"I've eaten a whole clove of garlic every day for the last three months. And certain other things too. You wouldn't like the taste of my blood."

"It wouldn't stop me." Then he added, "I smelled you before you even started up the stairs."

He let go of my forearm and grabbed the stake. He held it up in front of his eyes. He could see it quite clearly in the darkness. "Hm," he said. "How quaint."

"I wasn't sure of the best way. And a gunshot might have attracted the attention of the police."

He sat up, stood up. He was tall, thin, gangly even. Taller than me. His silver hair reached down to his shoulders. His eyes were dark and piercing.

"I'm Jacob," I said.

"Yes, I know. We all know. You've been watching my house from across the street. Four months now. Quite amusing, really." He reached out and took the mallet from my hand, examined it too, then tossed it aside. "Really amusing."

He studied me for a moment, circling me, cocking his head like a rooster, and sniffing with nostrils flared. At one point, he reached out and lightly touched my neck with fingers as thin and delicate as a courtesan's.

"Do you know Monsieur?" I asked.

"I know of him. I know your story as well."

"Where is he? I have to see him."

"If he'd wanted you to know his whereabouts, he'd have told you, wouldn't he?"

"I just want to talk to him. I need to know what I did that he—he just abandoned me. I want to apologize—"

"Hm," said the man.

I was feeling a little bolder now. He might still kill me. But not right away. "May I ask? Who are you? Can you tell me why Monsieur disappeared?"

"My name is ... well, my current name is Langham. Come downstairs now. I have to decide what to do with you."

I followed him down the stairs. I can't say that all thoughts of killing had left me, but I was quite aware now just how difficult it would be. Monsieur had once admitted that Nightsiders would go into a state of suspended animation resembling death for long hours after a period of extreme exertion. But—clearly, finding one in such a state was not going to be an easy task for anyone.

Once in the parlor, Langham had me sit in a tall comfortable chair. He sat opposite me. "I would offer you something, but my manservant is away at the moment."

I lifted a hand to politely demur.

"You know," Langham began. "You didn't have to make an attempt on my life to get my attention. You could have left your card. You could have requested an audience."

"I haven't had much luck with that—"

"Of course not. And personal ads in the newspaper are not exactly the best access to this community either. It was ... well, shall we say somewhat *gauche*?"

"You have to see it from my side—"

"Why?" He blinked. "Why should any of us make that effort? Why are you presuming that you're important enough to justify our attention?"

"If you really think that, then why didn't you just kill me upstairs?"

"I didn't want to make a mess in my private chambers. And besides, I was hoping you might say something interesting or amusing. So far, that has been a vain hope indeed."

"I'm not here to amuse you. I just want some answers."

"Well, young Master Jacob, I'm afraid you'll be leaving here without any."

"You're going to let me leave? Why?"

"Is there any reason why I shouldn't?"

"Aren't you afraid I'll tell someone what you are?"

"Really—?" He chuckled. "Please do so. I'm told that San Francisco has a ward in the general hospital, just for the study of the mentally ill." He examined his fingernails. They were long and sharp. "Besides," he said. "By this time tomorrow, I'll be gone. Pity about that, I rather liked this neighborhood. But...*c'est le mort.*"

"Ha ha. So you're not going to tell me anything?"

"Of course not. You haven't earned it."

"What do I have to do to earn it—?"

Langham shrugged. "I have no idea. You are of no concern to me. Now, please go."

I rose. I looked across at him. He sat impassively, waiting, studying me. I said, "If I ever figure out a way to kill one of you ... you'll be the first."

"I look forward to the adventure. You found your way in, I assume you can find your way out?"

Once outside, I stood blinking in the harsh glare of daylight. My thoughts and emotions were all in turmoil. I had no idea what to do next. I had not thought this far ahead. In fact, now that I thought about it, I didn't even know why I had wanted to kill Langham at all. An act of revenge? But Langham hadn't done anything at all to me.

A way to get The Community to take me seriously? To make them realize that I was a threat? Well, that hadn't exactly worked out either.

A way to get in touch with Monsieur? If The Community had been aware of my every move since leaving Seattle, then Monsieur would have had plenty of opportunity to come to me.

My entire effort—almost a year of planning and execution—and I couldn't even explain to myself why I had done any of it, except perhaps that I had been consumed by madness—a madness fueled by blind rage.

Now? I had nothing.

Even emptiness would have been something I could identify. I had ... nothing.

I don't know how long I stood there.

Finally, I headed back to my rooms across the street. I climbed the stairs. I sat down in my chair and watched the street because that was all I knew how to do.

After a while, Wellington—or whatever his name was, Langham hadn't told me—came down the street and entered the house. I never saw him again.

The very next morning, there was a "For Sale" sign in the window.

A few days later, when the real estate agent opened the house to the first prospective buyer, they found Wellington's lifeless body neatly laid out in the master bedroom.

"Wait a minute—" I have to interrupt. "You're telling me that Langham ... killed his daykeeper, discarded him, just like that?"

"Yes."

"What kind of man—monster—does that?"

"Someone who sees ordinary human beings as disposable. Langham was one of the oldest and most skilled of all the Nightsiders. I hadn't found him. He'd found me and put himself where I was certain to discover him. Actually, he had several locations. All bait. Because he was curious about me. He wanted a sniff. That's all."

"That's all?"

"It wasn't really about me. It was about Monsieur. He wanted to know what Monsieur had seen in me."

"I thought Monsieur had abandoned you—"

"So did I. At the time."

I had forgotten why I had begun the effort. I couldn't remember. Even Georgie-boy had slipped into distant memory. I had known him for such a short time, I found myself perplexed that his death had angered me so much. And then I found myself further perplexed that my anger had dissipated so rapidly.

One morning, I went out for a walk—San Francisco has the most remarkable park, it stretches across the western half of the city. I spent most of the day there, wandering its trails, allowing the sunlight to burnish my skin, smelling the essence of pine and evergreen, savoring the colorful cascades of blossoms—it was as if I had never seen daylight before. As if I had never experienced the glorious colors of the natural world. Perhaps I hadn't. I'd been so lost in myself, I'd forgotten to look outside.

Have you ever really looked at a tree? Or dirt? Or the bright blue sky? No, I mean really *looked*. I stopped, I stared in rapture, I was enthralled. I saw things I never would have noticed before, the fine veining in the leaves, the glistened drops of dew on the undersides of leaves in the shadows. I saw the fine hairs on a butterfly's legs. I discovered a world I had never known. Perhaps I had died in Langham's house—and come out the other side, reborn. I wandered that park like a man in a trance.

At last, as the evening lowered, as the day slowly faded to gray, my body began to ache and I realized that I had not eaten all day. The growling pangs of hunger finally forced me to head back toward the lights and bustle of the city—just beyond the edge the park.

I didn't want to leave the verdant shelter of the park. I had found peace here. But as the darkness began to creep out of the deeper shadows, I started getting uneasy and hurried toward the light beyond the trees.

Perhaps it was only the rustling of the wind through the leaves, but I had the sudden disconcerting sense that someone was watching me. I'd had that feeling as a recurring sensation ever since I'd left Seattle, sometimes very strong, sometimes just the barest intimation—even sometimes safely sequestered in my apartment.

Of course, now I knew that feeling was not just my imagination. Langham had said as much. And it made sense that I was still under observation—more now than ever. Perhaps it would have been more dramatic for a tall figure, all in black, to step in front of me just before I exited the park, but no such confrontation occurred.

Indeed, the streets were strangely deserted, there was no one I could see anywhere—and no one followed me out of the park. I hurried toward the nearest bright lights, a small restaurant across the street from the darkening forest.

I ordered fish chowder and sourdough—an easy meal, and one that reminded me of Seattle. And Georgie-boy. I was trying too hard to remember him, yes. But I remembered him as a flash of sunlight in my life—and I needed that now.

Someone sat down opposite me.

He said, "Hello, Jacob."

I looked up from my meal—

Monsieur.

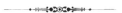

I lean back in my chair. I look to Jacob—there is a vast chasm between us. An unbridgeable gap.

"Are you making this up?"

"Why do you ask that?"

"I'm a writer—"

"Are you?"

"Somebody has paid to publish the stories I've told."

"But they're my stories—"

"That's the thing. I've cleaned them up. Tweaked them for dramatic effect. Given them structure, even a bit of meaning. I've told your stories, but I've told them better than you have."

"Yes, that's your opinion."

"The problem is—"

"What?"

"They're lousy stories."

"You think so?"

"I know so. There's no drama, no conflict, no confrontation. You wander from place to place, you're half-insane, you accomplish nothing, you discover less, and when you do run into a vampire, nothing happens. Here we are, how many tens of thousands of words into your narrative and you're still a desperate wannabe, crying in your soup. You haven't turned into a vampire, the real vampires apparently don't care about you, and as near as I can tell—you're a jerk." I catch myself. "I want to know the rest of the story, not this part. And if that's how I feel, then that's how the readers are going to feel."

"You watch too much television," Jacob says. "It's changed your perception of life. It's made you impatient. Everything has to be resolved before the last commercial. In the real world—no, that's wrong—in the world that exists out there, time moves at its own pace, not yours. And when you're immortal, you exist as a slow fire, not a burning flame. You ignite only when you choose to, not because you have to."

"Yes, all very poetic. But I'm bored."

"Yes, of course. Being a vampire would be boring—to you. Because you don't know how to...." Jacob trails off. "I have no word for it. Let me try it this way. You don't know how to experience the world around you on its terms—instead, you insist that life should hurry along because you don't want to wait. That's understandable. You know you'll die much too soon. I have no such concern. So I don't have to worry how long it takes to live each moment."

"Okay, fine. I'm a mayfly. Your term, not mine. So tell me the rest of the story. So you met Monsieur again. Then what?"

"See, there's your impatience again—"

"You were human once—"

"Yes?"

"So you should understand."

"I do. But that doesn't mean I have to oblige you. Now that I'm on *this* side of the transformation, I understand exactly why Langham and Monsieur and all the others behaved as they did."

I shake my head. I look around, frustrated. I grab the bottle and refill my glass. My buzz has worn off. Now I'm into headache-land.

Jacob looks at me strangely.

"What?"

"Do you have any idea how expensive it is to be a vampire?"

"I beg your pardon?"

"I don't have a day job, do I?"

"I never gave it any thought."

"Precisely."

"A vampire needs more than just a house—he needs a deep dark quiet place. That costs money. He needs to have it insulated against the daylight. Then there's all the mundanities of support—insurance, maintenance, property taxes, and so on. There's the cost of food and clothing and electricity, a furnace, an air conditioner, an occasional plumber, a house painter. So a vampire needs a daykeeper. There's even more expenses. Food and clothing for him. And you want the house to be comfortable, so there's furniture, perhaps a radio, a television, a stereo system. A computer and an internet connection? A satellite dish? It starts to add up. So where does all that money come from? Do you think I can steal enough from the people I feed upon to pay my monthly bills? Being a vampire is expensive. You have to have a self-sustaining income. A fortune big enough that you can live off the interest. You don't get into this club if you can't afford it—"

I replace the glass on the table. "So it's not enough to be a sociopath— you have to be a rich sociopath."

"Yes. That's why daykeepers are rarely graduated. As much as they understand the mechanics of taking care of a Nightsider, they don't understand the...the qualifications."

"But...Monsieur gifted you with a small fortune."

"Yes, he did. And not a small fortune. A large one."

"So...?"

Jacob smiles. "It was an interesting conversation, yes."

I looked across the table at Monsieur and I didn't know what to feel. I didn't know if I should be angry or afraid—or just happy to see him.

I didn't even know what to say.

So, I kept eating. I was that hungry.

"Jacob—"

"Go away." I dunked my bread sloppily in the chowder.

"You don't mean that."

"Yes, I do—"

"All right." He made as if to rise—

"No. Stay."

He sat again.

"Are you going to apologize?"

"For what?"

"For everything—"

"An apology? No. An explanation? Perhaps. That's what you want, isn't it?"

"All right—"

"What you did in Boston—I lied to you. I told you it wasn't anything to worry about."

"But all I did was ask Colonel Guignard if I could study his—his condition."

"You have no idea how much you offended him. The Community thrives on secrecy. We do not want to be studied. It would turn us into freaks—and we know how ignorant people deal with freaks. The Colonel was horrified by your request—he was so angered, he very nearly killed you right then and there. Only his friendship—well, relationship—with me held him back. You can't imagine the letters—and telegrams—that went back and forth about your situation. I had to beg the Boston Community to let you live. I promised that I would dissuade you from any further studies in that direction. And no, I couldn't dare let you know what danger you were in, you wouldn't have handled it well—you would have sought out the Colonel and tried to make amends, but that would have only made the situation worse. He wanted absolutely nothing more to do with you. So I lied. I told you it was nothing to worry about—and after I had called in every favor I could, and even issued a few threats of my own, I was able to secure your safety. And that's why the Colonel disengaged from all further contact."

"Oh," I said.

"There's more."

I waited.

Monsieur said. "Colonel Guignard is quite old—old enough to remember The Troubles in Paris. He saw the spying, the denunciations, the trials, the hysteria. That has made him...well, let's say that he's cautious. I think he overreacts, but he's survived a long time and I have to recognize that as evidence of lessons well learned. The Colonel believed, he still believes, that you are a threat to The Community. He had you watched. Everything you did in Boston, he knew about. And he reported all of it to me. He needed me to agree that you were a threat. If I had agreed, well—"

"I see."

"I was not going to agree," Monsieur said. "Perhaps Colonel Guignard doesn't understand loyalty. But I do. You were loyal to me, Jacob."

"What I felt—I thought it was more than loyalty."

"I know. And if I were human—I would have felt the same. What I felt instead—well, it wasn't the same, no. But it was something—enough that I could not let those idiots in Boston take you."

He reached across the table and put his hand on mine. "You have been under my protection ever since. No member of The Community is allowed to touch you. Or hurt you. Or turn you. Or kill you. Or anything. When you are under protection—well, that's why no member of The Community would even risk talking to you."

I thought about it.

"Do you understand now?"

I finally met his gaze. "I think so. It explains a little. But why didn't you—?"

"I couldn't either. That was part of the—the arrangement. I had to cut off all contact with you as well. I delayed it as long as I could, but— that business with Josiah. The Community felt you had become unstable. They forced my hand. If you were to continue to enjoy my protection, I had to—" Monsieur shrugged. "I had to disappear. It was time anyway. I had stayed much too long in Seattle. People were starting to notice. And wonder."

I thought about it. I didn't like it. But I understood. "So you did all that for me?"

"Yes, I did. And it wasn't easy. The Community now thinks that I'm... well, not a good member of The Community. I used up a lot of good will. But I owed it to you."

"But not Georgie-boy...?"

"I'm sorry about that, Jacob. But the umbrella of my protection didn't extend that far. And there were...there were people who wanted to send you a message. A warning."

"You'll excuse me if I don't think that's the best way to warn someone—"

"Perhaps. But it certainly demonstrates how serious they can be."

"Georgie-boy was—"

"He was not an innocent. He was taking small bills from your wallet. Small amounts that you wouldn't notice—"

"That still doesn't justify—"

"And he was still working with a pimp. They were planning to blackmail you—"

"That's not what he told the other street boys—"

"And you're going to believe them instead of me? The one who told you that Georgie wanted to go with you—that was Louis. He was next in line if you got tired of Georgie. I did you a favor—"

"You killed him—?"

"If I hadn't, someone else would have. I chose to do it because I felt it was my responsibility—the same way it's your responsibility to shoot your own dog."

"I'm not—"

"I know."

We sat in silence for a while. There was too much to say and I didn't know how to say it. I didn't even know if I wanted to say it.

So...we chatted about lesser things, unimportant things. Train rides. Property searches. The vineyards along the coast. Places to visit. Monsieur had not traveled as much as I had assumed. When you're a vampire, travel arrangements can get complicated. Your sensitivity to daylight limits your possibilities.

Finally, Monsieur pulled out his watch and looked at the time. "It's getting late. For you. Not for me."

"Will I see you again?"

"That's up to you," he said.

"What do you mean?"

"Would you like to live with me again?"

I considered the offer. "No. Thank you, but no. I don't want to be your daykeeper. I don't want to be anyone's daykeeper. I saw what Langham did to—whatever his name was."

Monsieur smiled—it was that same warm infectious smile that had teased my heart so many times on so many late Seattle nights while lightning flashed and thundered outside, and rain nattered on the roof.

"No," he said. "I wasn't asking you to be my daykeeper."

He waited patiently while the meaning of his words sank in—

"Oh," I said. And then, as I realized even more what he was offering, I said, "Monsieur, please. May I think about this?"

"Of course. But do not take too long."

"How long is too long. A week? A month?"

"The rest of your life," he said.

"Huh? I don't understand—"

Monsieur sighed, a sad sound, a sound of resignation. "You know so much and you understand so little. Jacob, my son, my beloved man-child—

if I still had a heart, you would have broken it a dozen times over. Be grateful that I remember enough of that flicker of life before transformation that I can still almost understand who you are. But you know too much to live.

"In the past, you were a diversion, a distraction, something to break up the monotony of immortality. Your oh-so-patient observation of Langham's little decoy house—that was amusing, even though it was never more than a game of cat and mouse—with you as the mouse, of course. But then—well, your daylight invasion and the things you said to Langham, your threats—as feeble and harmless as they were—he didn't like you before, he doesn't like you even more now. And he's not the only one. He's powerful. And he has a great deal of influence. I came to you tonight to tell you that there are many in The Community who now consider you too dangerous to be allowed to live. Too many. I am not understating the matter. I fear for you."

"Oh," I said.

Monsieur waited for me to speak.

"I could run. I'm very good at that. I could travel. I could go to Australia. Or Africa. I could get so far away—"

Monsieur shook his head. "No, you couldn't. You have no idea how far The Community can reach. You have no idea how many of us there are—or where we are. Or what we will do to protect ourselves."

"You keep saying 'we.' You agree with this—?"

"In principle, yes. In reality, no. But I cannot protect you any longer. There's only one way I can save you. This way."

"Then it's not really a choice at all, is it?"

"Yes, it is. It's a choice between existence or nullity."

I snorted. A skeptical sound. "I studied enough law. Join us or die? No, duress is not considered a choice."

"Jacob, you should be very concerned about this. You should be afraid."

And yet, sitting across from Monsieur, I wasn't. Curiously, the simple evidence of this conversation was enough to hold any possible terrors a safe distance away.

"Jacob, if you were to become a Nightsider, you would understand The Community much better. And they—we—would have no more reason to consider you a threat."

"The Community approves?"

"The Community will accept it—"

"You negotiated this? On my behalf?"

"Yes."

"I suppose I should appreciate that."

"You've been under my protection for a long time, Jacob. Why should I stop now?"

I reached across the table and put my hand on his. "Monsieur, I have hated you. I have feared you. I have grieved for you. And I have loved you. I have loved you too much—but there did come a day when I put that love aside because I believed you had betrayed me. Today, tonight, I cannot put aside all those other emotions as easily as I put aside my love for you. My heart doesn't work that way."

"I know that, Jacob. I know that too well. The difference between us is that I understand your heart—and you cannot yet understand mine. What I'm offering you—"

I pulled my hand back. "Monsieur, I do have some small understanding of what you are offering me. I lived with you for seven years. You know I was no innocent. You know how curious I was. You know that I prowled through every drawer and cabinet in your home. Even the ones you assumed were locked. And I didn't run away in horror. I was fascinated, I still am. I wanted to know everything—because in those days, I wanted the power to extract revenge on every man who ever abused me. As much as I needed their money, I hated them, even the most gentle and tender—not for who they were, but for who I was becoming, everything—what they were turning me into. Those first few days, I considered stealing everything from you. I even considered killing you and ransacking the house. But I was calculating enough to think that maybe I should play the long con. But the more I learned about you, the more interested I became in who you were and what you are and how you became that way. Yes. So the long con became the longer con and the longer con after that and then there came a time when I was no longer conning, but conning myself. And yes, you knew all this—and you let me live anyway—and ... Monsieur, there were days I hated myself because I did not expect my heart to betray me."

"But it did, Jacob. It did. And I watched it happen with enormous amusement at first. Later, I began to experience genuine pleasure and delight at your marvelous awakening. You were discovering your own soul, your own ability to live. It was like watching a flower unfold its petals to the sun—something I have not seen in more than a century, by the way. Only in paintings. Tell me," he said. "What was your favorite part of our life together? I ask because I would love to be able to do it again."

I had to stop and think. Finally, I said, "If I had to choose, it would be the time we spent in the evenings—when we sat by the fireplace and just talked about the events of the day. Nobody had ever talked to me like that before. Nobody had ever respected me as a human being until you did. And yes, I appreciate the irony now. Because of who you are—what you are—you treated me as an equal, even though you could never see me as an equal. Yes, you treated me as human, that meant you also saw me as … well, a snack."

Monsieur smiled. "A snack? No, a meal. But a meal I dared not touch. The anticipation was far too delicious, much more than the having could ever have been."

"I applaud your self-control."

"It was more than that. I truly hope to show you—"

I interrupted him. I could hear the anger in my voice. "My point is— you changed me. You changed my life. You opened me up to the possibilities of the world. You created me as a young gentleman, but a cruel kind of gentleman. I know that, sir. I am well aware that I do not connect easily with other human beings, perhaps not at all. I am well aware that I have behaved coldly and dispassionately in most of my interactions. My few attempts at affection have failed badly. So yes, Monsieur, I am well aware of the kind of man I have become, and it is due in no small part to your influence. So, if it were my choice to remain a mortal man, despite the danger I might be in from The Community—"

"It is a very real danger, I assure you."

"If it were my choice to remain a mortal man," I continued. "—then, given all you have taught me about the mechanics of existence, given what I learned at university, it is likely that I could be moderately successful, or even extremely successful, in all the day-to-day mundanities of the mortal world, but it is as equally unlikely that I would enjoy such an existence. It would likely be cold and lonely, without much affection—not because I am unworthy, but because I have never really learned to care about anyone but myself—"

"That's not true. You cared about Georgie. You cared about Josiah. You cared about me."

"And look how all those affections turned out. Every one of them was a failure. Josiah didn't care the way I did. Georgie didn't care at all, if I'm to believe you. And you betrayed and abandoned me—"

"I never did that."

"No—?"

"I couldn't tell you, I couldn't. It would have put you in immediate danger. If you had truly accepted the evidence of my death, if you had gone on to have a mortal life, The Community would have written you off as a reckless adventure on my part. I had no choice in the matter, Jacob. It had to be done that way, because if you knew I was still alive, you would have searched for me. The Community couldn't have that. The Community survives by being invisible. Your survival depended on your belief that The Community was truly out of reach for you. But no, your belief, your investigations, your persistence in the matter—well, it showed me how much you did care. And it showed The Community that you wanted to become dangerous. You have put yourself in danger, Jacob. If I didn't care, I wouldn't be here now. And if you didn't still care, you would have gotten up and left by now."

I didn't reply. Not immediately. And not just because he was right. But because I hadn't yet considered the *other* side of the question.

After a moment, Monsieur broke the silence. "You have no idea what I am offering you."

"You're right. I don't." I looked him straight in the eye. "I've observed. I've listened. I've studied. I've tried to imagine the experience. But I'm still on the outside, looking in. It is, at best, an intellectual exercise for me—"

"Yes," Monsieur agreed.

I took a deep breath. "Let me tell you a story."

"Go ahead. We have time."

"You know my past. My father died when I was thirteen, his fishing boat sank in a storm, his body was never recovered. There was no one to take me in. In very short order, I was homeless and hungry, I was begging on the streets. I had no understanding of the ways of the worldly. It did not take long—

"A man, a gentleman, a man who was clearly a cut above the fishermen and sailors I was familiar with, approached me on the street, invited me to show him a place where he could get a respectable meal. I led him to a place I knew, he offered to buy me dinner. I was hungry, I said yes. He asked me of my life, expressed pity for my situation, and offered me money if I would grant him a favor. Perhaps he assumed that I already knew what that favor would be. At the first, I didn't realize—but as he grew ever more friendly, and when he placed his hand suggestively on my knee, I understood exactly—"

"Excuse me, Jacob. But what is the point of this?" Monsieur asked.

"The point will be clear enough in a moment. If you will allow me to finish." I frowned at the interruption. It had derailed the train of my thought and it took me a moment to recover my place in my narrative. "You see, Monsieur, it was in that first moment of comprehension that I understood what was about to happen with a startling clarity. This was not a kindly gentleman looking out for the well-being of a forlorn street waif. No. From the first moment, he had been conducting a very skillful seduction. And I had stepped too eagerly into the illusions that he offered.

"But even as I understood that this was a seduction, I understood equally that I really had no idea what he wanted, only the vaguest sense of how couplings occurred. Perhaps this will seem odd to you, Monsieur, perhaps not—but the knowledge of how human beings mate was not something my father had ever discussed with me, nor had any other teacher. As a result, I was not only virginal, I was innocent in the ways of men and women, even more innocent in the ways of men and men. Up until that point, my only awareness of sex was that it was something done alone, in private, without a partner, and one should wash his hands afterward.

"I will not say that I led a sheltered life, that wasn't possible on the wharfs of Seattle, not in those days, but up to that moment, my life had been a strictly disciplined one, without too much access to the gutter knowledge of the street. My father had seen to that.

"My father had been a good man, a little crude in his ways perhaps, but he loved me unconditionally—because I was all he had left of my mother and I was her legacy. So perhaps he had been over-protective and as a result, I had little knowledge of ... matters of the heart, let alone matters of the bed. Only what I had read in books or in the newspapers, and the knowledge gained that way was either obscure or salacious.

"And that is my point. I speak to you, Monsieur, of the condition of virginity. Mine. Then and now. I understood then, in that critical moment, that I was about to lose mine. I could have demurred. I could have left the company of this gentleman and returned to the cold wet streets of Seattle. But he offered me warmth, companionship, a bed for the night, and sensing my reluctance, even a few coins for my pocket.

"As a child listening to the chatter of adults, I was aware that there were secrets only adults knew. As I became aware of my own changing body, I realized that I was becoming available to those secrets and that someday I too would have an opportunity to discover the mysteries of sex, that strange land so often whispered about by some, or loudly laughed about by others, or simply hinted at with a demurral, 'You'll understand when you're grown.'

"And right then, as that man put his hand on my knee—I understood. *This* was the moment. Or perhaps only a moment. All I had to do was accompany this man and I would cross that boundary into the land of those who *understood*—the ones who understood, but couldn't or wouldn't explain. Did I want to understand? Hell, yes, I wanted to understand. I was tired of not knowing. And...more than curious. Flight was still a possibility, yes. Always a possibility. I could run from this man, but—

"I was hungry, Monsieur. I was cold. I was lonely. The man was clean. He was friendly. He was even *perfumed* with that bay rum splash that barbers often used. And—I was curious. How do I know I was curious? I got an erection. So I went with him. Was it a choice? Or was it the spontaneous flush of blood to my organ? Does it matter? I went with him.

"And I was lucky that first night. He was tender and gentle and as an introduction to the strange new world of sensuous coupling, it could not have been better. He did not force himself, he did not ask me to do anything I was not willing. He looked at my body like a sacred work of art. It was a long sensuous night—and in the morning, as the first glimmers of dawn filtered through the curtains, I realized I was now a different person. I knew something. And the something I now knew had changed me. And I could never go back to being the person I had been before—because that was a person who didn't know what I knew now.

"I had finally crossed that strange unknown boundary and entered a domain of knowledge, a sense of the self that could now look back and realize why none of this could ever be explained. It can only be lived. Do you understand what I am saying, Monsieur?

"Let me complete the tale. When he came awake, I was nestled in his arms. We rocked together again, this time not as deeply or as intense or as long—but enough that it was a suitable coda to the night. It was an affirmation that the act had been special and generous and shared. He gave me money, tucking it into my shirt pocket, more than I had expected—and while I felt cheap and even a little resentful that he had done so, I was grateful that I would be able to eat that day and the next as well, if I was careful.

"I never saw him again, I looked for him often. I had enjoyed our encounter—and as the evening had unfolded, I had begun to secretly hope that perhaps he would find our coupling so enjoyable that he would take me home with him, and I would share his bed every night and we would have marvelous sexual adventures. But at some point in our affectionate wrestling, I saw that he had a gold ring on the third finger of his left hand—and I knew what that meant.

"Nevertheless, I still hoped that he would come back to the street from time to time, that he would find me and take me away for another sweet sensual evening. But no, he never came back. I never saw him again. Eventually, I had to realize that this man had taken me with no more thought than one would bring to a well-prepared meal. He had enjoyed himself, perhaps patted his belly, belched in satisfaction, then excused himself to the parlor to pour a brandy and light up a cigar. If he returned, it would not be for the same meal, but another, maybe better, maybe worse, it didn't matter. If one is hungry enough, then one meal is very much like another.

"And yes, if that was the moment that I began to understand the nature of sexual congress, then it was also the moment when I started down the path of another transformation of character—it was when my soul began to harden, Monsieur."

"Yes," he agreed. "Apparently, that process didn't take long. I met you when? A year later? Not even that. By then you had developed an impenetrable shell around your heart. Impressively hard. No one was ever going to touch you there again. Not so you'd feel it. It was part of what attracted me to you."

"Yes, well—you were wrong. You did touch me. The depth of my anger for you is a measure of how deeply I cared. When you left—when I realized you had not died, I began to wonder if perhaps you were just another kind of customer—just another perfumed gentleman, using a boy for an evening's comfort before moving on with no more thought than a five dollar bill and a kiss on the cheek. I hated you for that, the same way I hated him—still hate him—for giving me hope, and then throwing me back to the street."

"I told you, I had no choice."

"It doesn't erase the smoldering cauldron of anger that still burns in my chest, Monsieur. It doesn't."

"I understand that, but—"

"No, stop. You have already explained. And I have long since learned that people like you do not think like people like me. So what you do and why you do it will almost always be incomprehensible to people like me. There is no explanation that will change that. There is nothing you can say that will change my feelings. My feelings are what they are. Please don't speak, Monsieur—there was a reason I told you that story. And it wasn't just about the hardening of my heart. It was also about the choice you have put before me—

"You are inviting me to join you in your way of life. I stand before that doorway, that opportunity, that possibility, as another kind of virgin—innocent of all understanding, uncertain, unknowing, curious and yes, also afraid. Because—like the loss of virginity—if I cross this boundary, there is no return. But unlike the loss of virginity, which is a very human and very comprehensible experience, this is an experience both inhuman and incomprehensible. Perhaps it is even incomprehensible from your side as well. I cannot know unless I cross that boundary—and if I do, will crossing it change me so much that I will be unable to perceive anything except from that new perspective? Will I become a creature that enjoys being a monstrosity? Will I forget the humanity that I still cherish so dearly?"

Monsieur looked at me. "Do you really cherish your humanity that dearly? So far, it has not served you well. Nor you, it."

"However meager my humanity may be, dear sir, dear Monsieur, however cold and alone my existence has been, still it has been as much humanity as I am capable of. What would I be giving it up for?"

Monsieur smiled. "You would be giving up a swift and certain death—or perhaps maybe not so swift. Some vampires are not as gentle as others."

"That cannot be the only reason why you are inviting me to share your—just what are you inviting me to share? Your house? Your life? Your bed?"

Monsieur nodded. "I have invited you to come with me. That's the opportunity in front of you. Once you have crossed over, you will make your own choices. Once you become a Nightsider, you may feel differently about me. In fact, I'm certain that you will. I expect it will be a great adventure for both of us."

"I have to ask. Are you doing this just to save my life? Because if that's the only reason, then I would have to decline your offer—"

"Oh, hell no. I'm inviting you to join me, Jacob, because you're valuable. You've been trained—you've trained yourself to think like a Nightsider. You've demonstrated remarkable skill at investigation and observation. You've shown patience and commitment. You have a degree of education much better than most of the older members of The Community. You are street-wise in ways that others are not. With the additional skills and knowledge available to you on the other side, you will become a powerful force—"

"Is that true? Or is that part of your sales pitch—?"

"Of course it's true," Monsieur said. "I trained you, didn't I?"

He smiled at his little joke and I couldn't help myself, I laughed out loud.

"There's my sweet Jacob," he said. "I've missed you so much."

"And I've missed you too. More than I have allowed myself to say."

"So—you will join me then?"

"Well, yes ... I'm strongly considering it. Given the alternative, you do make a compelling argument."

"You're weighing the pros and cons."

"Let me ask you something, Monsieur." I hesitated, searching for the right way to phrase the question. "And please, consider your next words carefully. What can you say to me, what single argument can you make— yes, what is the most compelling reason you can give me for accepting your invitation to become a ... a Nightsider? What is the most compelling reason you can give anyone?"

Monsieur got up and came around the table. He sat down on the bench next to me and put his arm around my shoulder. He pulled me close so he could whisper in my ear, and what he said—after that, I couldn't say no.

———— • ⊹⊱✦⊰⊹ • ————

"Huh?" I look across the room at Jacob. "You can't stop there."

"Oh, but I can and I will." He points to his watch. "It's getting early. And I really want to get back to my coffin before sunrise."

"Wait! You have to tell me what he said!"

"I've given you enough clues. See if you can figure it out for yourself—"

And then he was gone.

Goddammit.

Jacob in New Orleans

Mardi Gras is a delirious frenzy, a seething mass, flung with green and purple beads. Ornate masks in silver and gold, glittering costumes, some little more than ribbons of cloth, bare flesh everywhere, naked chests and bellies, elongated codpieces and flapping breasts, with wild discordant music blaring from roving street bands—and everything lubricated with liquor and pot and darker drugs, a roiling torrent of sex and possibility, laced with overt hints of shame and hunger. And kink.

Every year, a few unwary celebrants disappear into the revels, never to be seen again. The state of Louisiana clucks sympathetically about the disappearances, but that's all the state ever does—cluck sympathetically. The people who disappear, maybe they wanted to disappear, maybe they left without telling anyone where they were going—and maybe they aren't all that important anyway. Nobody ever comes looking, nobody cares. And if there's a bit of danger around those unexplained disappearances—well, that's just part of the mystique, isn't it?

I have a pretty good idea what happens to the young men and women who disappear. I know what others have speculated, but I have more evidence than they do.

I don't know why I'm in New Orleans during Mardi Gras. I don't like crowds, I don't like the madness, the smell, the pushing, the bumping, the inconsiderate behaviors, and the outright rudeness of drunken men and women. I walk at a different pace than most people—most people walk like zombies, unconscious to everything around them, not noticing who they just stepped in front of, not caring if they stop suddenly for no apparent reason, and the four people behind them have to stop abruptly as well. I've been told that I am well on the way to becoming a cranky old man. "Yes? What was your first clue?" I'm already cranky.

But New Orleans does have its pleasures. Most people assume it's the beignets at Café du Monde. I prefer the po-boy sandwich at Coop's myself, but that's still a tourist spot, it's like eating at Disney World. You have to get out to the edges of the quarter—or beyond. You have to get well away from the off ramps before you start finding authentic Cajun or creole food, or that other cuisine that still doesn't have a name, but is distinctly whatever it is.

I have a room in a hotel on Rampart Street. In the back, above what used to be the livery and the slave quarters. It's quiet and at night I can sit and type. My most productive hours are just past midnight. Go figure.

I'm not a nightsider, but I'm living like one. My room has a balcony overlooking the side street, the parking lot, and the alley. Sometimes, after an hour or two of typing, I sit out on the balcony with a beer and watch the last stragglers wander back to whatever cribs and coffins they're going to crawl into. Perhaps one day, I'll see a nightsider come drifting through in pursuit of a meal—but they mostly hunt during the darkest nights and I expect to be moving on in a week or two. Just as soon as I finish this ... thing that's crawling out of my—

Is it crawling out of my keyboard? No, it's creeping out of my head, through my fingers, and into the keyboard. It's crap, whatever it is, a meandering existential conversation between an author and a character who refuses to do anything interesting but whine. But then again, J.D. Salinger built a whole career out of *Catcher In The Rye*, so who am I to nitpick?

I think I've hit the wall.

Not a block, not even a stumble—but a more profound moment of ennui, the realization of the shallowness of life, the inevitability of mortality and the fundamental question any author should ask: *why the fuck am I doing this anyway?*

Does the world really need this half-assed assemblage of words? It's just another distraction from humanity's headlong rush into its own self-centered extinction.

Probably not. But I'll type it up, send it off, cash the inevitable check, and return to the keyboard to do it all again—for the simple reason that I prefer eating to starvation. The occasional fuck is a useful diversion as well, but even desperation sex is a shallow comfort. Perhaps I still haven't recovered from the last one. "Can I call you?" "Dude, you're a McFuck, not a relationship."

Okay, that was on him, not me. It still scrapes.

Barefoot and bored, staring down at the street, I realize I'm judging everyone who passes, the drunks, the skanks, the whores of both sexes— they all look cheap and phony. They sing incomprehensible lyrics in voices slurred and uneven. Decorated with ranks of plastic beads, imitation silver and gold, the inevitable green and purple, some red and blue as well—all posing for each other in costumes that are little more than an excuse for rhinestones and glitter, and none of it conceals the underlying despair of their lives. Tennessee Williams was an optimist.

And I—

I am a self-centered, judgmental, arrogant, narcissistic, asshole, separated from the rest of my species by my own arrogant, narcissistic, assholiness.

Maybe I won't wait till I'm finished. Maybe tomorrow I'll pile everything into the back of the car and head west, north around the great cultural sinkhole of Texas, around to the baked earth of Arizona, or more likely the sparkling yellow canyons of Colorado. Anywhere but here. I'm starting to realize just how much this town depresses me. If it weren't for the food—

Someone on the street below, a familiar figure—he stares up at me with piercing eyes. His face is so flushed he glows, but I recognize him anyway.

Jacob.

Too much time has passed. Too much thought as well. I lean on the wrought-iron railing and look down at him.

"Go away."

"You're drunk," he says.

"And getting drunker—" I wave my beer at him.

"On that shit?" He holds up a bottle of something I can't identify. It's green. "This will get you there a lot faster."

"I don't trust you." I think about it. "Hell, I don't even like you."

"It's mutual. Can I come up anyway?"

"Yeah. Bring the bottle."

I meet him at the hotel's front door, he follows me back to my room, glances around with curiosity. "Nice big bed," he says. "You're here by yourself—?"

"I'm not exactly boyfriend material."

"That's a good thing—"

"Really?"

"Well, it depends on your point of view."

Jacob finds two glasses and splashes liquor into each. It's even greener in the light. "Here, try this—"

"What is it?" I sniff. It smells like licorice. Killer licorice.

"It's something to warm you up. You need it. It's absinthe."

"Absinthe? I thought that was illegal. Or poisonous. Or something—"

"Probably. But it's good for what ails you."

"How do you know what ails me? Or anybody?"

"I can smell your loneliness. It's self-imposed. It's because you're an asshole."

"Tell me something I don't know."

"You enjoy being an asshole."

"You want me to change?"

"Hell, no. I want you to get drunk with me. This will help. Absinthe makes the heart grow fonder. Or something like that."

"Did you just pun at me?"

"I wanted to see if you were paying attention." He's red-faced and giddy.

"You're already drunk—"

"A lot more than that," he admits. He's been waving the bottle around. Now he puts it down with a noticeable wobble. "It's one of the hazards of snacking at Mardi Gras. Not enough blood in the alcohol stream." He blinks across at me, takes a half-step. "If you're not too drunk, I could use a little taste—"

I hold up a hand between us. "I don't think so. Would coffee help?"

"Okay, yeah. You're a buzz-kill, but yeah."

There's a coffee-maker in the room—it's an anachronism in this ancient place, one of those weird little machines that uses plastic pre-filled cups, but the coffee is quick and not too vile. I fill a mug for Jacob, another for myself. He takes it with a nod, but barely sips at it.

"I've never seen you this way. You're all ruddy and flushed. And you're hot. You're burning up. Are you all right? What happened?"

"Nothing happened. I'm celebrating. Do you think it's all doom-and-gloom? Hell, no. It's Mardi Gras. Fat Tuesday. I'm getting fat." He hiccups. "Okay, I think I might have over-indulged. I might have—yes, I have— drunk too much tonight."

"So this is what it looks like?"

Jacob's smile darkens. "It's the annual rite of rejuvenation! National Vampire Week. Two weeks. Do you know how easy it is to feed here? Better than the Super Bowl, because nobody pays attention to anything they can't eat, drink, smoke, or fuck—show me your tits, here are some beads. Boys and girls—all free for the taking. Young and juicy, hot and delicious. You offer them a drink from your bottle of green, they never say no, they drink deep and get silly. It's too easy—you pull them into a doorway for a taste, just a little, not too much—and you get drunk too! The streets are full of flavors. Taste as many as you can. Nobody cares. There are vampires everywhere!"

He swings his coffee mug around, gesturing. "And here you are, stuck alone in your little dark room. Typing more of your feeble fables, while the rest of the world whirls around you. It's the perfect example of everything that's wrong with what's left of your pathetic little life. On the other hand, in here—it's probably safer. Or maybe not. Who knows what kind of monster you'll invite across your threshold?" He glistens with the thought. "And think about *that*, my little morsel. This is the first time you've ever invited me in."

Jacob turns slowly in the center of the room, arms outstretched. "You should fear me tonight, because tonight is the night I have no self-control. It's my party and I'll die if I want to." He winks at me. "Not die in the mortal sense, but die in the poetic sense—the metaphor—the little death of the human orgasm, that delicious moment of nirvana at the top of the mountain of fucking. The human climax. Let me die in your arms, my sweet savory boy. Metaphors be with you." He salutes me with his mug, then drinks enthusiastically. "I've had better—but I've had worse as well."

Abruptly, he falls silent. He plops into a chair and stares at me. "Yeah," he says. "Yeah."

"Yeah, what?"

"You're ready."

"I am? For what?"

Jacob giggles. "For whatever happens next."

"And what's that—?"

"What you've been waiting for—"

"I'm not waiting for anything—"

"The hell you're not—" He sprawls sideways across the chair, spreading his arms and legs wide in a position of casual availability. "You've been cruising me since day one, wondering what it would be like—" He adds, "You can't fool me, you know."

There's no point in denial. I might as well say it. "Okay, yes—I wondered what it would be like—"

"You wouldn't survive it." Jacob laughs. "But I promise, you'd die happy."

"You think so?"

"I know so. One way or another, you'll die screaming my name."

"Are those the only alternatives? I don't think I like either one."

"There is a third alternative...."

"Yes, I know. You've made it clear, more than once, that you don't think I'm right for it."

"No. I said you weren't ready for it."

"And you think I am now—?"

"Possibly."

"Except I don't want it. Everything you've told me—you've pretty much deconstructed the whole mystique. Frankly, it doesn't sound like a career opportunity with any advancement. Hiding in the darkness with a bunch of other paranoids is not on my bucket list."

"Oh, that's not all we do. Of course, there's Mardis Gras. But there's also Halloween. And New Year's. And the Super Bowl. And the circuit parties—those are always tasty. Las Vegas has its delights, so does New York. And then there are all the other ones that aren't so obvious. Passover, for instance. All those Seders, with all those Jews opening their doors, announcing to the world, 'If anyone is hungry, let him come in and eat.' All we need is the invitation and there we are. Actually, not—we don't need the invitation, but it's a tradition. For some reason, we honor it. Ahh, so many wonderful opportunities. Except August. That month is so empty. No holidays at all. Well, Dragon-Con. I suppose. But you get my point— life is delicious."

"Yes, if you like killing people."

"They're not people. They're—"

"They're people to me."

Jacob snorts in derision. "Not really. That's just what you want to believe. But you're up here, alone. Not down there with them. And you know why that is?" He doesn't wait for me to answer. "Because you don't see them as people—oh, maybe in your little idealistic fantasies, you want to see them that way. But in reality, even you can see how stupid they are—what's the quote? The great mass of men live lives of quiet domestication. They're enslaved to their own shallow beliefs, blind and unconscious, staggering to their inevitable graves like homing zombies. But that was never god enough for you. You believe there has to be something else, something more. You've been flailing away at the world since you learned how to type. People are cattle, you know that. Listen, you can hear them mooing. And so are you, my little mooncalf—you just can't stand being herded. You still think there's something else."

"I think I like you better sober."

"No. You put up with me when I'm sober. You've been terrified of me since the beginning."

"So why do you even talk to me?"

"I'm easily bored, I'm easily amused." Jacob looks at his watch. "It's getting early. Can I stay here tonight?"

"Aren't you afraid of the windows, the sunlight?"

"Look at me, I just ate. I'm flush. I'll be fine. As long as you keep the drapes closed."

"You're gonna sleep on the floor?"

"Hell, no. It's a big bed. I'm gonna sleep with you. I'll even spoon with you. Spooning only, no forking. Well, not yet anyway."

Jacob steps out of his shoes, switches off the light and moves to me like a ghost—or a ballet dancer, a shiver of gracefulness. He steps in close—crossing the invisible border, the boundary of personal space. If he leans forward he could kiss me—but he doesn't. Instead, he touches the top button on my shirt, a gesture of curiosity. He looks into my eyes to see if I will accept. He knows I can't refuse, but he looks anyway. A courtesy. Now, knowing that he can proceed, his fingers move slowly, but with certainty. He unbuttons that last line of resistance—it's the drawbridge, once it is down, entry is inevitable.

The next button and the next. Then his fingers trace delicately down the line of my chest, stopping only at my navel—he pokes his finger in, wiggles it a bit, explores my personal little concavity with an impish smile. Is this a preview of things to come?

He finishes unbuttoning my shirt, moves his hands to my belt, but then he hesitates and opens his arms, an invitation. It's my turn to unbutton him. He's wearing a black silk shirt, the fabric so fine it's like gossamer.

"Specially made," he says.

"Of course." If all your senses are enhanced, almost to the point of painful cacophony, the common fabrics must feel like sandpaper against the skin.

The buttons open with ease and I look at his naked chest for the first time. His skin is pale and golden, flushed and ruddy, a glistening landscape, as smooth as porcelain, and with the same eerie translucency of delicately sculpted wax. In the silvery glow of the pre-dawn darkness, with blue shadows embracing us, he's a vision both demonic and angelic. He licks his lips and leans in close, his hands sliding up my naked skin, his lips brushing mine, an electric tingle shooting through me—and abruptly I am flushed with surges of sensation, emotion, even lust—

"What did you just do—?"

"Nothing yet—"

"But—"

"Shh—" Jacob touches my lips to silence me. His finger is a promise. His eyes shine into mine.

A moment of panic. "—are you going to—"

He presses his finger harder against my lips. "I already ate. I'm beyond satiated. You have nothing to fear."

I believe him because I want to believe him. The whole time, I remember that he is a master-manipulator, a liar, a predator, a self-admitted sociopath—but I want to believe him, so I do.

He waits until I relax. Then he slips out of his black silk shirt, it slides off his shoulders and falls easily to the floor. In spite of myself, I'm mesmerized.

Jacob's body is trim, slim, and impossibly youthful. He is a contradiction of form—as smooth as a girl, but tautly muscled. Like a coiled spring, he's a possibility—he's the threat of pleasure, an avalanche of sensation so overwhelming that every moment afterward, any moment without it would be a slow dance with despair.

His touch is amazing. Unafraid, unashamed, curious. He slides his hands up to my shoulders, slips my shirt off, and lets it fall, an echo of his own movement. For a moment, we stand apart, surveying and studying each other. I'm suddenly acutely aware that I am out of shape—not yet flabby, but a little too fleshy. Too many hours sitting, not enough time walking, stretching, exercising—living.

But Jacob just smiles, admiring what he sees. "There's this about lust," he says. "It's not about beauty. It's about possibility."

His words trigger a flood of thoughts, a cascade of emotions. We stand shirtless in front of each other, admiring—always before, being naked was being vulnerable and being vulnerable was dangerous, because it was not only the risk of rejection, it was the possibility of pain. Now...

it's all that and more, but this time I crave it. I am caught in his gaze, helpless in his eyes.

Because—he wants me. And in that want, I have his power and strength, a core of fire that flashes and fills. It is this simple—he desires me as much as I desire him.

He unbuckles my belt, my pants. I unbuckle his. They all to the floor and we step sideways and out. I'm wearing white boxers, he's wearing black nylon tap pants with a hem of lace. Something from the lingerie counter. Jacob sees the surprise in my expression and laughs softly. But I get it. It's not just the enhanced sensitivity of his skin, it's that dark frisson that comes from living on the other side of the line. It's the freedom of being the unseen alien.

And then we're naked, but we still haven't touched. We move to the bed—Jacob pushes me down onto it, on my back—and then, oh so gently, covers me with his body, arm to arm, leg to leg. He grasps my hands in his, stretching me out on the cross of desire, and slowly, oh so slowly, he brushes my lips with his—he tastes my breath, a second time and a third. I'm impatient for the kiss, but he's in no hurry and—

I'm trying to figure out what he's doing. This isn't a kiss, it's a hesitation, a tease, more anticipation than connection—

"Shut up," he says.

"I didn't say anything."

"You're analyzing. You're looking for the words. You're not experiencing. You're too busy listening to the little voice in your head—"

"Huh?"

"That one. The one that's saying, 'What little voice? I don't hear any little voice.' That one. I'm telling it to shut up. Now kiss me. Kiss me like you intend the kiss to last forever—"

I start to kiss him—

"No," he says. "That's the impatient kiss. You're kissing like you're trying to make something happen. Kiss me like nothing has to happen, just the kiss—"

I don't know what to do.

Jacob says, "I'll show you. Don't do anything. Just let it happen."

He lies still on top of me. His hands hold mine above my head. He does nothing, but look into my eyes. "Shhh," he says. His body is hot against mine—and cold at the same time, like a chilled container with hot steam inside, it's a different kind of feeling—and finally, again, slowly he lowers his head and brushes his lips across mine. Once, twice, again—

And again and again, until I no longer expect anything, I just allow the sensations to continue. I relax beneath him and listen to all the tens of thousands of tiny tingles and sensations occurring in just the space between us, flesh against flesh.

I am naked beneath a vampire and we are both erect, almost motionless and the tension is incredible. It's not anticipation, it's something else, something I can't describe because I have no words for it, there are no words, only the simple perfection of the moment.

Until finally—my lips are tingling so intensely, the sensation is almost unbearable—Jacob stops and lifts just high enough to stare down into my eyes, as if to say something, but words are insufficient. His expression is more than enough.

I'm too stunned to do anything more than breathe. He has drained me of all power. All I can do is exist beneath him. He lowers himself onto me, into my embrace, and we stay in that moment, motionless and emotionless, simply recovering.

I can feel his heart beating against mine. And mine in unison, a mutual agreement—a silent pulse of heat, a wave that spreads outward from our common center, I can feel each pulse expanding from chest to belly to arms and legs, even finally to the tips of fingers and toes. I have never felt anything like this before and I will not move, lest I interrupt this incredible connection.

Jacob licks my ear, another prolonged exploration, and from there to my neck. I've never let anyone lick my neck before, I'm ticklish there, but with Jacob I'm so relaxed there's no threat of violation, he massages my neck with lips and tongue, gently tracing the carotid, the jugular—

"I could take you now," he whispers—

"I would die happy—"

"I told you so—" And then he shifts position, pulls away from neck, I wish he hadn't. I was enjoying it too much. But he says, "There. That's how it's done."

We roll onto our sides, facing each other, our arms loosely around each other. There's already a thin gleam of early morning high on the wall opposite the windows. A crack in the drapes. Jacob squints against the light.

"I'll fix it." I pull away from his embrace and pad naked to the window. It takes only a tug at the heavy drapes to restore the room to darkness. For just a moment, I wonder—if I were to throw them back, would Jacob burst into flame? Would he writhe in fiery pain? Or would his smooth and flawless skin simply burn red under the harsh yellow light? I'm not willing to find out. I feel strangely protective of my one-time lover.

A strange word that—lover. Especially here.

Because what we've done is really nothing at all. And yet, it's been the most intense experience of my life.

I slide back into bed and face him, naked again, aroused again. But no longer impatient. Arousal is only a condition, not a command.

"I get it."

"Get what?"

"What you said before."

"I said a lot of things."

"You said I wouldn't survive."

"Yet, here you are."

"Not the same."

"No."

"And not yet transformed either."

"Is this what you want?" Jacob smiles. "Last night you said that you didn't see much of a career opportunity here. You said that hiding in the darkness with a bunch of paranoids was not on your bucket list."

"I was being cynical."

"A cynic is an idealist who doesn't want to get caught." Jacob touches my nose lightly with a single forefinger, then down to my lips, and from there to my throat. His hand rests on that soft place at the base of my neck. "What is it you want, my sweet lonely boy—?"

I roll away, onto my back and stare at the ceiling. The dusty yellow ceiling with a pattern of water stains from before the roof was repaired. One of the brown stains looks like a dog head. Or maybe a wolf. A predator.

"The last time we talked, you told me that Monsieur had been stalking you, testing you, and finally came to you in San Francisco. He offered you the...choice."

"The gift."

"You turned him down."

"I did."

"Yet, here you are."

"Do you want me to tell you what he said?"

"I know what he said."

"You do?"

"I only look stupid."

"Yes, I know—"

I roll back to face him. "It was obvious. It has always been obvious." He waits for me to explain.

"You're capable of long periods of intense physical activity. And your senses are supremely enhanced—you can feel things profoundly. It doesn't take a genius to put it together."

"Go on."

"I'm guessing—no, I don't have to guess. He told you that sex with him would be astonishing. Didn't he?"

Jacob smiles, remembering. "It was." He lifts up on one elbow. What he said was, "You can't imagine what it feels like. There's only one way you will ever know."

Monsieur whispered, "There is no way I can describe this to you, because no human has ever had the experience. You have no language for this, Jacob."

Then he let go of my shoulder and pulled away, just far enough to look into my face and study my expression.

I didn't know what to say. I knew he was right.

"Have you studied the nature of language, Jacob? She's a cruel mistress. She enslaves us. She captures our lives and turns each moment of existence into a petroglyph, something scratched into a rock. The raw experience, the confection of sensation—it all gets crystallized and fossilized and leached of life. The words we use are distant reflections, mere shadows standing between ourselves and the light. Language denatures experience. Look at what the word *love* has done to the experience of two souls uniting—are we talking about emotional congruence or physical lust? Or merely infatuation masquerading as affection?"

Still, I sat silent, my hands folded in my lap, my face down.

"What I offer you, my beautiful boy, is time—enough time to discover what is really possible. These mayfly people, they flicker in and out of life so fast they have no time to learn what's possible, let alone achieve it. What I have—what we can have—is the chance to—" Monsieur stopped, frustrated. "I've run out of words. You can't know what's possible until after you've achieved it."

Finally, I look over to him again. "Monsieur, I do not doubt a word of what you are saying to me. And I have had enough experience to understand the way of life you are offering. I expect that I have had more experience than any human. So I believe I have some sense—as much sense as is humanly possible—that what you are offering is a rare and treasured gift, one that many would accept without hesitation.

"But I have had the misfortune of spending too many years in Boston, too many years alone in my rooms with nothing but a gas lamp and my books for company, my books and my journals—in which I have painstakingly recorded my thoughts on so many matters. I have had to consider not only my own inverted nature, but the nature of the species that produces men like me—and creatures like you.

"I have longed for a sense of..." I had to stop and take a breath. I wasn't sure what words would best express the churning dilemmas in my soul. "You know my history. If it had not been for your years of kindness, I don't know where I might have ended up. Perhaps dead. Or in prison. But you saw something in me worth saving, worth nurturing—you took me in, you cared for me, you fed me and clothed me and educated me. You gave me a love of learning, you gave me knowledge, you gave me success in the world—and I owe you everything. I owe you my life—"

"But—?"

"But the one thing you could not give me was the one thing no one can give another. It's the thing you have to discover for yourself—"

"And that is—?"

I had to laugh. "I don't know if there's a word for it. Soul, perhaps? Self? Identity? It's that feeling of knowing who you are." He waited patiently while I struggled to assemble my next few sentences. "All my life, I had this sense that I did not fit in, that I was not like anyone else around me. When you took me in, at first I thought we were the same, that we shared the same nature, an affection for our own kind, but then as I began to pay attention, I became painfully aware that—that there was another kind of difference between us, an unbridgeable gap, perhaps.

"When you sent me to Boston, I thought—no, I hoped that I would meet other young men like myself, that I would find a kind of companionship, a kind of community where I was not only understood, but accepted as well. And for a few short weeks, maybe even a little longer than that, I actually achieved that illusion of acceptance. But no, it was only an illusion—

"When I returned to Seattle, when I lived in Mrs. Grogan's house, when I took in Georgie-Boy, I thought for a moment that this was who I could be—but that turned out to be only a desperate grasp as well. It has only been in the year since then that—"

"Go on..." Monsieur encouraged.

I took a breath. "It has only been in the time since you abandoned me, in the time since The Community shunned me, in the time since I have been on my own, that I have discovered what I am."

"And that is...?"

"I'm a monster. Just like you."

Monsieur waited for me to continue.

I said, "The thing is—I don't know if I want to be a monster. Just like you. Of all the different opportunities, becoming a ... a Nightsider has always looked like the inevitable one. I've never really felt as if I had a choice to be anything else.

"And that's the dilemma that I am facing here, Monsieur. It is not that I don't love you. I do. The depth of my hatred for you—for what you have put me through—it's also a measure of how intensely I have loved you. And perhaps I might even love you again. On the other side. But do I want that? I don't know."

Monsieur smiled and nodded—it was his acceptance of my feelings. He already knew, of course. He might as well have been reading my mind.

"So..." I said. "I find myself confronting two questions."

"I hope that you can resolve them soon. It's getting early," Monsieur said, a deliberate hint that he was growing impatient, that this conversation must reach a conclusion while there was still time to retreat before the dawn.

"You offer me an enhanced physical capability, but have you also offered me any enhancement for my soul, for myself. Will I still hunger for knowledge? Will I still question the nature of existence? Will I look at the stars with greater clarity? Or will I fail to notice them at all?

"Because that is the real question here. Will this transformation be so complete that I will no longer have the ability to doubt, to question my choices, to even wonder if about the consequences of this choice and whether or not it was worth it? Are you even capable of answering this question honestly?

"Monsieur, tell me now—will I be such a monster? Will I enjoy being that kind of monster so much that I will not know how much of a monster I am?"

* ⊢═⟨●⟩○⟨●⟩═⊣ *

"What did he say?"

Jacob lies on his back, staring not at the ceiling, but at his memories of moments long past.

"He said the only thing he could say. He said, 'You asked if I was capable of answering your question honestly.' I can only tell you that if I was offered the choice to go back, I would not.' I said to him—but is that you talking, or the transformation?

"And he said, 'We are one and the same. As you will be.'" Jacob lifts himself up on one elbow to look at me. "There was only one way I could ever have my question answered."

"Do you regret it?"

"I do not. It is as Monsieur said. I am what I am."

I reach over and touch him, his chest, his porcelain skin. "But—the questions you asked. Were they answered for you?"

"Yes, they were. And no, they weren't—not in the way you understand them. But from the other side, yes. And I know how frustrating an answer that is for you. Because I was there once too." He leans across and kisses me. Not a vampire kiss. A human kiss. A human kiss plus Jacob. I nearly pass out from the intensity of it.

He laughs—not malicious. Joyous. "That's just a hint of what's on the other side. Do you want it?"

"Aren't you going to...finish your story? About you and Monsieur? What happened next?"

"What happened next? I can't tell you. That is, I can't describe it. It's what Monsieur said. There are no human words because there are no equivalent human experiences. I could give you the nightsider words, but you they'd have no meaning for you. If you want to know, there's only one way to get here." He touches my face, strokes my cheek with his hand—

"Why me? Why do you want me?"

"Why does anyone want anyone? Because I do. Because you want me."

I sit up in the bed and look at him. "No. You picked me out from the beginning. You told me your story—because you knew I'd write it. You knew I'd put myself into your story and write it from the inside. Except you never told me the rest, what it's like to be there, where you are. You teased and taunted and tickled, but all you ever told me was your journey to the moment of choice—"

"That's right." Jacob swivels around to sit opposite me. Naked and cross-legged. A marvelous view. But his words are blunt. "We never tell anyone what it's like to live on the nightside. You know the joke. I could tell you, but then I'd have to kill you. And eat you. I'm sure you'd be delicious."

"So that's the real choice you offer? Transform or die?"

Jacob shrugs. "In your case, you'll die happy. I promise that much. I've already given you a tease. So what's it gonna be?"

"You already know. You've been stalking me. I've been stalking you."

"Ahh, sweetheart—you've been lusting after my body." He spreads his arms and legs wide, sprawling backward across the bed. "Well, here it is. Here I am. Take your pleasure on me. Die happy."

I don't move and after a minute he rolls up onto an elbow, stares at me. "No?"

"No." I explain. "Yes, I would enjoy having sex with such a beautiful man. But we're beyond that now, aren't we? You want more than sex. You want the same thing I do. A relationship. That's why I'm asking. Why me?"

"Why not?"

"No. You said it at the beginning. Why would a man who's had more than a century and a half of life—why would he want a naïve sixteen year old girl? Or boy? I'm not even thirty yet. I'm still a kidult. I have nothing to offer you. I'm not your intellectual equal. I don't have the same depth of experience. If I say yes, I'll be agreeing to a century or more of being overshadowed by your strength, your knowledge, your power—"

Jacob sits up. He nods slowly, knowingly. He points, as if to an invisible blackboard. "There. That's it. Your insight. You're still untrained, yes—but with experience—" He shrugs. "With experience, you could be the equal of any nightsider."

"And if not?"

He shrugs again. "Vampire blood is the best of all."

"Really?"

"We're not immortal. We heal fast. But we can be killed." He traces the line of his carotid. "Slice me here, I'll bleed out in minutes. You wouldn't want to though—"

"Why not?"

"Because once you're known as a vampire killer, every vampire in the world will want your blood."

"You guys are that committed to revenge?"

"Oh, hell no. It's the blood. You'll have the most delicious blood in the world."

"How do you know that?"

"Because—" Jacob rearranges himself on the bed, curling up against me now, the comfortable position of two men who have just made love, and are now just chatting aimlessly about things of no importance—the resolution of the immediate dilemma has been casually set aside for later consideration. "Because—" Jacob says, "—of everything that happened afterward."

"Are you going to share that with me?"

Jacob almost-laughs, a chuckle deep in his throat.

"It's a long story."

"Tell me."

"I'd better not."

"Why?"

"Because you'll turn it into a great sprawling novel of history and bloodshed. The Vampire Wars."

"Mmm. You're probably right."

"I don't recommend it."

"Why not?"

"Too many of the survivors are still around. Nightsiders don't like publicity. I don't think you'd survive."

"What if I wrote it into the novel that the Nightsiders will likely kill me for writing the story? So that if I die suspiciously, everyone will know it's true?"

"I like the way you think," Jacob says.

"Is that why you stalked me for so many years?"

"I was waiting for you to ripen. One way or the other."

"Ahh." One way or the other. What a nice way of phrasing it. "So tell me about the Great Vampire War."

"It wasn't that great. It was mostly messy." Jacob pulls away so he can face me again.

"It goes all the way back to my time in Boston. And there's a lot of politics involved."

"Politics. Yes. Like you wouldn't believe. The Nightsider culture is a collection of individuals divided not only by geography, but time as well. You don't give up your past. It shapes you, trains you, hardens you. The man who was turned in 1732 does not think like the man who turned in 1832. Think about it. It's always going to be this group versus that group. More than ever among us, with so many different backgrounds. We have little continuity of purpose, and less sense of unity. We're strong and we're fragile—both at the same time."

"So...what happened?"

Jacob adjusts his position under my arm. "Well, let's just say that there were some members of The Community who didn't like me very much. Can't say I blame them. I was something of a brat. I still am. But that's part of the condition. You age really slow. I mean, look at me. I look as young as you. But they didn't hate me alone. They also resented Monsieur for inviting me into their circle of secrecy." Abruptly, Jacob stops. He twirls his fingers in the sparse hairs that decorate the skin above my sternum. "This is probably going to disappear. Most vampires are hairless."

"Really?"

"Uh-huh. It's those wolf guys who are hairy, remember?" He plays with my nipple. "You're going to be so hot—"

"You're assuming—"

"No, I'm not—"

I don't answer.

Jacob sighs, a deep exhalation. Neither exasperation nor resignation. Nor wistful either. Just a sigh. Impatience?

"Anyway," Jacob continues. "They didn't like me. They didn't like Monsieur. They hadn't liked him all that much before. Now they had another reason. Me. Monsieur used up all his favors protecting me from them."

"He really loved you then—"

"Vampires don't love. But whatever the equivalent is, yes. He did." Jacob turns slightly, so he can stare at the ceiling. "I think it would be fairer to say he had an investment in me. Time. Money. Teaching. So, yes. There was a certain connect. The others understood that—

"But Colonel Guignard in Boston, he'd never forgiven me. He was old. Very old. He saw my curiosity, my inquisitiveness, as an insult. I guess it gnawed at him. In his world, the way he was, what he was before he became what he was, if someone annoyed you—well, you made them disappear. I think he'd turned just after the French revolution, maybe even during the terrors, so that way of thinking was imprinted on him. You get imprinted you know—"

"Anyway, Colonel Guignard was determined to disappear me, but Monsieur said no. My questions had not been an insult, had not been a threat, and Guignard was out of line. So, of course, this triggered a schism. Another schism. One of many. It's a web of shifting alliances. Wealth. Power. Blood. Territories. We go from one war to the next. What's that phrase? 'Bitchy little schoolgirls?' Yeah." He stops himself. "No, there's a better one—empathy deficit. You're familiar with that description? That's us. We're sociopaths. We kill people. If we have any empathy left, we try to kill the ones who deserve it. But if someone annoys us—well, they deserve it. I annoyed the Colonel, and—" Jacob sighs again, remembering. "He had to get rid of Monsieur so he could get rid of me."

Abruptly, Jacob places his hand on my heart. "Your pulse is accelerating."

"It's a scary story."

"It gets worse."

"I'm sure—"

Jacob listens to my heartbeat a minute longer, then continues. "The fire—Monsieur's house in Seattle? That was the work of Colonel Guignard. Not directly. But an ally. Not the best ally, though. He couldn't keep his mouth shut. So Monsieur was warned, just in time. He still had friends. By the time the Colonel's agents arrived, Monsieur had slipped away. They didn't find out, not for a long time, that they'd failed. Monsieur let everyone think they'd succeeded. So he could plan his revenge."

"I assume you succeeded?"

Jacob laughs softly, deep in his throat. "Shakespeare was wrong. Revenge is best served hot and bloody."

"Are you going to tell me all the details—how you and Monsieur hunted down the Colonel? I could probably turn that into a pretty good horror novel. Maybe even win a Bram Stoker award."

Jacob smiles, nods. "It took a while. There's a lot to tell. You'd need to know the whole history to understand all the players and the sides they chose, but the important thing is that Colonel Guignard wasn't all that popular himself. I mentioned Langham, remember? The one I stalked and finally met in San Francisco? I still don't know how old he is. He didn't like Guignard. He didn't like Monsieur either, but he liked Guignard even less. But most of all, he didn't like Nightsiders killing each other. It was a bad precedent. Hell, it started a war—or continued one, depending on when you came in. Apparently, there had been a truce, at least since the Civil War. But then when Guignard ordered Monsieur burned, he crossed a line. So when Monsieur reached out to Langham, through an intermediary, Langham agreed to meet with us. By then, Monsieur had turned me—"

"You never did tell me how that worked—"

"And I'm not going to either." Jacob laughs softly in his throat. "There's only one way to know—" Another knowing chuckle. "Soon. You'll see."

"You're still assuming—"

"No, I'm not." He licks my neck. "Right there. You could be so delicious. But that would be a transitory pleasure. And I want more than that. There will be so much better with you on the other side."

I push him away, gently. "Finish your story."

"There's not much left to tell. We killed the Colonel. And his friends. There were three of them. And the arsonist, but he was just a human, hired for the job. But Monsieur gave him to me and I ripped his throat out—slowly. His screams were—" Jacob shrugs. "Wet. I think the best way to describe the sound is wet. And gurgly. Monsieur also let me have the one who killed Georgie-boy. Your heart—it's pounding again—"

"It's not every day I'm in bed with a murderer."

"I'm not a murderer. I'm a vampire. I was hungry. And they deserved it." Jacob pauses, thinking about whether or not he should go on. I wait patiently.

Finally, Jacob looks up at me and says, "Vampire blood is delicious. It's the best there is. You can't believe how rich and delicious. The older the vampire, the better. It's like fine wine. See its color, deep and dark—swirl it, smell it, sip it. Taste the balance, savor the blend—notice the nose, the texture, and finally allow the flavor to drift across your tongue, all the different places in your mouth where you assimilate the essences. Then, finally—drink with gusto. Don't guzzle, but enjoy. Monsieur gave me a taste of Colonel Guignard before he finished him off. I've been hungry for more ever since—"

"You're a vampire killer?"

"The worst kind. That's why there's a bounty on me—" Jacob's smile broadens. His teeth gleam. His eyes shine in the first hints of dawn.

"Should I pull the drapes?"

"Probably a good idea—"

I return to the bed and slip back into his arms. "So. How many vampires have you killed?"

"Enough. But only the ones who needed to be killed."

"And how do you decide that—?"

"Haven't you figured that part out yet?" He leans in toward me. "Come on, sweetheart. Guess—" Something malicious in his tone.

"Monsieur...?"

"Nailed it in one." Jacob grins.

"But why?"

"Well, I suppose I could say I was hungry. But that was only the smallest part of it."

The conversation fell into a necessary silence—but my thoughts roared in my head.

As much as I loved Monsieur—that was also how much I hated him.

Even worse—Monsieur knew exactly what I was feeling, every hideous thought, every exquisite desire. He studied me with those same piercing eyes, that familiar pale smile.

I was transparent to him, unrolled across the table like a parchment scroll, my squalid nakedness laid out and displayed, my innermost core illustrated in excruciating detail, every tortured facet, significant or otherwise, itemized and illuminated in all its glowing squalor.

Every act and every action—every lie and falsehood, every pretention, every sexual aspiration and achievement, every lustful moment, everything I wanted and everything I feared, everything—he knew it all. He'd known me that deeply ever since the first night. There were no secrets here.

So, yes, he knew how I felt. How could he not?

And yet, he still wanted me.

My thoughts churned.

He'd abandoned me. He'd done it deliberately. He'd waited to see if I could survive on my own. Like I hadn't already proven it surviving as a street-boy all those years until the night I'd reached into the wrong pocket—

But for Monsieur, mere love wasn't enough. He'd needed to see if I was *worthy*.

Well, I was—*I am*. But *he wasn't*.

The part he couldn't see—or if he could, he didn't care—but there was a growing core of realization inside my soul, a terrifying recognition of who this creature really was—just another nightsider. A sociopath with a condition. And while he was waiting to see if I was worthy of him—he had never been worthy of me.

I was loyal. He wasn't.

I had never stopped being loyal. But at the first warning of danger, he'd abandoned me, left me alone and vulnerable—I could have been killed—until he'd finally decided the situation might be safe enough for him to contact me. I only survived because Langham took an interest in me and lent me no small measure of protection. Otherwise, Guignard or one of his friends would have had me for a snack.

No, Monsieur was like all the rest, just another pitiless sociopath—but then again, so was I. He'd trained me too well. And that was the moment I came to the ultimate understanding. As I sat there, seething, the insight was inevitable. We deserved each other.

Monsieur sat across from me, quietly waiting.

There was a necessary process to my thoughts, an inevitable conclusion. He had known from the beginning. Transformation is not given, neither is it earned—it occurs only when every other alternative has been exhausted and obliterated. There must be no other possibility.

Monsieur knew this, every nightsider knows it—it cannot be understood until it is experienced. Everything else is naivete and ignorance.

All this time—from the very first day, perhaps even before that first dangerous moment when I tried to slip my hand unnoticed into his coat pocket—all this time, Monsieur had been waiting. So it was no matter for him to wait just a little bit longer while I seethed and churned in furious confusion, boiling away my thoughts until nothing was left but the raw kernel of insight.

Finally, I stood—

I began unbuttoning my shirt, loosening my belt, exposing my naked flesh to his patient gaze, his studying eyes—

It was the most terrifying moment of my life.

There are moments of terror in any man's life, but perhaps the most profound is the one that occurs when he stands at the threshold of fulfilled desire—that amazing hot-and-icy thrill that starts in the groin and surges upward like a wave of emotion. It's that delicious instant of recognition that the sheltering cloak of ignorance is about to be sacrificed on the altar of lust. It was the realization that *oh my god, I'm really going to do this—now!* On the other side of the moment, virginity becomes a lost memory.

This moment—naked before Monsieur—was all that and more. I was poised on the precipice, that elongated moment of anticipation before stepping through, falling into that chasm from which all thought of return would be impossible. I was about to become—

Monsieur wrapped me into his arms, a cold and frightening embrace—at the same time, delicate and tender. His fingers traced the line of my neck, then down to my nipples, my belly, and below, tasting my flesh with his touch.

Did I tremble, afraid to proceed, afraid to extend my own hands? Monsieur touched my arms, encouraging, inviting—he was not impatient, he was savoring the moment. We had both waited so long, neither of us needed to rush.

Can I describe that consummation—that little death, followed by the larger one? Can I speak to you now of that first amazing moment, the reawakening to life and the sudden awareness of the greater existence into which I had just been born? All these strange and new possibilities—?

I cannot. Because there are no words in your language that can evoke the experience, let alone capture its essence. No nightsider has ever attempted it. Why would we want to? Why would we want the daysiders to be aware of the possibilities?

I did not step immediately into the full knowledge of my new condition. That's another error, another misunderstanding. Just as a baby must learn to walk one step at a time before running is possible; just as the infant must learn to speak one syllable at a time, one word at a time, before he can assemble and convey his thoughts—so must the infant nightsider grow into his new life one step after the other, one syllable upon the next.

The details—there's another novel, a trilogy, a saga, an epic—again, there are few words in the pitiful language of daylight. There is another language, a language found in rapturous experience, but it would be as meaningless to you in your condition as are the languages of sex and sensuality to a prepubescent child. The experiences conveyed aren't just alien, they are unknowable.

Let me tell you of this instead—

Monsieur had been in hiding as well.

Not just from me, but from Colonel Guignard and his allies. And not just because of their various differences. Those were minor. There's a much more important reason why nightsiders keep secrets—especially from each other.

Yes, we do become uncomfortable when there are too many predators feeding on too small a herd. It creates unease, occasionally panic. The world becomes dangerous.

There is no real control over who gets turned, who gets brought into the community—any nightsider can create as many companions as he desires, but it's dangerous. Too many of the younger ones are careless and the discovery of one endangers all. It creates a frenzy, a hunt, a pogrom. Those who prey on The Community become powerful.

But those are manageable. Every nightsider has an exit strategy, usually several. The essential immortality of the condition carries with it a hallucinatory paranoia—everything is a conspiracy, no one can be trusted. You create plans behind plans. You spend a good part of your waking hours creating strategies for all contingencies. That's why it's so hard to find a vampire. He's already out-thought you.

No, the real danger comes from one's own brethren—isn't it obvious why? Because vampire blood is the most delicious of all. It has a flavor rich beyond belief, beyond description. Once tasted, it becomes more than a craving—it becomes an addiction. Once a nightsider has killed another, he becomes a threat to the entire Community.

It's the only taboo, the only real perversion we know.

• ‖ ⁼◦➤◦⊰ ⊱◦◄◦⁼ ‖ •

"But you—?"

"Yes. I did."

"Why?"

"Why not?" Jacob laughs and leans back. "After all those years of serving him, I deserved to be free. That's why." Jacob's eyes flash. "Any questions?"

I shake my head. I cannot look away. He's daring me to speak. Finally, I hazard the most noncommittal sentence I can construct. I choose my words carefully. "You're right. Being a vampire is a dangerous business."

Jacob laughs again Louder than before. "Well, there you have it. It's a community of sociopathic killers, a gaggle of selfish assholes yanked from time and history, all of them afraid of each other—and with good reason. There is no loyalty." He grabs me by the throat and leans in close. "Even if I were to profess my undying affection for you, you would still never be able to trust that one night I might find you so delicious I would succumb to my irrational hungers."

"Does that happen a lot?"

"More than any nightsider wants to admit." Jacob shrugs. "Usually when there are too many of us. When the herd needs culling. That's when the younger ones go to ground and wait until it's safe to come out."

"How often does that happen?"

"I've seen it twice. Two different cities. New Orleans is overdue. We'll have to get out of here soon, probably tonight."

"So you're not going to turn me after all—?"

Jacob stares into my eyes. "You still don't get it, do you?"

"Get what?"

"You can ask to be a vampire—it's not enough. You have to want it so badly, you'll demand it. And even then, you have to be worthy of it—worthy in the eyes of the one you challenge. It's a dangerous thing to demand. Like being a male praying mantis. You think you're going to get laid—the best sex you ever had in your life. That sounds like a good deal, but it's a gamble. You might get turned or you might get eaten, but you won't know which—unless you wake up afterward.

"This is a private club, my brave little bunny. Not everybody gets in. You have to be the right kind of sociopath, an interesting one. Otherwise, you're just another monster—and The Community kills monsters quickly, before the rest of the world knows they're real. Maybe you're ready, maybe you're not. Maybe you'll never be ready—"

Abruptly Jacob moves. Pushing me back, he sprawls on top of me. His naked flesh burns amazingly hot—a ferocious burst of energy that will leave him dormant for hours. He grabs my face and his kiss is overwhelming—

And then, just as abruptly, he lets go. He lifts himself enough to focus on my eyes. "You can't believe what it is to experience the world with hyper-developed senses, everything enhanced. You'll blaze like you're on fire. You'll soar through the night, you'll relish the incredible power of your body. The surges of strength. You'll run as fast as a cheetah, you'll leap like a bird. You'll slide through darkness like the hand of death. And finally—finally, the sex! You'll gasp with astonishment. Intense, overwhelming, unbelievable. It'll go on for hours. Days, if you want. Forever. Where you are, it's unimaginable. Where I am, I wouldn't go back, even if there was a way. From this side, from this side—you'll see how drab and dreary every moment of your life has been until now. Say yes...?"

Afterward...

I stayed with Monsieur for years. Decades. We traveled all over the country, and Europe as well—not always together, but always carefully coordinated. He traveled first. I followed. I continued the pretense that I was searching for him.

As before, I scoured through various records, apparently looking for various members of The Community. I pretended to be foolish and fumbling—

I made myself look like a threat. But not a dangerous threat, a clumsy one.

And sure enough, one after the other, members of The Community came after me.

And together we took them down and drank their blood.

I was the bait. Monsieur was the trap. Vampires are strong—but two vampires are much stronger than one, especially when their strength is powerfully coordinated. It was quick and violent and bloody.

And it was delicious. One after another.

Van Helsing had nothing on us. We were the greatest vampire hunters on two continents. Between us, we decimated The Community. Monsieur even fantasized about going after Langham.

But no—

One hungry afternoon, lying in bed, staring at the pressed copper ceiling tiles of our lavish hotel room in Paris—it was just a few months before The Great War—listening to the sounds of the raucous traffic filtering in through the heavy drapes, I realized I had become as strong as Monsieur. Perhaps even stronger. There was nothing left for him to teach. I had reached my potential. I think he knew it too, when I rolled over to face him. I began by licking him low, as I had already done so many times, working my way up toward his pale neck.

He was delicious too. The best yet.

• ⊹═⟨◆❍◗◖❍◆⟩═⊹ •

Jacob was right.

There are no human words for the experience. It was the most extreme pain and the most incredible pleasure I have ever felt. I shrank and grew simultaneously. I flamed and froze. I died and was reborn, both in the same moment. And none of those words even come close to intimating what happened. I was no longer me and I was the most amazing me I could be. It was everything promised and more.

There was a lot to learn. And Jacob taught me well.

We traveled all over the country—not always together, but always carefully coordinated. It's a skill, moving under cover of darkness. Think about it.

More than that, Jacob trained me how to kill quickly and efficiently. He taught me how to pick a victim, how to seduce him or her, how to make those last breaths the most exciting of their life.

A curious thing, Jacob had a surprising moral sense. Certain people were off-limits—parents, police, firefighters, doctors—but others were fair game. Predators, pimps, molesters. And certain others too—

When Jacob finally thought I was ready, we went after the bigger game.

The Community had gotten comfortable. There were too many nightsiders, and too many of them had become fat and lazy. They preyed on missing children, runaways, and disaffected. They deserved to die.

And yes, they were delicious.

We thinned the pack and made the world a better place—a better place for us as well.

Jacob was a good teacher.

Until there was nothing more to learn.

That was the day I killed him and drank him dry.

Because vampire blood is the best.

About the Author

David Gerrold has been writing professionally for half a century. He created the tribbles for *Star Trek* and the Sleestaks for *Land Of The Lost*. His most famous novel is *The Man Who Folded Himself*. His semi-autobiographical tale of his son's adoption, "The Martian Child" won both the Hugo and the Nebula awards, and was the basis for the 2007 movie starring John Cusack and Amanda Peet.

You can find more about him at http://www.gerrold.com.

CPSIA information can be obtained
at www.ICGtesting.com
Printed in the USA
BVHW07s0311050718
520783BV00009B/536/P